The Proof of Love

Catherine Hall

Portobello
BOOKS

For my mother and father, with love

First published by Portobello Books 2011
This edition published 2012

Portobello Books
12 Addison Avenue
London
W11 4QR

A CIP catalogue record is available from the British Library

9 8 7 6 5 4 3 2

ISBN 978 1 84627 300 1

www.portobellobooks.com

Typeset in Adobe Sabon by
Avon DataSet Ltd, Bidford on Avon, Warwickshire

Printed and bound by CPI Group (UK) Ltd, Croydon, CR0 4YY

'To become a child is to be very literal; to find everything so strange that nothing is surprising; to be heartless, to be ruthless, yet to be so passionate that a snub or a shadow drapes the world in gloom.'

Virginia Woolf, from 'Lewis Carroll',
in *The Moment and Other Essays*

'Mathematics, rightly viewed, possesses not only truth, but supreme beauty – a beauty cold and austere, like that of sculpture, without appeal to any part of our weaker nature, without the gorgeous trappings of painting or music, yet sublimely pure, and capable of a stern perfection such as only the greatest art can show.'

Bertrand Russell, from 'The Study of Mathematics',
in *Mysticism and Logic and Other Essays*

Now the silence was broken as he waded, each step forcing the water to ripple out away from him, slapping hard into granite. He felt neither the dark cold nor the pressure of it, moving blindly forward, cradling the little weight in his arms.

He passed from shallows into shadows, and then was claimed by moonlight. He stood for a minute, looking at the vast, sleeping mountains and fields that glittered under silver dew.

'I'm sorry,' he said quietly, and laid his burden down.

One

THE SUN WAS ALMOST AT ITS PEAK WHEN DOROTHY WILKINSON noticed the black speck moving down the mountain. It was nearly noon and she was hungry for her lunch. Sitting in the shade of an oak tree, she opened her knapsack and took out a hard-boiled egg. She picked off its shell, dipped it into a newspaper twist of salt, then took a bite, chewing thoughtfully as she watched the ant-like figure inch its way along the narrow road. It was too big to be a sheep, not big enough for one of the rare cars that dared attempt the challenge of the pass. Taking another bite, she leaned back against the tree, waiting. As the speck crept around a bend, it became a shape: a large-framed, old-fashioned bicycle, ridden by someone hunched low over the handlebars as if he were hanging on for his life.

'Bloody idiot!' she muttered to herself, half admiring, half amused.

Taking a ham sandwich from its greaseproof wrapper, she went on eating as she followed the bicycle's jerky progress, moving forward a little, stopping abruptly, its rider lurching over the handlebars, then setting off again, a few yards at a time. She found herself tensing, as if she were riding it herself, holding her breath in anticipation of every jolt.

Let go! she thought, and as if its rider had somehow heard her, the bicycle suddenly began to pick up speed, wobbling at first, gathering momentum, then moving faster until it became almost a blur. It raced down the hill, looping around the snaky curves of the road, disappearing into dips then hurtling back into sudden view. As it came over the final hurdle, a humpback bridge, it left the road and flew through the air, crashing back onto the tarmac to shudder across a cattle grid. After a brief and painful squeal of brakes, everything was mercifully still.

*

At the bottom of the hill the rider stood, blinking and dazed, not quite able to believe he had at last come to a halt. His shoulders heaved as he filled his lungs with gulps of air, tasting the melting tar, giddy with the terror and exhilaration of his descent. For a moment he did not move, feeling only the thudding of his heart, then turned to look at where he had come from. Jagged crags reached for the sky, the opening between them no more than a crack, the road curving along the contours of the mountain. It made him dizzy to remember it.

Flexing his hands, stiff from gripping the handlebars, he turned back. He had the curious sensation of being in a landscape that he almost but not quite recognized. The valley stretched out in front of him, scooped out of the mountains and carpeted with fields split by dry stone walls: an infinity of rocks. Oak trees grew along their edges, dividing them from the hills.

4

The road wound along the valley bottom like a river, glittering in the sun. A little further from where he stood was a track that led off it, up into the fells. A sign was propped against the wall where it met the road, uneven letters on a slab of grey-blue slate, leaking little rivulets of paint.

Eggs for Sale, 10p/doz.

He wheeled his bicycle forward and looked inside the rusting biscuit tin. It was filled with brown eggs, twelve of them, flecked with dirt and wisps of feather. Picking up the jam jar that stood next to it, he shook it, listening to the dull clink of coins against glass.

He was cautious by nature, but there was something that he liked about the dripping letters, the jam jar and the eggs. He found them oddly reassuring. Besides, he was tired, from the heat and from his journey, and from the thoughts that had filled his head as he cycled, thoughts he had come north to escape. Turning the handlebars, he began to push his bicycle along the dusty track.

*

Hartley Dodds was finishing his lunch when the dogs began to bark, hurling themselves against the door of the barn in which he had locked them. He sat at the table, methodically chewing his last mouthful of potato. The barking was accompanied by a low, warning growl from the old dog chained up outside, rumbling under the rest of the cacophony. As the growling grew louder, he put down his knife and fork, then drained his mug of tea. The others watched as he stood up, wiped his mouth with the back of his hand, walked across the room and flung open the door. The barking stopped immediately.

Squinting in the sunlight, he jerked his head in the direction of the awkward figure standing in the middle of the yard. The man came forward, glancing nervously at the tethered dog, keeping his bicycle between himself and the snarling animal. He was oddly dressed for summer heat, in walking boots, a heavy tweed jacket and flannel trousers held in at the ankles with bicycle clips. His hair was dark with sweat, his face flushed. As he came closer, he took a handkerchief from his pocket and patted his forehead in an oddly formal gesture, as if to make himself presentable.

*

The two men looked at each other warily. The farmer stooped in the low porch, his dark eyes pools of suspicion. Lines were etched into his skin, his features carved by the elements over a lifetime of working outside. Battling his environment had aged him; deep furrows ploughed between his eyebrows and down each side of his mouth. His clothes might have been worn by his father and his grandfather too: heavy hobnailed boots, dark trousers, a checked cotton shirt, well mended but fraying at the collar and cuffs.

Standing opposite, sweat trickling down his back, the newcomer felt raw and out of place. He was beginning to regret his decision to turn up the track, made on the flimsy reassurance of a box of eggs. He knew that when he spoke he would stammer, and he knew it would not be interpreted kindly. The farmer's expression remained impassive as he explained that he wanted to spend the summer working. But when he quickly added that he did not need to be paid for it, the farmer looked at him thoughtfully, assessing the breadth of his shoulders under the folds of his jacket. At last he nodded.

'There's a hut on't fell. Me brother sleeps in it at lambing time. You can have that.'

*

The farmer led the way as they climbed halfway up the mountain that reached high behind the house, walking in silent single file

6

along the narrow path. By the time they arrived, the newcomer was panting, his shirt heavy with sweat.

The farmer grunted. 'This do you?'

An eager nod.

'Tea's at five. I'll tell me wife to lay another place.'

He turned and set off back down the path, striding through bracken that reached almost to his waist.

*

The newcomer pushed gingerly at the peeling door, uncertain of what might lie behind. It opened onto a single room with rough, unplastered walls. Half-burned twigs and ash littered the makeshift fireplace, spilling out across the earthen floor. The only furniture was a narrow iron bedstead, covered with a woollen blanket and a rolled-up sheep's fleece at its head to serve as a pillow. Next to it, on the floor, was a candle stub stuck onto a saucer, charred matches melted into the pool of wax around it.

He let out a long sigh of relief. The room was small, but to him it was wonderful. He walked over to the bed and sat down, shrugging off his knapsack, then his jacket. For a while he was motionless, feeling his muscles begin to relax as he listened to the sheep bleat in the valley below. Then he folded his jacket neatly and hung it over the bedpost, undid the buckle of his knapsack, loosened its drawstring and took out its contents: a change of shirt and underpants, razor and soap, a well-washed towel, a penknife and a small stack of books. He stood up, holding the books in his hands, and looked about the room. On a small shelf above the fireplace was a ram's horn, curled in on itself like a shell. He arranged his little library on the shelf in order of size, lining the edges up neatly, using the horn as a bookstop, making adjustments until the tip of it faced the room directly.

He was tired from his journey, long days in which the landscape had slowly changed from flat plains to marshy midlands to peaks, as if England grew higher the further north he went. He had ridden through small towns and sullen suburbs, along back roads and bridleways, canal paths and country lanes, his heart pumping as he pushed down on the pedals, his mind always working, picking at his preoccupations. He had slept in pubs and hostels, in ditches and on benches, waking each day to unaccustomed sunshine. It had been warm on his face in the mornings, then hot on his shoulders as it rose high in the sky, beating down on him as he pedalled towards his uncertain destination.

Now he lay down on the bed, his body sinking into the thin mattress. Old sweat, tobacco and wood smoke rose from the blanket to mingle with the fusty smell of wool. From where he was lying, through the doorway, he could see the back of the farm, the tight-stretched washing line in the garden, its row of white sheets bleaching in the sun. Beyond it, on the other side of the valley, was another range of mountains, peaks misty in the afternoon haze, a flock of sheep grazing on its lower pastures. He traced the rocky frontier of a dry stone wall, taking pleasure in its neat construction. He had made the right choice, he thought. Here there would be no distractions. It was the perfect place to grapple with the problems he so badly needed to solve. For the first time in weeks, Spencer Little smiled to himself, and promptly fell asleep.

*

Later that evening, Hartley Dodds was playing dominoes at the Black Tup.

'He says he's a student. From down south. At Cambridge University. Doing maths.'

Titch Tyson matched a six to a six. 'Clever bugger, eh?'

'I reckon the lad's a bit cracked. Silly sod came over the pass on a pushbike. In't middle of the day! He wants his head looking at. We haven't had a summer this hot as long as I can remember.'

'And what's he doing here?'

'He says he's on his holidays. Funny sort of holidays, if you ask me.'

'He says he wants to think,' Thomas Dodds said quietly.

Hartley shook his head at his brother. 'He could do his thinking anywhere. That's what he's meant to do at his college. He doesn't need to come here for that.'

The three men reached for their tankards and took long draughts of beer.

'Anyhow, he doesn't want paying,' said Hartley. 'It's a free pair of hands.'

Titch added another domino to the line that had started to spread over the table.

'What does Mary reckon to it?'

'Eh?'

'About having a student staying with you.'

'Not much. She'll not mind.'

He grinned slyly. 'I wouldn't go leaving my wife alone with a clever bugger this late at night.'

Hartley spluttered into his pint.

'Don't be daft, man.'

Thomas coughed and rose to his feet. 'I'll get another round in.'

Two

When Spencer woke, the hut was filled with warm light creeping under the door. The air, thick with dancing dust and the smell of warm bracken, tickled his nostrils, making him sneeze. Throwing back the blanket, he scrambled out of bed and then, pulling on his trousers and boots, stumbled to the door and pushed it open.

To the side of the hut was a little stream, half dried up but running clear. The previous night he had taken off his clothes and washed in it, soaping himself one limb at a time, shy under the moonlight. Now he squatted next to it and splashed his face and neck, enjoying the cool of the water as it trickled down his chest. Lifting his face to the sun to dry, he closed his eyes, thinking back to the day before.

There had been no concession to the heat at supper as Hartley and Thomas silently ate their way through plates of greyish stew and boiled potatoes, mopping up what was left with thick slices of buttered bread and washing it down with mugs of coffee. They ate mechanically, as if it made no difference what was put in front of them, simply that there was plenty of it. Hartley's wife, Mary, a large-boned, nervous woman, made sure that there was, repeatedly jumping up from the table to fetch potatoes and bring more to drink. She left her stew unfinished the instant the men had wiped their plates clean of gravy, rushing to the kitchen to bring out apple crumble and custard.

Afterwards, as Mary washed the dishes, Thomas sat, saying nothing as Hartley asked the questions that Spencer had been dreading, about who he was and where he had come from. He had to listen hard to catch Hartley's thick accent with its clipped, almost guttural pronunciation, mixed with words that he could not understand but guessed were some form of dialect. He answered as best he could, hoping the conversation would soon move away from him and on to other topics, itching for the moment when he could return to the hut and to his books. They had agreed he would start work on the farm the next day.

Back at the hut, he had sat outside, reading until it was too dark to see. Going back indoors, he lit the candle and then finally, gratefully, lay down on the bed. Strange noises drifted over the valley: high-pitched animal shrieks, and later on, an odd, eerie harmony, carried on the breeze. He had not wondered about it for long. Exhausted by his journey and the effort of talking to strangers, he fell asleep before the smoke from his blown-out candle had disappeared into the darkness.

*

Without a watch he did not know the time, but the sun was hot enough to make his back damp with sweat, pulling beads of moisture out of his skin. Slipping on his shirt, he hurried down the mountain. As he came around the side of the house he hesitated, bracing himself, but the barn doors were open, the dogs long gone.

He stood for a moment, looking at his home for the summer. Buildings huddled around a cobbled yard, a barn stretching along one side of it, the house standing opposite, whitewashed and low. A small tractor was parked in a corner next to a mass of rusting machinery and a Land Rover, spattered with mud, its number plate tied on with string.

A bold mass of marigolds in a trough spilled out into the shabby farmyard. He found the sight of them reassuring, like the eggs at the end of the track. Ducking quickly into the porch, he pushed open the door.

The inside of the farmhouse was a gloomy contrast to the sunshine. Moving blindly forward, he hit his head on something hard. A high-pitched voice came from the shadows.

'That's how Dad bashed all his brains out, on that beam.'

A little girl was standing in the doorway to the kitchen, squinting at him through thick glasses. She was a skinny child, dressed in faded blue shorts, an old red T-shirt and wellington boots. Mousy hair fell to her shoulders, a lopsided fringe tickling her eyes. A dog sat next to her, following her gaze.

'Are you Spencer?' the girl asked. 'Mam said you'd be down for your breakfast.'

'Oh,' he said. 'Y-yes. Yes, I'm Spencer.'

'My name's Alice.' She patted the dog. 'And this is Shadow.'

She had not been there at supper the day before. As she disappeared into the kitchen, he remembered Hartley asking Mary, 'Where is she?' and her muttered response, 'At her lesson.' He guessed it was Alice whom they had meant.

He sat down on a wooden settle and looked around the low-ceilinged room, made dark by the smallness of the windows set deep into thick walls, the slate flagstones and ancient wooden panelling that stretched from floor to ceiling. Sticky lengths of yellow flypaper hung from the beams, dotted with tiny corpses. A rag rug marked the space between a cavernous blackened fireplace and a sofa, once upholstered in velvet, its pile now reduced to greyish webbing. China plates balanced, dusty, on the shelves of an old dresser, its surfaces crammed with piles of paper and an assortment of odd nails and screws.

A radio, wedged among the mess, spilled out music. The noise and energy of it seemed out of place in the subdued cool of the farmhouse. He recognized the song from the roadside cafés of his journey; rhyming and jolly with a syncopated beat.

Alice came back into the room, frowning with concentration as she carried a plate piled high with sausages, bacon, tomatoes and baked beans, topped off with a fried egg. She set the plate down on the old oak table, its surface pitted and uneven from generations of use.

'Here you are,' she said.

She went back to the kitchen and returned with a mug of tea and a rack of burnt toast. Sliding onto a chair, she looked at Spencer closely, as if she were trying to work something out. He felt himself flush under her scrutiny.

'Thank you,' he managed, eventually.

She flashed him a gappy smile. 'It wasn't me,' she confessed. 'Mam left it in the Rayburn to keep warm. I made the toast though, and the tea.'

He wondered how late he was. 'What time is it?' he asked.

Before she could reply, a succession of chimes came from the radio.

'It's eight o'clock in the morning,' a voice said, breezy and bright.

'And this is Radio Carlisle. That was Frankie Valli and the Four Seasons, with last year's big hit, *Oh What A Night*. And what season are *we* in? That's right, it's still summer and it's sunny all over again. It'll be a good day all the way through. Get ready to hit ninety degrees.'

Alice went over to the radio and switched it off. 'I'm not allowed to have it on in the morning. Dad doesn't like it. He says it hurts his head, so we only listen to the weather. But sometimes I keep it on anyway, when he's not here.'

Spencer sawed into a sausage. 'When did you have breakfast?' he asked.

'When Mam woke me up. It was before Dad and Uncle Tom went out. They're on the intake. I'm to bring you there when you're finished.'

'What's the intake?'

She looked at him curiously. 'Don't you know?'

He shook his head.

'But you're a teacher! That's what Mam said.'

'Well, yes, some of the time. But I don't know anything about farming.'

'Miss Todd always knows the answers.'

'Who's Miss Todd?'

'She's my teacher. But school's closed now for the holidays. Are you on your holidays too?'

'Yes. Well, I don't have to teach, at least. But I still have to do my own work.'

'Is it like homework?'

'I suppose so, yes.'

'I didn't know teachers did homework.'

Spencer thought of the ladders of conjecture that led nowhere, the wrangles that he sweated over late at night, sequences of numbers, the world in which he spent most of his time; an abstract world, a beautiful but elusive place in which he was often lost. He had come to the valley hoping to find a clearer way through it.

'It's not really homework. It's sort of – my job. Only, I never stop thinking about it. I do it all the time.'

'What's the name of your school?'

'It's not actually a school, it's a university.'

'What's a university?'

'It's where people go after they've been to school.'

Alice frowned. 'Dad didn't. He worked here with Grandad. I don't think Mam went either. Or Uncle Tom.'

'Not everyone goes to university,' Spencer said quickly. 'Some people get jobs instead.'

'Where is it, your university?'

'Cambridge.'

'Where's that?'

He thought about it. 'Near London.'

'London!' Her eyes sparkled behind the thick glasses. 'I know all about London from my book!'

'Well, it's not very far from there.'

'Is it like here?'

'No,' he said, carefully. 'It's not. It's very flat.'

*

After breakfast, Spencer followed Alice along a path that led up to the mountains at the top of the valley. She kept up a steady stream of chatter as they walked but did not seem to need a response, and he was glad of it. He was not used to children, could not remember the last time he had talked to someone younger than the undergraduates he supervised. With them, the conversation was of abstract things and followed logical routes. Alice talked about whatever occurred to her, flitting from subject to subject, not seeming to care if they were connected or not. She passed unharmed between the spiky gorse bushes, moving quickly, sure-footed, her dog close to her heels, its pink tongue lolling out of its mouth as it panted in the heat.

'I've had Shadow since she was a pup,' said Alice. 'Uncle Tom gave her to me when I was six. She's the only slape-haired dog we've got.'

'What's slape-haired?'

Again she gave him a look as if she couldn't believe he didn't know.

'Smooth, like this.' She ran her hand over the dog's back. 'All our other ones are rough-haired. Shadow's nicer than them. And she's the only girl we've got left, since Moss died. She's going to have her own pups soon, her first ones ever. Look!'

The dog's swollen belly swung below her as she walked, bulging and hairless, a row of black teats either side. To Spencer it seemed almost indecent and he looked away hastily.

'They'll be born by the end of the holidays. I'm going to make her a nest in the barn when she whelps. You can help if you like.'

They passed from bracken into scrubby, yellowing grass.

'This is the intake,' she said. 'It's just a bit of the fell. It's got a wall around it to keep the sheep in, that's the only difference. Look! There's Dad and Uncle Tom.'

She ran towards them, Shadow at her heels. The men went on working, mending a gap in the dry stone wall. Spencer observed them, amazed by the ease with which they lifted great boulders from the ground.

Both men were tall, but Hartley was broader, thicker set. He gripped the stones firmly with great blunt hands, their fingernails blackened and split. Thomas stooped slightly, his body spare and lean, head bowed, intent on what he was doing. There was something about the self-containment of the brothers that made them powerful, as if together they might be capable of anything. Spencer was suddenly nervous, mindful of being late.

They had taken off their jackets and laid them on the grass. Three dogs lay close by, panting, keeping guard. As he approached, they bared their teeth and growled. Shadow kept her distance, circling around them, staying near to her mistress.

'I've brought him, Dad,' called Alice.

Hartley nodded in Spencer's direction. He looked different from the day before, his skin grey under the weathered redness, dark eyes bloodshot and swollen. As he turned towards them, a blast of stale, sour alcohol hit the summer air.

'I'm sorry I'm late,' said Spencer.

Alice was whistling tunelessly, Shadow following close behind. As she passed her father, he reached out and batted her away like a fly.

'I thought I said to keep that bitch away from the dogs,' he said. 'And I told you to keep out of my way, too.'

He nodded shortly at Spencer. 'Now then,' he said, 'let's see what you're made of. You'll have noticed there's plenty gaps in these walls. Sheep are always scrambling over. Holidaymakers, too, if they get the chance. If you're any good at mending them, you'll always have work round here.'

Spencer looked down at the valley bottom, wondering how many stones had gone to make the grey granite margins of the farm. He liked the thought of putting them back together, making the whole greater than the sum of its parts.

Hartley bent to pick up a boulder. 'Right. You pick your stones by size. Biggest ones go at the bottom and then you build it up. You've got two sides and a middle, see. You build up both sides at the same time, then you fill in't middle with small stones. But you don't want to let yourself get carried away and build up too far. You've got to think of your wall in rounds.'

'Rounds?'

'Aye. You know, like layers. That's how you build it up. And mind you don't just chuck any old stones in't middle. You want enough of them so they don't all shake down later. If that happens it'll just collapse. Then you'll have the job to do all over again, and you don't want that.'

Placing the boulder across the wall, he stepped back, looked at it critically, then adjusted it slightly.

'Now, can you see what I've done?'

Mystified, Spencer shook his head.

'Lad! I thought you were meant to have brains! I'm bonding it together. You don't want to just put the stones on top of each other, otherwise they'll fall down soon as they're pushed. You put your new stone on top of two underneath, to make it good and strong. Like brickwork. And every so often you put a big stone through it, against the way of the others, to hold it together. Do you see?'

'I think so,' said Spencer slowly.

'You'll be all right. It's you who's good at maths, isn't it, eh?' He barked with grim laughter. 'It's nobbut yan on two and two on yan, and that's all there is to it. We'll see how you get on.'

*

They spent the rest of the day on the intake, sweating under the hot sun. The brothers did not speak as they worked, and their break at ten and lunch at noon were silent affairs as they sat at the table, unthinkingly swallowing the food that Mary brought to them. By mid-afternoon, at teatime, Hartley was recovered enough to talk, managing to have a discussion with Thomas on when to start making hay, and as night drew closer, his mood seemed to improve.

18

When the last jobs were finished, at almost eight o'clock, he went to the kitchen, bending to put his head under the cold tap, which he let run, sluicing off gritty rivers of dirt and sweat. Scrubbing his finger-nails with a brush, he worked up a greyish lather and rinsed it away, then took a tub of grease from the window sill and massaged it methodically into his hands, taking care to cover every inch of skin, flexing his swollen fingers and cracking his joints. Then he and Thomas disappeared upstairs, returning soon after in clean shirts and, despite the stifling heat, their jackets. Grabbing a handful of coins from the dresser and dropping them in his pocket, Hartley nodded in Mary's direction, then the brothers left.

Spencer tried to help her with the dishes but she wouldn't let him, shaking her head as she stood in the doorway to the kitchen as if to bar him entry. She kept herself distant, standing over the old stone sink, scrubbing and scouring, restoring order, straightening the chairs that the men had left askew and sweeping up the dirt they had brought into the house on their boots.

The marigolds in the trough by the porch were hers. After she had finished in the kitchen, she filled a bucket with the water she had used for rinsing the plates and poured it over them. She worked her way through the plants, pinching off dead petals and leaves, and gently taking away greenfly. Her features softened as she bent over the flowers, her shoulders dropping as if, for the first time that day, she was doing something she enjoyed.

She did not know that Spencer watched her then. Nor did she know that he watched her later that night, when a hush fell on the valley and the air was still. After supper, he walked back to the hut. Taking his notebook from the mantelpiece, he went outside and sat on a rock. For a while he worked intently, trying to capture his train of thought, until his fingers grew sore from gripping his pencil. Putting it down, he raised his head from his book and looked over to the back of the farmhouse, unpainted and ugly, its render coming off in chunks, the washing line across the scrubby garden hanging slack without its sheets.

It was then that he noticed a woman leaning against the side of the house, lifting her face to the evening sun. He knew it could only be Mary, but it looked nothing like her. She had changed out of the dowdy skirt and blouse she had been wearing at supper into a red dress with a low neckline and a pair of high sandals. Her hair was brushed and curled. As he watched, she took out a cigarette from the packet she was holding, put it to her lips and lit it. She held in the smoke for a moment, then exhaled, a long drift of it hanging in the still air. She smoked it slowly and deliberately, savouring it to the end, then ground it out under her sandal. She stayed there a long while, almost an hour, basking and smoking until the sun went down.

*

Later, Spencer came to understand the noises that he had heard the night before. It was almost midnight when he heard them again, drifting up the side of the mountain. Cautiously he got out of bed and opened the door. As he stood waiting for his eyes to become accustomed to the light, the noise grew louder and clearer, until he could make out little snatches of melody.

The full moon lit up the fields and made the road glint silver. After a while, he noticed two dark figures moving unsteadily along it and then he understood. The figures were Hartley and Thomas; the noise was them in song.

Three

THE NEXT MORNING HARTLEY SAT AT THE TABLE, SMELLING of the night before, speaking to no-one and slicing into his sausages with weary viciousness. After breakfast he nodded to Spencer.

'You'll be on your own today,' he said. 'Thomas and me are off to town. Get yourself back up on't intake and carry on with them gaps.'

On the intake Spencer found a demolished stretch of wall, its stones scattered across the grass. Taking off his jacket, he laid it on a rock and began to pick up the stones, making neat piles according to size. Some were little more than pebbles, others heavy enough for him to have to roll them. He thought of Hartley lifting the boulder with ease, holding it casually as he explained how to build the wall, and grimaced, telling himself to try harder.

When he had finished sorting the stones, he stood and looked at them, pleased. The piles were something tangible, proof of the effort he had put into making them. A breeze blew across the fellside, bringing cool relief from the sun, and for a moment he stayed still, letting the wind lift his hair, enjoying the feel of it on his scalp.

Going over to the pile of larger stones, he picked one out at random. It was heavier than he had imagined and he staggered a little, then righted himself and carried it over to the wall. His muscles began to ache and pull as he stood wondering where to put it, and at last he had to let it drop. It hit the ground with a dull thud, tearing up the grass.

He left it where it was and looked at the wall, then back at the stones, calculating how to fit them together. This time, he picked out his first piece carefully, a large hunk of granite. When it slotted into place, he felt a thrill of satisfaction. Selecting a second piece, he shuffled it into position, then lifted a third.

'It's nobbut yan on two and two on yan,' he said under his breath, relishing the phrase.

He worked quickly, standing back after laying on each stone like an artist assessing a canvas. After a while, he began to notice the shifts of colour in the rocks, shades of grey from ash to lead, interspersed with blue and white.

The sound of whistling came drifting on the breeze, faint at first, then louder. Turning, he saw Alice. She broke into a smile and waved.

'Hello,' she called. 'That's a nice wall you're making.'

He wasn't used to easy praise. 'Is it?'

His voice, thickened by embarrassment, came out brusque, but Alice continued.

'Oh yes. It's hard, you know. It takes people yonks to get it right but you're good at it already.'

Her friendliness was disarming.

'Thank you,' he said.

She went up to the wall, running the back of her hand against the stones. 'I like the way it fits together.'

'Yes, that's what makes it interesting, the tessellation.'

Reaching into the cloth bag that hung from her shoulder, she took out a pencil and an exercise book.

'How do you spell that?'

He was taken aback. 'What?'

'Tessel . . . that thing you said.'

'Tessellation?'

'Yes.'

'Oh, right.'

He spelled it out and she wrote it down letter by letter, the tip of her tongue protruding between her teeth. 'Thanks! What does it mean?'

'Well, what you said, really.' He paused. 'It means things slotting together, putting shapes next to one another, so they fit neatly, without any gaps.'

'But there are gaps. I can see them.'

'Yes,' he admitted. 'You're right. There are a few.'

'I see what you mean, though,' she said. 'You're good at explaining, like Miss Todd.'

She made another note.

'What are you doing?' he asked, intrigued.

'When we go back to school we have to write about what we did in the summer holidays. We do it every year. I'm keeping it all in here so I don't forget any of it. No-one ever comes to stay with us, so I'm going to write about you. I'm going to tell them everything.'

He shot her a nervous glance.

'Don't worry,' she said. 'I'll make you really interesting.'

As he carried on with his work, he was aware of Alice watching him. Her scrutiny was unnerving, an uncomfortable reminder of the

23

stares he had come so far to escape. He felt a hot flush of shame, recalling the long walk to his seat in the college dining hall at break-fast, conscious of eyes upon him and the muffled sniggers as he passed.

She doesn't mean anything by it, he told himself.

After an hour he was tired, his muscles tense and sore. Leaning forward, he rested his head on the wall, feeling the rough granite cool against his cheek, then closed his eyes. The darkness was a relief. He began to drift, his mind strangely light, thinking, for once, about nothing at all.

He flinched when the small hand touched his shoulder.

'Spencer? Did you fall asleep?'

With an effort, he opened his eyes. 'Oh,' he said. 'It's you.'

'I'm sorry I woke you up.'

He blinked, embarrassed at having being caught napping. He hoped she wouldn't tell Hartley.

'Can I help you?' asked Alice. 'Go on, let me. Please.'

'I don't know . . .'

'You can do the outside bits and I'll fill in the middle.'

He couldn't think how to refuse. 'All right,' he said, and was rewarded by a gappy grin.

She scampered about, picking up small pieces of rock and using her T-shirt like a sling to carry them. Climbing up on a boulder, she slotted them between the outer walls, arranging each piece with care, her brow furrowed with concentration. When she had finished she looked at him, triumphant.

'See,' she said. 'Tessellation.'

He smiled. 'Yes,' he said, 'it is.'

*

At supper he was hungry and ate like Hartley and Thomas, indif-ferent to flavour, craving fuel. That night he ached, his muscles

24

stretched beyond their limits, skin tight from the sun. He had long since learned to distance himself from his body, to consider it simply as a means of transport for his mind. More recently he had come to distrust it. Now, he saw he would be unable to ignore it, reminded daily of its strengths and its limitations.

Despite his exhaustion, he could not sleep, his thoughts springing alive. His insomnia was something to which he had become accustomed. He was used to long nights spent lying still, his eyes open in the darkness, his brain unpicking problems. Sometimes, in the moments before dawn, he would come to a solution that had evaded him in the daytime. Tonight, though, his mind was restless, refusing to cooperate.

Perhaps I should start counting sheep, he thought, grimacing into the darkness.

Instead, he decided to go walking. Slipping on his clothes, he made his way outside, stopping for a moment to let his eyes adjust, then climbing high behind the hut to the top of the fells. Bathed in strange midsummer moonlight, the landscape was transformed into an otherworldly setting, a place of strange possibility in which the bleached skeletons of dead sheep reached out, jagged, from dried-up streams, and foxes flitted with their prey. He was fascinated by the animal remains, picking up skulls and other bits of bone to examine them, trying to imagine the layers of cartilage and muscle, ligaments and veins that once had covered them, turning them over in his hands, intrigued by how they fitted together. He chose a fine ram's skull for his mantelpiece, its long, curled horns intact.

Wandering along tracks trodden bare by generations of sheep, he explored the crags and gullies, jumping from rock to rock, gradually growing in confidence. The sky seemed very far away, arched high above the hills, and very clear. He stopped to look up, gazing at clusters of white stars, trying to make out constellations, drawing imaginary lines between them.

After a while he became aware of a distant rustling. Gradually it grew louder, punctuated by a swishing, thwacking noise, and the sound of someone talking. An elderly woman came into view, striding towards him, beating at the bracken with a stick. Her ferocity was at odds with her appearance. Dressed in a faded yellow frock and battered walking boots, she looked frail, flesh falling away from thin arms, bare legs scratched and bruised and crossed with veins. White wisps of hair escaped the old-fashioned kirby grips that tried to contain them, standing up around her head in a fluffy cloud.

She seemed not to have noticed Spencer, and went on hitting the bracken, muttering to herself. Not wanting to frighten her, he gave a polite cough. Immediately she stopped and looked up at him. Her eyes were a pale, piercing blue.

'Oh!' she said. 'It's you!'

He was startled.

'I don't think we've—'

'It *is* you, isn't it? You came on your bicycle over the pass. I watched you do it. Thought you were absolutely mad to be riding in that heat.'

Spencer recognized the clipped tones of quadrangles and dining halls, formality and privilege.

'I'm Dorothy Wilkinson,' she said. 'And you are?'

'Spencer . . . Spencer Little.'

'And what are you doing here?'

'I – I find it hard to sleep. In this heat, I mean.'

She nodded. 'It's the best time to be out and about. Peace and quiet and a breeze, too, if you're lucky. In the day, it's like Piccadilly Circus up here, with all the tourists. You can't hear yourself think. At this time of night, it's just me and George Gordon.'

She grinned at his puzzlement. 'Byron. He's very good as a

walking companion. It's the rhythm, you see. He's got pace. Ha! I never got on with the Lake poets: Wordsworth and Southey, that sort of chap.'

She waved a stick-like arm in the direction of the mountains. 'I can see all this for myself. I don't think anyone could ever come close to describing it.'

She shrugged off her ancient khaki knapsack and undid the drawstring. Scrabbling inside it for a moment, she brought out a pair of wire cutters, glinting sharp.

'Besides, it's safer at this time of night.'

'S-safer?'

'I'm on the run from the farmers. They keep putting up barbed wire and closing off the paths. The public has right of way of course, but they think they can get away with it. Well, it won't wash with me. So whenever I find a fence where there shouldn't be one, I snip it.'

He thought of the fury that flashed across Hartley's face at the least provocation and felt a sneaking admiration for the tiny woman standing in front of him, brandishing her wire cutters like a weapon.

'They may suspect me,' she confided, 'but they can't prove it.'

She looked at Spencer, cocking her head to one side like a bird. 'You're working for Hartley Dodds, aren't you? At Mirethwaite?'

He was instantly nervous. 'How did you know?'

She shrugged. 'You'll have noticed that this is a very small place. You can't keep much to yourself. Unless you're very good at secrets.' A brief flicker of vulnerability passed over her face. 'You won't mention the snipping, will you?'

He shook his head. 'I promise.'

'Well, I must be off.' She pushed her cutters into her knapsack and swung it onto her shoulders. 'I have promises to keep, / And miles to go before I sleep.'

She set off through the bracken, batting it away with her stick. 'That's not Byron, by the way,' she called over her shoulder. 'It's Robert Frost. Another of my favourites.'

The next morning, Alice sidled up to him, looking uncharacteristically nervous. She had taken to following him, appearing whenever her father was absent.

'Spencer,' she began, then hesitated. 'Spence—'

There was an almost imperceptible pause. He had never had a nickname, had not been the sort of child to inspire intimacy. He was not a man to whom people felt close. Now he found Alice's gesture oddly pleasurable. He accepted it by pretending not to notice.

'Yes?'

'You know how I helped you with the wall the other day?'

He nodded.

'Now can you help me?'

'What with?'

'I'll show you.' She picked up a couple of empty ice-cream tubs from a shelf in the porch and gave one to him. 'Stay,' she said firmly to Shadow, who settled down in a patch of shade, resting her head on her paws.

She led Spencer to an orchard planted with apple trees laden with small green fruit. Rust-coloured hens picked their way through it, stepping delicately, beaks close to the ground, seeking out food. They had stripped the orchard floor, treading it hard and flat, dotting it with greyish curls of excrement. Spencer watched as one of them scratched out a well in the cracked soil, fluffed up her feathers, then lowered herself, ladylike, to take a dust bath in the sun.

Alice pointed to a row of tall sycamores at the end of the orchard, standing next to a stream. Thick roots reached high out of the ground, forming an intricate lattice wrapped in velvet moss.

'That's where they are,' she said.

'What?'

'The eggs. It's where the hens like laying. I'm supposed to collect them, but I don't like doing it. I'm scared.' Frowning, she moved closer to him, her arm brushing against his thigh. Unused to being touched, he felt himself flinch.

'I didn't think you were scared of anything!' he said quickly, to cover his unease.

'I'm not,' she said, primly. 'Apart from hens. They're nasty – you'll see.'

As they went towards the trees, the hens came rushing, heads bobbing, their bottom-heavy bodies moving surprisingly fast.

Alice hid behind Spencer, scrabbling furiously in her pocket.

'Quick! Throw this!' She pressed a handful of grain into his palm. 'Please, Spence! Get them away from me.'

The hens had surrounded them, pushing forward with hard, curved beaks, their yellow eyes bright and questing. Spencer flung the grain as far across the orchard as he could and they swarmed towards it in a pack. As they pecked at the ground, their heads moving in quick, stabbing jerks, Alice grabbed his hand, pulling him towards the trees.

'You go that way. They hide the eggs so you have to really look.'

She was quick to find them, reaching carefully into the roots with her small hands. He was less successful.

'There, Spence, next to your foot.'

Within minutes, their tubs were full and they went back to the house. Alice brought a bowl of water and showed him how to wash the eggs, dipping them gently into it and rubbing them with a damp cloth.

'Are you all right?' he asked.

She blushed. 'It's just that I don't like hens,' she said. 'They're pecky and I don't like their eyes. They're always staring.'

'So why do you have to collect the eggs?'

She looked up at him from under her fringe. 'Because Mam sells them for me.'

He thought of the sign at the end of the lane, and how it had inspired him to turn towards the farm.

'What do you mean?'

'She got the hens so I could keep doing bally. Dad said there was no money to pay for it and I had to stop going.'

'Bally?'

She looked at him quizzically. 'Bally. You know, bally dancing.'

Standing up straight, she brought her heels together, turned out her feet and raised her arms in front of her body, up to shoulder height.

'This is first position.'

Sweeping her arms down regally, she sank into something that looked like a curtsey.

'And this is a demi-plié. That's French.'

Spencer looked at Alice in her faded shorts and wellington boots, glasses slipping down her nose. It was hard to imagine her as a ballerina.

She went over to her bag, which was hanging on the back of a chair, pulled out a book and passed it to him reverently. On the cover was a photograph of a girl, about the same age as her, wearing a white tunic and pink satin shoes, and posed in front of a mirror. The title curled and pirouetted across the top.

Ballet Shoes, by Noel Streatfield.

'I got it from the library van,' said Alice. 'I've read it five times. It's all about three girls who are sisters, well sort of, orphans, actually, who live in a house in London and they go to the Children's Academy of Dancing. It's the best book ever. They've got boarders who stay in their house and are nice to them, a bit like you, really. Anyway, I do bally with Miss Mannering and it's sort of the same but we haven't got proper costumes and we don't go to auditions or do Christmas pantomimes. Selling the eggs was Mam's idea, so we could pay for my lessons. She got the hens for free from a lady in the village. They were scratching up her lawn so she didn't want them any more.'

She shot him a sideways glance. 'Dad says it's a waste of money but it isn't. And Mam doesn't think it is either. I'm going to dance at the show. You can come and watch, if you like.'

'What's the show?'

'It's at the end of the summer, just before we go back to school. There's sheep trials and wrestling and Punch and Judy. Everyone goes. Mam makes cakes for the tea tent, Dad shows his tups—'

She saw Spencer's confusion. 'Tups are boy sheep and yows are girls. Uncle Tom sometimes shows a crook. And Shadow won a ribbon last year.'

She pointed at the line of rosettes pinned to the dresser, shiny red, white and blue. 'But she can't be in it this year because of her pups, so I'm going to make an animal-vegetable instead.'

She came back to the table and went on washing the eggs, balancing them carefully on a tea towel to dry.

'We never used to bother washing them, but Mam thinks we'll sell more if they're clean. She said the holidaymakers would like it.'

He was reminded of Dorothy Wilkinson comparing the fells to Piccadilly Circus. Their encounter the previous night seemed so unlikely that he had begun to wonder if it had really taken place.

'Alice,' he said.

'What?'

'Do you know an old lady called Dorothy Wilkinson?'

She nodded, her eyes wide. 'Oh yes. She lives on the other side of the valley, near the waterfall. She doesn't have a husband, she just lives with her cat. The house is all dark and closed up. Dad says she's an old witch. She looks like a witch too. Once when she smiled at me in the shop, I saw her teeth. They were all crooked and a funny colour. Just like a witch.'

Four

Apart from his nocturnal wanderings, Spencer stayed close at first to the farm. He liked the way that Hartley and Thomas worked, their conversation confined to the job in hand and the weather, a combination of practical sentences and silences, punctuated by short nods and slow exhalations of breath. Their economy of phrase was something he understood, and which appealed to him. They did not invite him on their outings to the pub and he was grateful, preferring to spend his evenings in the hut, working on his maths. He had not forgotten his last, painful meeting with his supervisor. He had sat tense and ashamed as the professor had spoken, his words wounding and precise, making his disappointment clear.

'You know there are others working on this problem? And that there is only one fellowship available?'

He had paused, looking at Spencer thoughtfully.

'I'll need to see substantial progress by the start of Michaelmas term. I hope I can count on you to provide it.'

Spencer had nodded quickly then left, flushed with humiliation. Back in his rooms, he had sat for a long time, cursing the way he had allowed himself to be distracted from his work, losing those last few precious weeks at the end of term. The fellowship was what he had always wanted, the only future he had planned. He had resolved not to let it slip away.

The farm was his retreat, the place where he would find his proof, and now, each night, he worked on his thesis, absorbed in it again, not noticing the hours pass, engrossed.

*

After Spencer had been at the farm for a fortnight, Hartley started to give him jobs to do on his own. The latest was sawing up trees that they had felled for firewood a few days before.

'I thought someone might buy them,' Hartley had said. 'They're not buying much else, but they'll need logs in't winter, at least, for burning.'

Thomas had cleared his throat. 'Do you remember, the choke on't chainsaw broke last time we used it. I haven't had chance to fix it.'

'I'll ring Lance Lutwidge and ask if we can use his. He's still got my bracken sprayer. The lad can bring it back with the saw.'

He had sent Spencer to the neighbouring farm, a mile or so away. The farmyard was like the one at Mirethwaite, but where that was ramshackle, doors looped on with bailer twine, weeds straggling up through the cobbles, this farm was well looked after, its buildings maintained, its cobbles swept clean. There was a spare, almost military feel to it, no marigolds in troughs, the empty washing line stretched tight.

A dog that lay curled up in the porch, its black fur shot through with grey, lifted its head but did not growl.

'Are you going to let me past, old girl?' Spencer had asked, approaching it cautiously.

The dog's ears pricked at a noise behind him. Turning, Spencer saw a man not much older than himself.

'How do?' the man had said, looking at him suspiciously.

Straightening up, he held out his hand. 'H-hello,' he said. 'My name's Spencer. Spencer Little.'

The man frowned. 'Aye?'

'I – I'm working for Hartley Dodds. At Mirethwaite. J-just for the summer.'

He looked Spencer up and down, as if assessing his suitability for the job.

'And he said he'd spoken to someone called Lance Lutwidge to ask if we could borrow a chainsaw for a few days. I-is that you?'

'No,' replied the man, his voice curt. 'It's my father.'

Stepping past Spencer, he had called into the house. 'Dad? Hartley Dodds's sent someone for our chainsaw. Says he wants it for a few days. That all right?'

There was a pause, and then a deep voice came from within. 'Aye. But he'd better bring it back sooner than last time, else he won't be having it again.'

The man jerked his head towards Spencer. 'You hear that? We'll want it back when he's finished with it.'

He nodded eagerly. 'Y-yes, of course.'

There was another pause as he hesitated, building up the courage to ask his next question. 'He, er, said you've still got his bracken sprayer and I should bring that back too.'

For a moment the man had said nothing, then nodded shortly. 'They're both in't barn.'

As Spencer had followed him across the yard, he saw someone else, a younger, blond-haired man, pushing a wheelbarrow full of manure, who stopped, giving him the same brief look of assessment as the man he had just met, then a second glance that was harder to interpret. Spencer had hurried after his guide, anxious to avoid any trouble.

Now he negotiated the ancient tractor and trailer across the field, parking just outside the wood. Six majestic oak trees lay where they had fallen, crushing whatever lay in their path. He walked the length of one of them, running his hand over the rough bark, feeling it catch against the skin of his palm. As he reached the upper branches he noticed a bird's nest and bent to examine the broken eggshells that lay on the ground, their yolky residue stuck to the grass.

Turning back to the trailer, he lifted out the heavy chainsaw, then took out a file and began to sharpen the links, buffing each one until they glinted sharp and clean. Carefully, recalling Hartley's instructions, he flicked a switch and put in the choke, then turned the accelerator to half speed. When he tugged on the starter cord, the machine roared into life, making shudders pass through his body as the chain went on spinning to a blur, belching out thick fumes.

Pulling out the choke, he held the saw against the tree trunk. It glanced off, slipping to one side. He tried again, pressing harder, and soon it found its place, settling into the bark. The valley echoed with the whine of steel against wood, which rang in his ears as he guided the chainsaw down. Sawdust spilled out bright against the weathered bark. He struggled to keep the saw straight as it cut through the dense wood, and it took longer than he had expected, but at last the tension broke and the tree split in two, releasing the sweet smell of sap.

He worked methodically, cutting until the trunk was divided into equal parts, then went back to each portion, carving it into logs. Sawdust swirled in the air but he barely noticed it, absorbed with trying to make the logs identical in size.

Lost in what he was doing, when he next looked up he was surprised to see Alice, standing next to a large, florid-faced man. Switching off the chainsaw, he wiped his forehead, sticky with sawdust and sweat, and nodded in their direction, vaguely annoyed at the interruption.

'You're cutting up the bluebell wood,' said Alice, sadly.

'They'll grow again, Alice, you'll see.' The man's voice was smooth and authoritative, as if he were used to being listened to. Spencer noticed he was wearing a dog collar.

'The vicar's here to see you,' said Alice.

'Indeed I am,' he said. 'How do you do? I'm delighted to meet you, I must say.'

He held out his hand.

'I – I'd better not,' said Spencer, showing his own hand, caked in chainsaw oil and sawdust.

The vicar smiled. 'Don't worry. I've got used to it, living around here. My name's David Loxley. And you must be the famous Spencer Little.'

The only people he had met outside the farm were Dorothy and the two men at the neighbouring farm. The men had not seemed the sort to gossip. It must have been Dorothy, he thought, and felt slightly disappointed.

'Alice told me all about you on our way over here.'

'I told him you're a teacher,' Alice said. 'Not in a school but at Cambridge University and you came here on your bike, all the way from there, and it took almost a week, and Cambridge is very flat.'

He saw the pride in her eyes as she reeled off her list, and couldn't bring himself to be angry.

'I'm a Cambridge man myself,' the vicar confessed, with barely concealed satisfaction. 'Peterhouse, '47 to '50. You?'

'Jesus,' he said shortly. 'Since I was an undergraduate.' He did not want to continue the conversation. 'I'd better get on with those trees.'

Stepping forward, the vicar clapped a hand on his back.

'Well, I look forward to welcoming you into the congregation. Our service is tomorrow, at half past nine. Mary'll be coming; she'll give you a lift. There are lots of people you should meet. We don't often get visitors – at least, not visitors like you.'

Spencer hesitated.

'I – I don't, I mean, I'm not especially . . .'

The vicar wagged a finger at him. 'In a place like this it's not so much about what you believe. It's about joining in. Come for coffee afterwards at the vicarage. It's always rather jolly.' He smiled broadly. 'Well, I must be going. See you in church.'

As he left, Alice made a face. 'I don't like him very much,' she said.

Spencer was inclined to agree with her. 'Why not?'

'He does assembly at school sometimes. He goes on and on and no-one ever knows what he's talking about.'

'Well, I suppose I'd better go to church. Since he came especially.'

'Don't worry,' said Alice. 'I'll come too.'

*

As he went on chopping logs, Spencer thought of the chapel at his college, and the time he had spent there alone at the organ, lost in the swell of sound that filled every corner of the ancient building. Music had always been a comfort, his only pastime apart from maths. His passion was Bach. He had spent hours at the piano, practising scales and arpeggios, training his fingers to cover the keyboard, learning to decipher the dense notation, a respite from the mass of symbols that filled the pages of his notebooks. As a child, he had mastered the rules of the minuet, then the preludes, moving on to his favourite form, the fugue, delighting in its patterns and precision. Countless times in Cambridge unable to wrangle his way out of a problem, he had crept to a music room, or, if it was empty, to the chapel, knowing that the complexities of a sonata or a concerto would distract his brain enough for it to unravel, allowing him to think clearly again. Playing Bach unlocked his mind.

But he had never gone to the chapel for services on Sundays, slipping out of college early instead, crossing town in time to see the choristers marching in a crocodile, disappearing two by two into the chapel at King's. Standing outside, he had been transfixed, listening to the voices that rose, sublime, above the organ, high into the Cambridge air, pure notes, one floating up above the rest. He had allowed himself just a brief moment of pleasure as he listened, imagining the choristers in the ornate wooden choir stalls, their faces raised to the vaulted ceiling, then he would hurry past on his way to the faculty, to his own pursuit of transcendence, the thing that lifted him up and away, both from himself and from everything that surrounded him.

And so the invitation to the performance of Bach's Mass in B Minor had come as an unexpected delight.

His conversation with the undergraduate had turned to music by chance. Spencer had always kept his rooms tidy, but since starting to supervise students in them, he had taken extra care to keep his few possessions in their place. It felt somehow odd, strangely intimate, that undergraduates came there to be taught, and so he left nothing around that would reveal too much about himself. The sheet music on the coffee table was an aberration, thrown down hastily when he had arrived late for the supervision, but towards the end of the hour his student had smiled and picked it up. They had spoken about Bach, finding common ground as they mentioned their favourite pieces, and a shared delight in the hidden patterns of his music.

'I – I suppose it's the way the notes fit together,' Spencer had said slowly, encouraged by the nod of recognition. 'He takes the rules and redefines them, takes them somewhere further than they'd ever been before. It's so logical, so perfect that it seems inevitable, but it's still surprising and still beautiful.'

He had sat in his room for some time after saying goodbye to the student, feeling elated. The lonely solace that he found in maths and music had been taken over by something entirely different. He was not used to that sort of conversation. Maths had been both his companion and his escape. He had chosen it over friendships, content to keep to a world of his own, believing that his work would not be helped by discussing it. But this was a different kind of discussion, one with someone who shared his two passions, and that had made him search for new ways of putting his thoughts into words. He had found it oddly pleasurable.

When he found the invitation in his pigeonhole, a Xeroxed flyer with a scribbled note on the back, he had felt a strange exhilaration. The week until the concert passed slowly, and when the day finally arrived he found himself dressing carefully, taking time to choose from his limited wardrobe. Shaving beforehand, he had looked at himself closely in the mirror, worrying over his reflection.

He had hurried across town to King's, checking his watch, anxious not to be late. Clocks chimed eight, disrupting the still air of a May evening. He was in the chapel by quarter past, sliding into his seat with apologies that were quickly and kindly dismissed.

The performance was polished, the music and surroundings sublime, but Spencer could not concentrate, spending the concert in an agony of distraction, disturbed by how they sat so close that their legs almost touched. Afterwards, they had drinks in a nearby pub, their conversation alternating easily between maths and music, and then walked back to college, parting at the porters' lodge, agreeing to go to another concert the following week.

Back in his rooms, as he brushed his teeth, Spencer had gazed into the mirror again, noticing a light in his eyes that had not been there before.

Mary seemed surprised and not altogether pleased when Spencer asked if he could accompany her to church.

'I'll be leaving at nine o'clock,' she said, 'so don't be late.'

'Holy Joe's found himself a new recruit then, eh?' said Hartley, shaking his head.

'I'm not religious,' Spencer mumbled, but that night he rinsed out a shirt in the stream next to the hut and draped it over a rock to dry. The next morning he put it on, smoothing out the creases with his hands as he hurried down to the farmhouse.

Mary had made an effort too, exchanging her worn clothes for a dress printed with poppies. She seemed ill at ease, already sweating, dark patches spreading under her arms as she combed her hair, looking into the old, blotched mirror that hung on a nail by the kitchen door. Alice had also dressed for the occasion, exchanging her shorts and boots for a blue dress and sandals, her hair brushed down flat.

By nine o'clock they were in the ancient Land Rover, jolting along the track, Spencer perched on the hard seat, its stuffing erupting from holes in the leatherette. The vehicle had seemed dilapidated enough from outside, splashed with dirt, a small sweep of windscreen carved out by the wipers. Inside, it was covered with a thick coating of dust, which lay in deep drifts at the base of the gearstick, clogging the buttons of the radio and obstructing the dashboard dials. Like the farmhouse dresser, every surface was hidden under mounds of old envelopes with their contents stuffed back inside, cracked biros, boxes of animal medicine and loops of string. Wisps of wool fluttered in the grill that separated the seats from the back, which, judging from the smell, had recently been used to transport frightened animals.

'Can you open the window?' asked Alice, who was sitting between Mary and Spencer. 'It stinks in here.'

Spencer slid the inner pane behind the outer, then traced his finger along the fine layer of moss that had started to grow on the rubber window casing, feeling its soft springiness.

They turned onto the road and began to make their way along it. He looked about, trying to distract himself from his anxiety at leaving the seclusion of the farm. The valley seemed different to how it appeared from his vantage point of the hut, the trees suddenly taller, mountains rising high into the sky, looming grey like enormous shadows folded up against one another.

After a minute, he felt Alice's elbow digging into his side.

'That's where Miss Wilkinson lives,' she said. 'Up there, next to the waterfall. Can you see?'

He looked over to a white streak of water tumbling down a fissure in the crags. Below it was a cottage, painted white with black window frames like the farmhouse. A row of trees stood sentinel outside, blocking the garden from closer view.

'How do you know Miss Wilkinson?' said Mary.

It was the first thing she'd asked him since his arrival, apart from if he'd like second helpings at supper.

'Oh,' he said. 'I met her on the fell. She was very nice to me.'

'Was she? She's—' Mary stopped herself. 'Well, she's a bit difficult sometimes, that's all.'

Spencer thought of Dorothy brandishing her secateurs, her white hair sticking out around her head as she talked furiously about footpaths and rights of way.

'She'll likely be there this morning,' Mary continued. 'She usually is.'

Soon after, they passed Dorothy on the church lane, dressed in the same faded frock and walking boots as when he had first met her, striding determinedly, stick in hand and knapsack on her back.

The church was set next to a river with views up to the top of the valley and down, its graveyard surrounded by a low wall. Bells rang out as they walked up the little path through the graves. Inside it was simply furnished, with rows of plain wooden pews facing a lectern and an altar draped with a white linen cloth. Jugs of wild-flowers stood on the window ledges, already dropping their petals.

An elderly woman was playing a muted melody on the organ. Spencer walked between Mary and Alice, listening to the rise and fall of the music, remembering the feel of organ keys beneath his fingers in the college chapel and trying to ignore the weight of the congregation's eyes on his back. Mary kept her face expressionless, looking straight ahead. Suddenly he understood why she had been reluctant for him to join her and knew that he should not have come. Mary hurried Alice into a pew and Spencer slid in alongside her.

The vicar's opening words made him flush with embarrassment.

'This morning, I'd like to say a special hello to a stranger in our midst. Spencer Little is staying with Hartley and Mary Dodds at Mirethwaite Farm for the summer. We welcome him into our congregation.'

The vicar smiled benevolently. Stifling a giggle, Alice nudged Spencer.

'And now let us sing our first hymn – number 437: "Love Divine, All Loves Excelling".'

Despite the cool of the church Spencer found it stifling. He had grown used to the emptiness of the fields, wide skies opening endlessly over his head at night as he wandered over the fells, a perfect contrast to his other world, claustrophobic and cloistered by its high walls, its rituals and routines. He liked his hut, the wind that blew through its walls, its narrow bed, space only for himself, preferring its simplicity to the set of rooms on a solid stone staircase, his name painted on a list at the bottom for everyone to see. He had liked his anonymity, and now he resented the vicar for breaking it.

The rest of the congregation were turned out like Mary and Alice, in their Sunday best. He observed them as they sank to their knees in prayer, the women in summer dresses, creased from sitting, the men in trousers and jackets, and wearing ties. They didn't look like farmers, he thought; their faces were less tanned and cracked than the Dodds brothers', their shoulders narrower in their suits.

As Mary prayed, her hands together and eyes closed, her face relaxed, losing its habitual frown and becoming almost girlish. Her breathing was so slow that she could have been asleep. He guessed that church was one of the few moments in the week when she was free of the jobs that kept her busy long after Hartley and Thomas had gone to the pub.

As people got up from their prayer cushions and settled back into their seats, the vicar began to preach. His sermon was on Joseph's interpretation of the Pharaoh's dream. Standing at the lectern, he read from a leather-bound Bible, his voice filling every corner of the church.

"'I was standing on the bank of the Nile, and there came up from the river seven cows, fat and sleek, and they grazed on the reeds. After them seven other cows came that were poor, very gaunt and lean . . . These lean, gaunt cows devoured the first cows, the fat ones . . . I saw in a dream seven ears of corn, full and ripe, growing on

44

one stalk. Growing up after them were seven other ears, shrivelled, thin and blighted by the east wind. The thin ears swallowed up the seven ripe ears . . ." And Joseph said: "There are to be seven years of great plenty throughout the land. After them will come seven years of famine; all the years of plenty in Egypt will be forgotten, and the famine will ruin the country . . . This is what the Pharaoh should do: take one fifth of the produce of Egypt during the seven years of plenty . . . This food will be a reserve for the country against the seven years of famine, which will come upon Egypt. Thus the country will not be devastated by the famine."'

Rocking back on his heels, the vicar paused and looked around at the congregation.

'There are valuable lessons to be learned from Joseph. In our community, which relies on the weather for its livelihood, times are hard.'

Spencer felt Mary shift in her seat.

'The heatwave these past weeks is by no means comparable to seven years of drought, of course. But I think we can draw the conclusion that being prepared is the key to getting ourselves through it. And being ready to ask for help. I'd like to remind you that the vicarage door is always open to those who want to talk.'

At the end of the service, Mary stood up promptly and moved as quickly as she could towards the back. Spotting the vicar at the doorway, saying goodbye to the congregation, Spencer kept close to Mary and Alice, trying to sidle out of the church unnoticed.

Mary went past with a brief handshake, but when Spencer attempted to follow, the vicar clasped his hand in both of his.

'I'm so pleased you managed to join us,' he said. 'I'm looking forward to getting to know you. You're coming for coffee, of course, at the vicarage. It's just a few people from the village. We're very friendly, you'll see.'

The vicarage, gabled and rambling, stood at the end of a drive flanked with fleshy rhododendrons. Mary stopped the Land Rover in front of the porch.

'We'll see you for dinner at half past twelve, then,' she said.

'Aren't you coming too?'

She gave him a brief, apologetic smile. 'I can't, I've things to do.'

'We wouldn't need to stay for long.'

'Can't we go, Mam?' said Alice. 'We've never been in there.'

'Dinner won't cook itself,' said Mary. 'That roast needs looking after.'

Alice waved as they drove away, pressing her small face against the window. He waved back, feeling again a stab of apprehension.

*

Standing in the doorway to the drawing room, he recognized the scene, the hum of people released from shared duty and given something to drink. He felt conspicuous, and was surprised to find himself wishing that Alice were with him, her small, straightforward presence a buffer between him and the others in the room.

'There you are!' The vicar waved from behind a table laden with glasses. 'Let's get you a drink. There's coffee if you want, but most of us are on the sherry. Complete alcoholics, the lot of us! There's not much else to do on a Sunday around here.'

Flinching at the volume of his voice, Spencer nodded. 'Y-yes please. A sherry would be, er, marvellous.'

The vicar took a glass and poured pale sherry to the brim.

'Let me make some introductions.'

He ushered Spencer towards a group of women standing by the window.

'Ladies, this is Spencer Little, whom you might remember me talking about in church. He's with us for the summer, from Cambridge. He's doing research at the university. That's all I've managed to get out of him so far, but perhaps you'll have more luck. Spencer, this is Valerie Horsley, Margaret Vickers and Janet Todd. I'll leave you in their capable hands. Beware of Margaret, she's on the prowl for volunteers.'

As the vicar moved on to the next cluster of people, brandishing the sherry bottle, Spencer took a sip of his drink, his mind anticipating the inevitable questions. He braced himself for the interrogation.

'Don't believe a word of what he says,' one of the women chuckled. Short and plump, she was fizzing with energy. 'I'm Margaret. Pleased to meet you.' She shook his hand vigorously. 'Although I *am* looking for volunteers, of course.'

There was a brief pause and then she gave another little laugh, tinged with reproach. 'For the fete. The village fete.'

Spencer realized that he had been expected to ask.

'Oh,' he said. 'W-when is it?'

'August. Will you still be here?'

'I – I think so.'

'Well, we must get you involved. Everyone joins in. It's tremendous fun.'

He remembered Alice telling him about her animal-vegetable and Hartley's tups.

'I think I've heard about that. With the competition for the sheep? It – it sounded like quite an occasion.'

Margaret's face fell. 'Actually, no,' she said rather coolly. 'That's the show. It's different. The show's for the farmers. The fete's more of a village thing, to raise funds for the church and the school.'

He took another, larger sip.

'Anyway,' she said. 'We'd love to have you on board.'

'I'll have to see. To check with Mr Dodds, I mean. We're very busy on the farm.'

'Well, there's always the evenings. And if you're not free then, there's always lots to do just before the day itself. We can always use another set of hands to set up the marquee.'

'Oh, leave him alone,' said the lean, well-dressed woman on her right. Unlike the other women she was wearing make-up, her lips painted an immaculate red. As she turned towards Spencer he caught a whiff of strong perfume. 'There's plenty of time for him to get involved in the wretched fete if he wants.' She flashed him a glossy smile. 'Although I'd think carefully about it, if I were you. It seems to get people rather caught up in it.'

Margaret bristled. 'Oh Valerie. I just thought it would be a good way for him to make friends. He can't spend all his time up at the farm with Hartley Dodds and that brother of his.'

'And Mary,' said Valerie, raising a perfectly arched eyebrow. 'We mustn't forget her.'

She was looking at Spencer with something that seemed like amusement. Avoiding her eyes, he looked out of the window. A farmer was sitting on a tractor, cutting grass in the field beyond the vicarage. He wished they could exchange places.

'Hello,' said the third woman, in a friendly voice. 'I'm Janet Todd. I teach at the school in the village. What's your subject?'

'Maths,' he said, glad of the change of topic.

'Maths!' said Margaret. 'Then you could help with the money, sorting out what we take on the stalls. It's really quite tricky. We can never find people to cover that side of things.'

'Are you a student?' asked Valerie.

'Y-yes. I'm doing a PhD. I'm sort of between that and trying to get a research fellowship. But it all depends on my thesis.'

48

'And what's your research about?' Janet asked politely.

'Oh,' he said. 'Well, it's pure maths. It's to do with logic.'

He launched into a description of his thesis, pleased to describe it, as if talking about it made it tangible again, something he could achieve. His tongue loosened by the sherry, he began to talk not just about the details of his research but how it fitted into the study of mathematics as a whole, and how he hoped it would further the field.

After a while, he looked up, and suddenly became aware he had lost his audience.

'Well, anyway . . .' he said, deflated. 'I don't usually . . . I mean . . . It's pretty abstract. Easier to do than to explain.'

'It must be very complicated,' said Margaret.

'It's actually about making things simple,' he said. 'Or trying to.'

Valerie smiled at him again, a complicit, rather intimate smile. 'It's rather nice to hear someone be so passionate about what they do for a living.'

There was a pause.

'And how's young Alice enjoying her summer holidays?' asked Janet.

His mind was still preoccupied with his work. With an effort, he managed to bring his attention back to the women.

'You must be her teacher. She told me about you.'

She nodded. 'She's a bright girl, always asking questions, or looking for answers, even if they're ones she's invented herself. She's a funny little thing. I'm very fond of her.'

'So am I,' he said.

He could see why Alice liked this woman, with her gentle manner and soft voice.

'She'll like your company,' Janet went on. 'A real mathematician! It must be a lonely life for her, up at the top of the valley. And her father's not always an easy man.'

'He's a drunk!' said Valerie.

Spencer suddenly felt an odd allegiance to Hartley. 'He's been all right with me,' he said.

There was another pause, longer this time. Turning his glass to catch the sun, he watched light refract through the crystal. Following its path, he spotted Dorothy in heated conversation with a tall man dressed in a suit.

'Would you excuse me?' he mumbled to the three women.

As he made his way across the room, he was intercepted by the vicar.

'Ah, there you are!' he said. 'Did the ladies look after you? You must come down to the village more often. You'll go mad staying up at the farm all the time. My wife and I often have people round for bridge. Do you play?'

Spencer shook his head. 'I'm afraid not.'

'Well, I'm sure a clever chap like you would pick it up in no time. And I'd be glad of the company. I like to reminisce. I know it's a cliché, but those university years really were the happiest days of my life! Do tell me, though – I don't understand why you chose to come up here, of all places, and why now? Cambridge summers are rather lovely, as far as I can remember. The town must be practically deserted with all the undergraduates away for the holidays, except for the really keen ones. You'd almost have the place to yourself.'

The sherry was suddenly sour in his mouth. 'I – I wanted a change, that's all.'

*

After leaving the vicarage, Spencer and Dorothy walked back along the river.

'I don't agree with cars,' she said. 'They're no good in a place like this. They don't fit. I always think if people want to come here, they should come on foot. It's the only way to understand the landscape.'

Spencer looked up at the mountains, their contours softened by a blanket of lush green bracken. A sudden breeze sent ripples across it as if it were water. Birds, startled, rose into the air, clumsy at first, then settling to hover on the current. In the fields the grass was high, dotted with spots of colour: yellow ragwort and buttercups, burdocks and clover, red and white. The air was thick with the heady scent of the meadowsweet that grew close to the river, butterflies dancing over lace-like flowers.

'Yes,' he said. 'I think you're probably right.'

'There's no probably about it,' she said. 'But they keep on coming. More and more cars, year after year. It's too lovely for its own good. "That fatal gift of beauty", as Byron would have it. At least you had the decency to come on your bicycle.' Abruptly, she changed the subject. 'I wouldn't get mixed up with that lot at the vicarage, if I were you. Busybodies and gossips. I have my battles with the farmers, but at least they keep to themselves.'

'The vicar came to Mirethwaite especially to ask me to church,' Spencer said.

She shook her head dismissively. 'The vicar's a terrible snob. It's only because you're at Cambridge. Do you think he would have bothered if you'd been one of Hartley's labourers?' Her lips came together in a sly smile. 'But his sherry's not bad, I must say.'

They walked on in companionable silence, crossing humpback bridges and climbing over stiles, Dorothy agile as she scrambled up and down the steps, Spencer slower, unsure of where to put his feet. After a while they arrived at her cottage.

'Thank you for escorting me this far,' he said.

For a moment, Dorothy looked as if she were about to blush.

'I was coming this way myself,' she said. 'The rest of it's easy. Just follow the river.'

As they looked at each other awkwardly, not knowing quite how to say goodbye, a terrible howl ripped into the peace of the afternoon, a strange animal shriek. A second later, the cursing began, a torrent of obscenities spat into the summer haze. The swearing was interspersed with long, high whistles and one word, repeated in a low, warning monotone.

'Fly . . . Fly . . . Fly . . .'

Spencer felt his forehead grow damp with embarrassment.

'Ah,' said Dorothy. 'The Dodds are gathering the intakes again.'

'What?'

'I really don't understand how one of them hasn't had a heart attack before now. Thomas is the one who's shouting. Hartley's controlling the dogs.'

'Thomas? But I—'

'It's like this every time they go to bring the sheep down from the fell. They're terribly stupid animals, you know. If one goes off in the wrong direction, the rest all follow. So Thomas loses his temper. Strange that it should be him, he's usually such a shy man. Actually, I find it rather impressive. He's marvellously inventive with his cursing, don't you think?'

Spencer walked back to the farm, dreading what he might find. Hartley's outbursts were frequent but short-lived, unpleasant but expected. This new side to his brother was unnerving. But when he arrived, the sheep were huddled together in a pen, shifting and bleating, contained by gates secured with knotted string. In the house the men were sitting at the table, silent as usual, waiting for their Sunday lunch.

'H-hello,' he said, uncertainly.

Alice jumped up from her seat and ran over to him.

'Spence! You're back!' She looked at him closely, searching his face. 'Spence, are you posh?'

He was taken aback. 'What do you mean?'

'Only posh people are allowed in the vicarage. That's what Mam says.'

Mary came in from the kitchen carrying a joint of beef. Her cheeks were red from the heat of the kitchen, but underneath was a blush.

'Alice! Don't be so silly.'

'But—'

'Alice,' Hartley said in a low voice. 'I'll have no more of that.'

Five

SPENCER DID NOT GO BACK TO CHURCH THE FOLLOWING
Sunday, nor did he return to the vicarage. It was a world he found
at once familiar and oppressive, reminding him of awkward evenings
in drawing rooms, holding on to a glass as security, desperately
searching for something to say. He found no comfort in community
and had no wish to be the latest topic of conversation, dreading the
thought of what the women had talked about after he had left with
Dorothy. He resolved to keep to the farm, the fields and the fells,
avoiding the gossip of the village and keeping his own company,
working for Hartley by day and on his thesis each night, letting it
occupy his brain and find form in the space of the mountaintops.

Alice had become a regular presence as he went about his farm
work, dancing alongside him, Shadow at her heels. He had come to
like their conversations, long and meandering, about everything and

nothing at all. She listened intently, noting down what he said in her scruffy notebook. Realising that she was quick with numbers, he began to set her simple problems to resolve as he got on with what he had to do. She scribbled away, head down, frowning, before shouting out the answers, her face turning pink with pleasure when she was right. He taught her mathematical tricks, ways to remember her times tables, and riddles in logic, enjoying how she greedily absorbed it all.

She always appeared quickly, without warning, whenever Hartley wasn't there, as if she had some sixth sense about his movements. One afternoon, when Spencer had been left to load the trailer with logs, she materialized just as her father had gone around the corner.

'What are you doing?' she asked.

He jumped. 'A-Alice!'

She smiled. 'Hello, Spence. You look dead serious.'

He raised his eyebrows. 'I'm thinking.'

'I can't think on my own without telling someone else. It's too hard.'

Spencer smiled. 'Sometimes it is, you're right.'

'What are you thinking about?'

'Maths. Numbers.'

'How do you think of a number?'

'What do you mean?'

'I mean, what do you see in your head?'

Spencer looked out at the fields, parched grass standing still, undisturbed by the faintest flicker of a breeze, boundaried by the dry stone walls that ran like arteries over the body of the valley. He thought again of Hartley showing him how to build them.

'It's nobbut yan on two and two on yan, and that's all there is to it.'

'Spence?'

'It's not so much that I see numbers . . .' He searched for the best way of putting it. 'It's more like – I feel them.'

'Feel them? How?'

'I don't know, really. They're just – well, I suppose, *in* me, I don't have to see them to do things with them.'

'What sort of things?'

'Well, I put them together, I suppose. On their own, they're not so exciting, it's what they do when you put them together. It's about how things are connected, the consequences of their relationships.'

'What's con-seq-uences?' She stumbled over the word.

'Oh – it's something that happens because of something else, one thing that leads to another.'

She looked doubtful.

'Well, it's like when you're writing in your book. If you just had lots of letters all jumbled up, that wouldn't mean much, would it? But once you start putting them together to make words or sentences, you can tell a story. Then it's interesting. There are stories you can tell with numbers too.'

'What kind of stories?'

'Well, they usually start with a problem that I'm trying to solve.'

She looked up at him and grinned. 'You're trying to find the answers! I like finding answers too.'

'Sort of. Most of the time it's about writing a thing called a proof. Like if you were writing a story about someone, you'd talk about what she's like, and what happens when she meets other people, and what that shows about her, and what it shows about the world. You'd build up to something big that happens to her. And that would show your reader something new about the world, or your heroine, something that you didn't see at the beginning. That's what I do. I write about numbers and what happens between them, and I try to show what that means in a way that someone else can understand.'

'How do you know when you've got it right?'

He thought for a second. 'I feel it. Suddenly it makes sense and it all fits into place. It might be something very complicated, but it's also obvious. It seems inevitable.'

'What's inevitable?'

'It's when you can't see how something could be anything different.'

'Then what? What do you do with it after that?'

'Well, nothing, really,' he admitted.

'So why do you do it?'

'Because—' For a moment he paused, trying to think of how to explain it. 'I suppose I find it beautiful.'

Her eyes were wide. 'Beautiful like a bally dancer?'

'Beautiful like . . . a story, perhaps, when you've picked exactly the right words to tell it.' He thought for a moment. 'Actually, that's not quite right. It's a little bit different, I suppose. If you read a story and you think it's really good, you can tell me why, but that doesn't mean you're right. Other people might not like it. They could argue that you're wrong. With maths you can prove that something's true and no-one can come along later and say that the world's changed and what you said isn't true any more. They might not like the way you've put it, but if your proof's right, they can't change the truth of it. It's pure – it's uncontaminated. Maybe that's the best way to put it.'

'What's uncontaminated?'

'It means not messed up by anything else. Most things are affected by things people do or what they say, like people changing their minds about what's beautiful. Maths isn't like that. It's permanent.'

Alice frowned. 'But why does it matter, if you don't do anything with it afterwards?'

'Well, I suppose it's that pure mathematics exists for itself. It's just what it is. Like those fells over there. They're beautiful, aren't they? But they're just beautiful for themselves. You can put sheep on them if you like but that's not why they're there. It's a bit like that with maths. Maybe one day someone will come along and use your little bit of knowledge to add to theirs, and they might use it for something practical, but it doesn't matter if they don't, it's still true and it's still there.'

'Pure mathy-matics!' she said, rolling the phrase off her tongue with relish. 'I like that. It sounds clean.'

He smiled at her. 'That's exactly what it is. It's the cleanest thing you'll ever find.'

She was quiet for a minute, frowning, thinking hard. Eventually she looked up at Spencer triumphantly. 'I can tell you something about numbers. Something you don't know.'

'Oh yes?' he said. 'What's that?'

'I can count like Grandad used to with the sheep,' she said. 'It's how they used to do it in the olden days. Do you want to hear me do it?'

'Go on, then.'

She sat up straight, squaring her shoulders and nodding her head as she began to chant.

'Yan, tyan, tethera, methera, pimp. Sethera, lethera, hovera, dovera, dick. Yandick, tyandick, tetheradick, metheradick.'

She paused, looking at him from under her eyelashes. 'Bumfit,' she said quickly, and giggled.

Spencer smiled. 'What's that?'

'Fifteen,' she said. 'It makes me want to laugh before I even say it. There are loads of other words too, not numbers, just the ones Dad and Uncle Tom say all the time. But Mam doesn't like me

58

talking like that. She says I have to learn to speak properly, otherwise I'll be stuck here for ever, like her.'

He was surprised. 'Is that really what she says?' He wondered again about Mary's nightly cigarettes and the low-cut dress.

Alice reached out to stroke Shadow, tickling the top of her head. 'I don't want to stay. I want to see all the other places that I've read about in books. And the things you talk about, too. I'll take Shadow with me. Maybe we could come to your university? I could read stories in your library while you do your mathy-matics. That would be nice, wouldn't it?'

Spencer smiled at the thought of Alice striding through the Cambridge streets, Shadow at her heels. He imagined her in the library, reading intently, her dog curled up under the desk. Stranger things went on there, he thought.

'*Are* there girls in Cambridge, Spence?'

He wondered why she was asking.

'G-girls?'

'Well, ones more grown up than me, I mean.'

'Oh! Yes,' he said. 'Yes, there are now, in some colleges, anyway.'

'At your one?'

'Y-yes, a few.'

'Well, maybe I could go there then and you could be my teacher for mathy-matics.'

Looking at Alice, he tried to imagine her as an undergraduate, hearing her high, clear voice questioning, arguing her point in a room off an ancient courtyard. He wondered where he would be then. He would either have made his name or he wouldn't be there at all, that small, precious spark of possibility lost for ever. His chest tightened with anxiety.

'Well, we'll have to see,' he said. 'You can't go until you're eighteen. Lots of things might have changed by then.'

'You'll still be my friend though, whatever happens,' she said. 'I'll still be Alice and you'll still be Spencer. That won't change.'

'Pure mathy-matics,' she repeated, dreamily, as they made their way back to the farmhouse for tea. 'Pure mathy-matics. I like the way it sounds.'

*

Mary was baking when they got there, bent over the rough slate worktop, rolling out pastry. A spicy smell, of currants and cinnamon, nutmeg and ginger, drifted through the house. Alice sniffed appreciatively.

'What're you making, Mam?'

Mary looked up, flour smudged white on her cheeks, crusts of dough stuck to her hands, turning her fingernails opaque.

'I'm filling the deep freeze,' she said. 'There's some pies and a crumble, and a fruitcake. I've made a sponge for tea. I left the raspberries for you to put on top.'

Alice let out a loud whoop of pleasure. 'Thanks, Mam!' Running to her mother, she wrapped her arms around her waist.

'Get off, you daft thing!' Mary said, sounding pleased.

Disentangling herself, Alice went over to the sponge cake, resplendent on a patterned plate. Putting her finger to her lips, she shot Spencer a glance, then dipped it into the thick layer of whipped cream and put it quickly into her mouth. Wiping her hand on her shorts she took the bowl of raspberries and, standing on tiptoe, carefully arranged them on top of the cake.

Mary was looking into a cupboard, sorting through what was inside.

'Damn it,' she said.

60

Alice looked up guiltily. 'What?'

'I've run out of sugar. I was going to make jam with the leftover raspberries. Otherwise they'll go off.'

Spencer had felt a strange sympathy for Mary since the time he had seen her smoking outside in wistful solitude. He thought of what Alice had said about being stuck at the farm for ever and wondered what other life she might have wanted. She worked alone and apart, digging in the garden, tying plants to canes, watering her marigolds in their trough. Her hands were raw from scrubbing and peeling, her bottom lip cracked from her habit of nervously chewing it. Hartley spoke to his dogs more than to her, giving little more than a grunt as she brought food to the table. Spencer had tried to compensate, complimenting her cooking, but it brought little more than a blush and an uncomfortable silence, broken by a snort from Hartley.

'I – I could get some from the shop,' he said. 'I could go on my bike.'

The surprise on her face was gratitude enough.

'It won't take long. Just tell me where it is and I'll go now.'

*

It felt good to be back on his bicycle, which had leant, untouched, against the barn since the day he had arrived. Although it had only been three weeks before, his muscles had begun to forget the action of cycling. He pushed down on the pedals, enjoying the pressure in his calves as they tensed. The narrow road was flanked by rambling, overgrown hedgerows, a mass of foliage and flowers, pale briar roses twisting upwards to the sun, wound around with sweet-smelling honeysuckle. Spencer breathed in, savouring it. Cycling to him had meant freedom from the first time he had managed to wobble along on a tricycle as a child, and he felt it now as he began to pedal through the green tunnels of the hedgerows, then faster, down the centre of the deserted road, enjoying the breeze as he pushed forward, slicing through the heat, and counting the telegraph poles as he passed them, spread out at regular intervals. As he made his way along the valley bottom, he passed Dorothy's cottage, the little track that turned off to the church, the vicarage, hidden behind its bank of rhododendrons, and then the farms; huddles of white buildings clustered on fellsides, ugly corrugated iron barns next to piles of old machinery, rusting in yards. Some of the farmers had already cut the grass, which lay in great swathes over the fields, blond stalks bleaching in the sun. He decided to ask Hartley when they would be making hay at Mirethwaite.

He thought of Hartley again as he rode past a pub on the corner. A lone girl in a black skirt and white blouse was clearing glasses and straightening chairs on the little terrace at the front. Bright blue umbrellas balanced through holes in the middle of rickety tables, advertising Skol lager. A sign swung from the front of the building, festooned with Union Jack bunting.

The Lion and Lamb. Free House.

Spencer wondered if that was where Hartley and Thomas went at night to drink. The bunting seemed somehow too frivolous to appeal to them. In his imagination they went somewhere smaller, more spartan, where the clientele took their drinking seriously, and did it inside.

As he cycled on and the valley widened, the farms were replaced by houses, each in its own well-tended garden. Gradually, they became closer to each other, until they were a village. It was a village with no discernible centre, no duck pond or green, just a collection of houses clinging to the road. There were two buildings that were not houses, standing opposite each other: a tiny post office and a shop with a red-and-white-striped awning.

Village Stores, a sign said. *Props. S.M. and J.F Dickinson.*

Spencer leant his bicycle against the post office wall and crossed the road to the shop. He bent to pat a dog, slape-haired like Shadow and curled up on the threshold, and looked at the hand-written advertisements stuck up in the window: babysitting, painting and decorating, manure and day-old chicks for sale.

As he went inside, the two women standing in front of the cheese counter turned and smiled as if they recognized him.

'Hello,' said one of them. 'Nice to see you again. You haven't been around for a while.'

'Give him a chance,' murmured her friend. 'The poor thing probably doesn't even remember who we are.'

Spencer looked at them, one short and plump, the other elegant, looking at him with mocking eyes. He was suddenly aware that his shirt was crumpled and dusty, patched with sweat after his ride. He ran his hand over his hair, trying to work out where he had seen them before. It was at the vicarage, he realized, just as the short woman spoke again.

'I'm Margaret Vickers. And this is Valerie Horsley. We met at the vicarage. We talked about the village fete.'

'Correction,' said Valerie. '*You* did. Don't drag me into it.' She raised an eyebrow. 'So Mary's got you doing her shopping, has she?'

Spencer looked at her, noticing the perfect symmetry of her features, lips painted the colour of red wine, exotic among the tins of soup and packets of dog food, sprouting onions and bags of potatoes. He hated the insinuation of her questions, the way she sought out gossip like a dog on the trail of fresh meat. He thought of the two deep frown lines etched between Mary's eyebrows and a spark of something like rebellion flashed through him.

'I'll tek yan packet of sugar,' he said to the shopkeeper, ignoring the other two women.

Coming out from behind the counter, she took a bag off one of the shelves.

'That'll be fifteen pence,' she said, looking at him with curiosity. 'Unless you want to put it on Mrs Dodds' account.'

Shaking his head, he handed over the money and left.

*

Cycling back along the valley, Spencer felt a strange exhilaration. He had not planned to speak in dialect, had not realized he had picked enough of it up to be able to do so, but the words had tumbled out of his mouth. They had at least seemed to silence Valerie and put a stop to her prying. He pushed down hard on the pedals, cycling quickly, feeling the wind rush past his ears. Flinging back his head, he shouted out the numbers that Alice had taught him – 'Yan, tyan, tethera, methera, pimp!' – and let out a joyful, reckless whoop.

*

Back at the shop, Margaret was flushed with confusion.

'What happened to him? He seemed such a nice young man when we met him at the vicarage.'

'Perhaps I touched a nerve,' said Valerie.

'What do you mean?'

'When I mentioned Mary.'

'Mary?'

'You never know. It's a strange place, all the way up there. And you must admit, he's better looking than Hartley. And Thomas,' she added thoughtfully.

'Who is he?' asked the shopkeeper.

'His name's Spencer Little,' said Margaret, eager to pass on what she knew. 'He's a student at Cambridge. Does research or something. I'm not sure what in.'

'Maths, he said.' Valerie smirked. '*Pure* maths.'

'And he's spending the summer with Hartley Dodds. Working. For free I heard. Just in return for board and lodgings.'

The shopkeeper shook her head. 'Why would he want to do that? And why would anyone decide to stay all the way up there? It's the last place I'd choose.'

'I don't know,' said Margaret. 'It's very odd, if you ask me. I mean, going from Cambridge University to Mirethwaite Farm? It must be a bit of a shock. I can't see what they'd talk about at night.'

'They don't talk, probably,' said Valerie. 'Hartley and Thomas are always in the Tup. Mary's the one in need of conversation.'

'Valerie!'

'Well you saw how he reacted. A man doesn't react like that unless he's got something on his conscience. Not in my experience.'

'Or if he's provoked,' said a dry voice.

Dorothy Wilkinson was leaning on her stick, looking at them closely.

'Dorothy!' said Margaret. 'You almost shocked the life out of me. We didn't know you were here.'

'Evidently.' She turned to the shopkeeper. 'A quarter of the Wensleydale, please, and three slices of ham.'

As the shopkeeper was cutting it, Dorothy went about the shop, picking up tins of corned beef and tomato soup, a packet of water biscuits and some porridge oats. At the till she stowed them away in her knapsack and counted out coins from a small plastic bag.

Lifting her knapsack onto her back, she picked up her stick and turned to leave. As she reached the door she stopped for a moment.

'He's a nice young man,' she said quietly. 'I won't stand for things being said against him. And you should know better, Mrs Horsley.' She gave Valerie a long look, opened the door and walked out.

There was a pause, broken by Margaret tittering rather uncertainly.

'Well, Mr Little knows how to pick his allies,' she said. 'Dorothy Wilkinson and Hartley Dodds!'

'An old witch and an old drunk,' said Valerie. 'Can I have ten Silk Cut, Jean? I need a cigarette.'

*

The women were not the only ones to wonder about Spencer. Over the next few days he began to drop little bits of dialect into everyday conversation, storing up words that he heard Hartley use and mixing them into his sentences whenever he could. The language of the farm started to form connections in his head as new words fitted themselves to familiar objects. He liked the rough sound of it, the way that speaking like that made him feel as if he were someone else. It brought him closer to the farmers, he decided, and would keep him away from village curiosity.

Hartley, however, was wary of Spencer's new habit.

'I cannot understand the lad,' he said one night in the Black Tup. 'I mean, he must have brains but he acts like a daft bugger half the time.' He took a swig from his tankard. 'There's plenty other places a lad like him could have gone. What's he doing here?'

'Hartley, man, you never know why off-comers decide to do anything,' said Titch Tyson. 'He'll have his own reasons.'

'But usually folk don't come on their own. They've got friends of their own sort. He doesn't ever leave our spot, just goes from working to his hut, then he's back again in't morning, ready for work as early as us. I can't make sense of it.'

'He's a good worker,' Thomas murmured.

'Oh aye,' said Hartley. 'He'll work all day, do whatever you give him, all the roughest jobs that come round. But that's what I mean.

I cannot fathom why. Seems like a waste of his time. And t'other thing is, he's started talking funny – you know – in Cumbrian. The first time he did it, I thought he was taking the piss. I thought he was laughing at us, but there he was, no smile on his face, he just looked as if he meant it.' He took a long swallow of beer. 'It's strange, like, the lad can hardly speak at all, most of the time. Then he starts talking like me father! I don't know how he manages to be a teacher, like, never wanting to say owt.'

'Maybe it's not that sort of teaching,' said Titch Tyson.

'Maybe not. But I still can't fathom it.'

Six

As the summer wore on and the temperature climbed, Hartley's mood worsened. It took him longer to recover from each night's drinking, his face permanently reddened from alcohol and sun. He began to give Spencer harder, dirtier jobs, each one worse then the last.

The day after the sheep had been brought down from the intakes, Spencer and Thomas separated them according to sex.

'Tups on't left, yows on't right.'

'Tups and yows,' Spencer said to himself, remembering Alice's explanation. 'Males on the left, females on the right.'

As the sheep trotted through the narrow corridor between the pens, making dust rise from the hard soil, Hartley counted them out loud in the rhythmic, rhyming way that Alice had taught Spencer, mixing up the old-fashioned dialect with modern numbers. As

Spencer listened, trying to guess the meanings of the words he didn't know, Thomas managed the gates, directing the males to one pen, females to another, expertly hooking them about the neck with his crook when they went the wrong way, jerking back their heads and sending them scuttling back. They bleated, nervous and hot, unsettled by the dogs, which circled, their eyes narrowed, noses close to the ground.

When they had finished, one pen was crammed with ewes pressed tight together, tufts of grey wool escaping through the gaps in the fence. In the other, twenty rams stood, their great horns curling close to impassive faces. Their coats were darker than their female counterparts, great tufts of wool, and they stood as if they knew their worth, chests thrust forward, heads held high.

'You needn't look so pleased with yourselves, bonny lads,' muttered Hartley. 'There's work to be done on you.'

He turned to Spencer. 'Right, then. It's not easy, this. But a clever bugger like you should be able to handle it. What do you think?'

Spencer found the glint in his eye unnerving. 'What would you like me to do?'

Hartley smiled unpleasantly. 'Well, it's a matter of topping and tailing. Taking them to't barbers. Starting at the arse end. See this one here?'

Reaching out, he grabbed the nearest ram by the horns and straddled it, facing its tail, gripping its bulky body between his thighs. As the ram struggled, Hartley sat firm, putting all his weight onto the animal until its front legs buckled and it sank to its knees. Spencer flinched as Thomas picked up a pair of rusty shears, two rough blades fashioned out of a single piece of iron, and passed them to Hartley, whose gnarled fingers gripped them tight. Reaching down, he lifted the ram's tail.

'See all that muck stuck onto him? That's daggings.'

Spencer bent to look. Strange cocoon-like shapes, stiffened and black with excrement, hung heavily under the ram's tail.

'We have to clip them off. The blowfly'll get to them otherwise. Tups are hellish bad for blowfly.'

He was deft with the shears, snipping quickly until the ground was strewn with heavy, matted hunks of wool.

'Got it?' said Hartley. 'That's the barbering.'

Spencer nodded.

'But we're not finished with him yet. I'll need you to give me a hand with this bit.' Taking hold of the ram's horns, he jerked its head back. 'Can you see how they're growing into its cheek?'

Spencer looked at the great ridges of horn curling back past the ram's ears and around to its face, pressing into the sides of its nose and rubbing naked patches in its wool.

'Poor bugger can't see a bloody thing,' said Hartley. 'We'll have to saw them off.'

Thomas passed Hartley a length of wire, bladed with sharp snags. Each end was wrapped around a peg of wood.

'We'll wedge it against the wall, then you hold its head while I cut.'

Hartley took the ram by the scruff of the neck and half carried, half dragged it over to the wall. Immediately, the animal seemed to regain its spirit, kicking and struggling, frantically twisting its head from side to side.

'Hold its backside,' Hartley panted. 'Tight as you can. We don't want it moving.'

The ram was stronger than Spencer had imagined, using all its bulk to shove him away, but eventually he managed to pin it against the wall, using his weight to hold it down. Standing over it, his knee pushed against its neck, Hartley put the wire on one of its horns.

'You have to do it quick enough. Otherwise it'll jam, and you'll never get it going again. Hold him still.'

Spencer gripped the ram's head as Hartley pulled the wire tight and began to saw. As he worked his way into the thick horn, the smell of burning rose into the air. He frowned, concentrating hard, his knuckles white as he seared into the horn, trying to go fast enough to cauterize it. Blood began to trickle down the ram's face and he began to pull faster. It began to struggle again, trying to get to its feet. Spencer could hardly bear to look at the animal, its eyes rolling and terrified. The smell was stronger now, chokingly thick, but Hartley sawed on, grimly focused on his work. At last, the wire cut through the bottom of the horn and it dropped to the ground.

'Get us a cobweb!' Hartley shouted, and Thomas ran to the dipping shed. When he came back, his hands covered with dusty threads, he draped it onto the wound.

'Always works,' said Hartley. 'Couldn't tell you why, but it does.'

The ram blinked, as if surprised to be able to see again. Thomas went over to the horn and picked it up.

'This one'll be good for a stick.'

Feeling slightly dizzy, Spencer stared at the severed horn.

Thomas brandished his crook, crowned with a smooth curve of bone.

'You boil up the horn first, 'til it's all soft,' he said shyly. 'Then you bend it round, and wait for it to get hard. Put it on a good strong bit of hazel, whittled down, and it'll be a good'un.'

'He knows what he's on about,' said Hartley. 'His crooks win prizes every year at the show.'

The ram had stopped struggling and lay, passive, next to the wall.

'Right, then,' said Hartley, and held out the piece of wire to Spencer with a casualness contradicted by the flint in his eyes.

71

Spencer took it, his mind racing. He felt the weight of the unspoken challenge hanging in the air. Hartley wanted proof, he knew, that he could take it, that he was willing to do it, that he was something more than just a visitor from the south, playing at farming on a whim.

He looked down at the ram, slumped and submissive, weakened by the humiliations that Hartley had inflicted, unrecognizable as the beast that had stood puffing out its chest just minutes before. He hated to continue, but knew the only way to prove himself was by making it suffer.

Slowly he pulled the wire taut, tugging at the wooden pegs to test its resistance. It was sticky with blood.

'Wipe it,' said Hartley. 'You want it to be clean. Otherwise it'll stick.'

Gingerly, Spencer wiped the wire on his trousers as Hartley picked up the ram and turned it over, exposing the other horn. They exchanged positions. Pushing his knee into the ram's neck and feeling its tendons give under his weight, Spencer shivered. He pulled at the wire again, gauging how to move it. His mind took over, as he began to calculate. It had taken Hartley about two minutes to sever the horn, each movement back and forth had taken about a second: one hundred and twenty movements to count down. His calculations soothed him, making the task something abstract, reducing it to a proposition.

But his hands shook as he began to saw.

'Keep it fast and steady, lad, and don't stop,' said Hartley. 'That's all you need to remember.'

A fine grey dust began to spill from either side of the wire, falling onto the ram's cheek. Resisting his instinct to blow it away, Spencer sawed on. As he got through the outer layer he reached the quick: deep pink, like the skin under a fingernail, then the red of flesh. Blood began

72

to trickle down the horny ridges, dripping, noiseless, into the dust. He was sweating now, his hair sodden, stinging, salty drops falling into his eyes. Blinking them back, he tried to focus on the wire, moving back and forth, blurred now, faster. He could hear nothing but the pounding of blood in his ears, in strange accordance with his hands, which seemed no longer to belong to him. With an effort he told himself to concentrate, silently repeating Hartley's words.

Don't stop, don't stop, don't stop.

It was then that he noticed the sheep looking at him from behind the stump of the horn that Hartley had cut off. It stared at him, unblinking, a long, dark glare, as eloquent as if it had spoken to accuse him. Spencer stared back, captivated and guilty.

At that moment, the ram gave an almighty buck, flinging back its head and scrambling to its feet. Spencer, caught off-guard, lost his grip on the wire, which remained jammed into the horn. As the ram shook its head from side to side, furiously trying to get rid of it, blood began to pour out of the horn.

'Bloody hell-fire!' Hartley, thrown to the ground, leapt to his feet.

The three men backed away as the animal struggled, beating itself against the wall, blindly trying to put an end to its pain. The blood kept coming, fast, gathering in dark pools.

'It's the artery,' Hartley muttered. 'You cut too close to the head. That's where it bleeds most. There's nowt we can do. By the time I get the gun it'll be dead.'

Spencer stared at the writhing animal in helpless horror. The muscles in his forearms were tight with the tension of sawing and his jaw ached from being clamped shut to hide his fear. But the pain was nothing next to the shame that was beginning to fester inside him: shame for his clumsiness, for having taken on the job to prove himself, and having failed.

The ram was suffering for its own pride, too. As if in agreement, it convulsed once, twice, then, looking at him once again with what seemed like reproach in its eyes, it hung its head and died.

As he looked down at the sheep lying twisted in the dust, he heard the unmistakable sound of Alice singing. The next moment she was with them, Shadow close behind.

'What happened?' she asked.

During the long pause that followed, Spencer braced himself for Hartley's fury. But when the farmer spoke, his voice was thick with remorse.

'Cannot be helped, lad. I shouldn't have got you to do it. Or I should have told you not to go so near the head. I've messed it up myself before now. Doesn't make you feel much good, does it?'

Spencer shook his head, feeling tears pinch at the unexpected sympathy.

*

Thomas brought a wheelbarrow and they lifted the heavy body into it, then trudged across the field to an oak wood. As they grew closer, crows began to circle, rising from the trees, cawing loudly, a harsh cracking noise that echoed in the silence.

'Bastards,' said Hartley. 'They're after its eyes.'

'What?'

'The crows. They peck them out. From lambs, mostly, in the fields. But they'll go for this one now.'

Spencer thought of the ram, standing proud and virile in the pen, then struggling and staggering, bewildered and bleeding. He looked down at the wheelbarrow, the animal's fleece spilling over the sides, its legs sticking out stiffly at angles, hooves stained an unnatural red. The crows seemed a cruel addition to its indignity.

The men pushed forward, passing through a gap in the trees. As they stepped inside, Spencer felt a chill. The wood was so dense that the sunlight could hardly break through. Fungi flourished: strange folds sprouting from tree trunks and rubbery clusters of fine-gilled toadstools, blotched with menace.

With some difficulty, Hartley steered the wheelbarrow between the trees, crushing the toadstools underfoot. Shaken by the jolting, the ram's head fell to one side. Its mouth opened, exposing a row of yellow teeth ground to stumps, like the ones in Spencer's collection of skulls.

As they reached the far side of the wood, the air was filled with a sour, choking stench. It was a dangerous, dreadful smell, and Spencer's instinct was to turn back and get as far away from it as he could. But Hartley pushed on, stepping into it, his face set, gripping tightly on to the wheelbarrow handles. They followed him, Thomas silent as ever, his shoulders hunched, hands thrust deep into his pockets, Spencer still awkward and ashamed, Alice for once silent too. Shadow slunk after them, keeping close to Alice's heels.

When Spencer first caught sight of the pit he covered his mouth with his hands, trying to block out the reek of decay, so thick that he could taste it. He wanted to cover his eyes, to prevent himself from seeing the mass of bodies flung into the shallow grave, lying at angles, backs contorted, legs snapped, dangling broken and loose in differing states of decay. Grey wool heaved and buzzed with blue-bottles that hovered close, sucking at rotten flesh. Other scavengers had been there before them; a ewe lay on her side, her swollen belly ripped apart by sharp teeth, unborn lamb half eaten, crawling with fat white maggots. More lambs were consigned to a pile in a corner, their limp white bodies bearing the same insignia, two gaping eye sockets rimmed with splashes of old blood. Crows perched on low branches, hunched and waiting, ready to gorge.

'Give us a hand,' said Hartley, jerking his head towards the pit. 'Alice, you stay back, and keep that dog away an' all.'

Together Hartley and Spencer lifted the heavy animal, each taking hold of two legs. Spencer looked at its face, lopsided with its one remaining horn, half-split and jagged, and felt quiet pity. He hung his head as they swung the body once, twice, then let it go to fall onto the pile of carcasses with a soft thud.

*

That night Spencer went back to the only thing he knew could steady him. He had not worked at his research for days. The ache in his muscles each evening testified to his achievements on the farm, results that were visible in the solidity of a wall, or in a pile of well-chopped logs. His lack of progress on his thesis was painful to compare.

What had happened that afternoon had unsettled him. The ram had died because of his ineptitude, his inability to refuse Hartley's challenge.

'You weren't good enough,' he muttered to himself as he walked up to the hut.

Stripping off his shirt, he knelt by the stream and dipped his hands into the cool water, letting it trickle through his fingers. He pushed them into the silt, rubbing away the traces of blood, then splashed water on his face and his chest, washing away the sweat that clung to his skin. Rocking back on his heels he closed his eyes for a moment, feeling the sun on his torso, letting it dry him.

He sat down with his back to a boulder and opened out a penknife. For a moment he turned it over in his hand, feeling along the blade with his finger, testing its sharpness. The tip caught a little, drawing a single drop of blood, and he winced, not in pain, but in memory of the ram, struggling wildly as it bled.

The pencil he worked with was blunt and worn. With the pen-knife, he whittled it until he had made a perfect point. He stayed there for a long time, working steadily, methodically, making notations with his pencil. It was as good a cure as it had always been. As he slid into another world, his memories of the day began to evaporate. This other world was far away from the visceral horrors of the afternoon, somewhere abstract, somewhere clean, a place where he could find simplicity, where everything was either true or false, right or wrong. That night he retreated into the familiarity of restoring order, finding patterns, moving towards possible solutions and potential proofs. There was no trace of his usual physical awkwardness as he worked, his movements fluent and calm as he covered the pages with dense, precise script.

He was too engrossed to notice the sky turn burnt orange, streaks of yellow unfurling along the horizon, or the enormous blood-red sun, descending regally into the sea. When it was finally dark he looked up, bewildered, out of place and time.

Seven

THEY WERE SITTING AT THE TABLE, ABOUT TO START LUNCH, when Hartley's voice came from the yard, thick with fury.

'If I catch you doing that again, I'll bray you to hell and back.'

There came a thud and then a high, strangled cry.

'I won't have it.' Another thud.

A door slammed, a bolt rattling across it. The next minute Hartley strode into the room, his face flushed with anger, frowning horribly.

The others stayed silent, Alice fiddling with her cutlery, while Thomas sat, impassive, taking another gulp of coffee. Spencer looked down at his plate, wondering at the scene depicted on it: an ornate Chinese temple next to a bridge over a river, a willow tree, its branches waving in the breeze, a boat passing in the background. It seemed an odd choice for the Mirethwaite table. He resisted the urge to trace his finger along the zigzags of the little fence, not wanting to attract Hartley's attention.

As Hartley stalked into the kitchen to wash his hands, Mary came out, carrying a Pyrex dish that was pillowed high with pastry. Taking a knife she cut into it, releasing a waft of chicken, then served it out onto the Chinese-patterned plates.

Hartley came back into the room, abruptly pulled out his chair and dug a spoon into the bowl of potatoes that sat, steaming, in the middle of the table. Picking up his knife and fork, he attacked his pie, tearing the pastry and spearing pieces of chicken with barely controlled savagery, thrusting them into his mouth and swallowing, almost without chewing. The others ate without speaking, the only sound the scrape of cutlery against china.

When Hartley had finished eating there was a pause, a moment in which Spencer held his breath. Then he spoke, his voice grim with purpose.

'That bitch of yours is going in wi't tups.'

Spencer wondered what he meant. One look on Alice's face suggested it was something terrible.

'Dad!' she wailed. 'No, not Shadow. She's not done anything bad. I'd know. She's always with me.'

His dark eyebrows came together in another frown, deeper than before. 'Well, she *isn't* always with you, is she? Because when I found her this morning, you weren't there.'

'Sh-she ran off while I was feeding the hens,' Alice stammered, shrinking back in her chair.

'You should've gone after her,' said Hartley, spitting out his words. 'Because when I found her she had blood all round her mouth. You know what happens when a dog gets the taste for it. None of the sheep'll be safe. You've seen it before. Remember Shep?'

79

Alice nodded, hanging her head. 'You shot him.'

Hartley shook his head. 'Aye, I did, because I had to. If they get the taste for blood they never lose it. You cannot trust them.'

'But Shadow's never done it before. She's always been good.'

'Doesn't matter. She's done it now.'

Alice was close to tears, her face pink, her breath catching.

'Maybe – maybe it was a sheep that was already dead. Maybe she went back to the pit and got that tup from yesterday. Then it would be all right. It doesn't matter if they're already dead.'

'I haven't got time to find out.'

'But Dad – please! Give her a chance.'

'I am giving her a chance. I could take her out and shoot her now. If I had owt about me, that's what I'd do. But I won't. I'll put her in wi't tups. They'll trample her down. Teach her some respect.'

'Dad—'

'She needs to be battered about a bit. She needs to learn. It's the only way she will.'

'But what about her pups?'

'She's right,' said Mary. 'You can't put her in there while she's pregnant.'

'I can do what I like,' said Hartley. 'I've let her away with enough. She should never have been petted like this. You've ruined her, Alice. I don't know what Thomas was playing at, giving you a dog of your own.'

Alice was shifting agitatedly in her chair, her face wet with tears, glasses slipping down her nose.

'She'll be hurt. Dad, please!'

He leaned forward. 'I'll have no more of this, understand? Or you'll feel the back of my hand. There's nowt else to be done. She needs to have it beaten out of her. We've still got tups penned in at the dipping shed. She can go in with them this afternoon.'

'Where is she? Have you put her in the barn?' Alice's voice was high with panic. 'I'm going to see her.'

'No you won't.' said Hartley.

'I will!' said Alice, defiant suddenly.

Leaping to her feet, she ran past him, slamming the door behind her. He made as if to follow, but Mary said quietly, 'Leave her.'

There was something in her voice, something different from her usual reticence, that startled Spencer. A muscle went in her jaw as she looked steadily at Hartley, challenging him to get up from his chair. He stayed where he was, staring back at her, knitting his eyebrows, breathing hard.

'We should have put the lass in wi't tups too when she was small,' he muttered. 'Might have knocked some sense into her as well.'

Spencer remembered the strength with which the ram had struggled and bucked when he was cutting its horn. He had a sudden horrible vision of Alice's small body in the sheep pens, trampled underfoot, and shuddered.

'She needs to learn,' Hartley continued. 'She can't just do what she wants. She's getting too many ideas. First thing that's going to stop are them bloody dancing lessons. Money's tight and this weather's not helping. We'll not be making much hay this year, with the grass all burnt off. There'll be none to sell and we'll even have to buy it in for winter. We can't be spending money on nowt.'

'No,' said Mary, through gritted teeth.

'Listen, woman, there's no need for it. Why the hell does she need to learn to dance, anyhow? Where's it going to get her?'

'She likes it. And it does her good to get away from here.' Mary shook her head. 'It would do us all good.'

'What are you saying?'

'You know what I mean.'

'That's enough,' snapped Hartley. 'I've decided, and that's that.

81

She'll stop going. And we'll use the money for things we need.'

'On drink, more like,' muttered Mary under her breath.

Hartley stood up and pushed back his chair. A vein in his temple was pulsing hard, beads of sweat standing out on his forehead. As he moved towards her the chair leg caught on a flagstone. He stopped it with his hand and set it straight with a bang.

'Right,' he said, his jaw clenched. 'I'm going to get that dog and teach it to behave.'

He turned and strode out of the door. Thomas got to his feet, nodded at Mary and Spencer, and went after him.

Spencer looked over at Mary. She was shaking, gripping the edge of the table, her knuckles white. He felt out of place, an awkward witness to the scene, caught between wanting to leave the room and to make sure she was all right. He had a sudden irrational desire to stretch out his hand and brush back her hair, which had fallen over her face.

'A-are you all right?' he said cautiously.

She didn't respond. He listened to the clock tick, loud in the silent room, and counted ten beats, shy about what to call her. Until now he had avoided addressing her directly.

'M-Mrs—' He tried again. 'M-Mary?'

She turned her face to him, her eyes very dark against the paleness of her skin. For a moment they looked at each other, saying nothing.

She was the first to drop her gaze.

'He's not always like this,' she said quietly. 'It's the drink. And this heat. It's making him go sour, like gone-off milk.' She shook her head. 'But it's not fair on Alice. He's got this idea in his head that the dancing's too good for her. He's never liked it. I thought I could get round him by making the money myself, but now he wants to take that too.'

82

Spencer thought of the pride in Alice's eyes as she showed him her demi-plié, the little spark of hope as she explained about her lessons.

'I-I could help,' he said. 'I've got a bit of money. It could keep her going for the summer.'

Mary shook her head. 'I couldn't take it from you. It wouldn't be right.'

'But it wouldn't be for you, it'd be for Alice. I'd like to help. I'm very . . . Alice is a good girl.'

'That's nice of you, Spencer,' she said with a sigh. 'But I can't. He'd know. It'd just make him worse. Anyway, it's not really the money. He just doesn't like her doing it.'

'But—'

A bellow of anger came from the yard. Exchanging glances, Spencer and Mary shot to their feet.

Hartley was standing outside the barn, staring at the open door.

'She's taken the bitch,' he said, kicking at the wood. 'She's run off with it. Where the hell has she gone?'

They said nothing, watching the colour rise in his face.

'When she gets back I'll thrash the living daylights out of both of them. She won't be doing this again in a hurry.'

He kicked the door again. 'And if a thrashing doesn't teach that bitch a thing or two, the tups will. I'll not forget to do it.'

Turning to Spencer and Thomas, he jerked his head in the direction of the sheep pens.

'Right, Tweedledum and Tweedledee. We'll get on with that dagging while we're waiting.'

*

As the three men worked their way through the flock, clipping off stinking clumps of wool, the air was thick with Hartley's resentment. He gripped the shears hard, viciously snipping at the animals' hindquarters. Often he went too close, catching flesh and making the sheep jump and buck. He handled them roughly, his fury barely contained.

Spencer found himself staring at Hartley's thick fingers as they cricked back a sheep's neck, powerful fingers used to getting what they wanted, by force if that was what it took. He thought of the yelps that they had heard from Shadow before lunch, and dreaded what would happen to her and to Alice when Hartley found them.

It was very still that afternoon, and very hot. Sweat poured down Spencer's back as he worked, soaking his shirt. He wished he dared take it off and work bare-chested, but Hartley and Thomas never removed the least bit of clothing, refusing to undo their shirts any more than a button, oddly proper and contained. His collar rubbed at his neck, tufts of gritty wool gathering in the creases of his skin, which he knew would be raw by evening.

The sheep were fretful, sensing Hartley's mood, shifting and pushing, bleating nervously, releasing anxious streams of excrement. Crows perched in the hawthorn trees that grew next to the pens, their claws wrapped tight around the spiky branches, peering at the scene below.

It was the crows that gave the first hint that something was wrong. Bending over a sheep, clipping carefully around its tail, Spencer heard a cracked, urgent cawing. He looked up to see a flurry of wings as the birds rose from the trees, beating a hurried path towards the bluebell wood. The sheep seemed to feel something too, calling to each other, shifting about, pushing at the fences that contained them. Even the dogs had stopped their snarling, their noses raised, sniffing at the air.

Spencer let go of the sheep that he was holding and straightened up. As he stood, trying to make sense of the animals' agitation, he saw a figure on the intake, standing very still. The next moment, the figure began to run down the hill, limbs flying, tumbling over gorse bushes and rocks. In the same instant that he smelled the first whiff of smoke, Spencer realized it was Mary.

For a moment he didn't move, tasting the smoke, wondering where it was coming from. Then he saw it, little drifts of grey rising up through the bracken. As he watched, flames began to flicker, then push across the ground in swathes. It was mesmeric, almost beautiful, the air shimmering above the fire in a haze.

A shout from Hartley brought him to his senses.

'Get the beaters!' he yelled, running to the gate at the bottom of the intake and throwing it open.

Spencer and Thomas were there immediately, following him to a stack of paddles piled against a wall, squares of black rubber cut from tractor tyres and nailed onto stakes. As they approached the fire, beaters in hand, Spencer could hear it greedily eating through the undergrowth that lay beneath the bracken, parched from weeks of sun. It was a low, busy noise, punctuated with popping and cracking as the fire devoured its way forward. Now he was glad of his shirt, as protection against the heat, ten times stronger than the afternoon sun, a dry, intense heat that seared into his eyeballs.

'Spencer, head it off at the top,' shouted Hartley. 'Thomas, take the right and I'll go left.'

They split up, attacking the fire at its edges, trying to contain it, pounding the heavy beaters against the hard ground. Each time Spencer brought down the beater, hot ash rose up, filling his mouth with grit, and soon his hands were blistered and raw from gripping the stake. Their efforts made no difference as the fire continued to spread, little licks of flame escaping, leaping off to start a new blaze. As soon as they managed to extinguish one, ten others sprang up, the fire multiplying like a mythical creature across the intake.

'Shouldn't we call the fire brigade?' Spencer suggested, panting, to Hartley.

Hartley raised his arm, wiping his face on his shirtsleeve, leaving streaks of ash across his forehead.

'No point,' he said. 'Nearest station's an hour away. It'll have gone all over by then, if we don't get it put out.'

They went on beating, racing the fire, which had taken hold and was burning fiercely, flames leaping high as they reached a thicket of dried-out gorse. The smell of charred rubber from the beaters began to add to the acrid smell of smoke.

Standing back from the blaze, Spencer heard something very faint, muffled by the crackle and hiss. He listened harder, straining to hear as the sound came again, louder. Suddenly he realized what it was: a child's wail, punctuated by a dog barking.

'Alice!' he shouted.

The others seemed not to hear him, continuing to beat against the flames. He thought quickly, trying to imagine where she might be hiding. When the sound came again, he suddenly knew where she was, the place she would have chosen to keep Shadow out of Hartley's hands.

She had shown him it the week before, leading him up the intake, taking him via a circuitous route 'so you don't remember exactly where it is, Spence'. By the time they had reached the cluster of boulders, high up near the boundary wall, he had been out of breath. She had made him close his eyes as they approached, busily pointing out obstacles, guiding him over rocks and branches, her small hand in his.

'Bend your knees,' she had said, 'so you don't hit your head.' They went into somewhere shady, out of the sun, smelling faintly of sheep.

'You can open your eyes now.'

He was in a dim space, almost a cave but not quite, created by two great boulders balanced against each other.

'This is my den,' Alice said proudly. 'Isn't it brilliant? Do you like it?'

Spencer nodded. 'It's wonderful.'

Busily, she unpacked the basket she had carried with her. 'I got some plums off the tree and some strawberries so we can have a picnic.'

She snapped off a head of bracken, and made plates out of two fronds, balancing little piles of strawberries on them, and then passing one to him.

Sitting on the floor of the cave, which Alice had carpeted with more bracken, Spencer had eaten the sweet-tasting strawberries. Shadow lay between them, panting heavily, her long pink tongue lolling out of her mouth.

'I thought she could have her pups here,' Alice said. 'But I'm worried in case they might fall over the edge.'

'It might be better for her to have them in the barn,' suggested Spencer. 'Then you can go and see them whenever you like.'

'I know,' she said. 'It's just that I like this place, that's all. No-one else knows about it, not Mam or Dad or even Uncle Tom. Only us.'

Throwing down his beater, Spencer began to run. The fire was spreading quickly now, up towards the boulders at the top of the fell. The wail came again, louder, and he picked up speed, his muscles straining as he ran, ignoring the heat that rose through his boots, dodging the blaze of gorse bushes. As he grew closer he saw Alice and Shadow standing on top of the rocks that went to make her cave, fire closing in around them.

'Spence!' screamed Alice, waving frantically. Shadow was barking and running about in circles.

'I'm coming,' Spencer shouted. 'I'm coming. Don't move. Stay where you are.'

Picking his way between the rocks, he began to climb, his palms burning on the hot stone. At last he pulled himself up to where Alice stood. Her glasses were filthy, her cheeks wet with tears, streaking the ash that caked her face.

'You're here,' she sobbed, throwing her arms around him. 'I knew you'd come. I'm sorry, I just wanted to save Shadow. I wanted to keep her away—'

Clumsily he patted her head. 'We need to get *you* away from the fire.'

'And Shadow.'

'Of course.'

Reaching down, hoping he would be strong enough, he hooked an arm around Shadow, lifting her to his hip.

'You need to get onto my back,' he said to Alice, bending down.

She ran a couple of steps and then jumped, clasping her legs around his middle and putting her arms around his neck.

'Now hold on tight,' he said. 'I'm going to try to run. It'll be very hot. Try not to breathe in too much smoke. It won't last long, I promise.'

He went to where the fire burned high, hesitated, then, taking a deep breath, stepped into the flames. Alice screamed.

'It's all right,' he shouted. 'Just keep holding on.'

Her small arms tightened around his neck, almost choking him as he blundered through the fire, weighed down by his double load. Shadow was as heavy as Alice, her swollen belly soft against his side. Alice continued to cling to him, her small body pressed against his back, her cheek against his neck. He could feel her breathing as he made his way, half running, half stumbling, down the intake. It would take a hundred and fifty steps, he thought, to get to the bottom. Not allowing himself to look anywhere but the path, he counted them, forcing himself to stay focused, taking his mind away from the heat.

One . . . he almost tripped over a rock . . . One, two, three . . . five . . . eight . . . thirteen . . . twenty-one . . . thirty-four . . .

As he grew closer to the intake gate he saw Mary standing, her hand over her mouth.

Fifty-five . . . eighty-nine . . . a hundred and forty-four . . .

He reached her. Shadow immediately wriggled free from his grasp, then slunk under the gate to safety. Alice, in contrast, didn't move, her arms around his neck.

'Alice, love,' said Mary, white-faced. 'Are you all right?'

She said nothing, burying her face in Spencer's neck.

Gently, he bent his knees. 'Come on Alice, you're safe now. You can get down.'

Mary moved over to her and stroked her hair.

'I'm sorry, love. I'm so sorry.'

Hartley and Thomas arrived at the gate, breathing heavily.

'Is she all right?' said Hartley, sounding shaken.

Mary was silent.

'Yes,' said Spencer. 'I think so. Alice?'

She wouldn't look at Hartley, but nodded, pushing her nose against Spencer's collar.

'There's nowt to cry about now, Alice,' said Hartley, his voice almost tender.

She shook her head, saying nothing.

'Best take her down to the house. I reckon we'll able to stop it going any further. There's the intake wall, it won't cross that. Thomas and I'll make sure it doesn't, anyway.'

Spencer nodded.

Hartley looked at him. 'Thanks, lad. You did a good thing.'

As he and Thomas went back up the hillside, beaters in hand, Spencer and Mary made their way back down the lane to the farmhouse. Mary continued to say nothing, her head down, lost in thought. Alice was heavy on Spencer's back, nuzzling into his neck, her glasses pressing against his skin.

As they reached the end of the lane he turned to look at the fell. Hartley and Thomas were at the intake wall, still bashing at stubborn flames. The fire had carved a black scoop out of the fell, dark and startling against the green of what little bracken was left. Wisps of smoke rose at intervals from the smouldering undergrowth. As they walked down through the sheep pens they saw the tops of fences frosted with ash like a layer of grimy snow.

In the dark cool of the farmhouse, Alice agreed at last to climb off Spencer's back. Mary sent her to have a bath.

'I want you to go and get cleaned up. Then you're going to bed.'

'But Mam! It's still light. I'm not a baby. And I'm not ill.'

'You've had a shock.'

It was Mary who looked as if she were in shock, her eyes burning in her pale face. Her hands shook as she twisted a handkerchief, wrapping it around her fingers, then unwinding it to start all over again.

'Go on,' said Spencer gently to Alice.

She loitered in the doorway at the bottom of the stairs. 'What about Shadow? I have to make sure she's all right.'

'I'll do it. I'll put her in the barn. I'll give her something to drink.'

'Will you do it now?'

'This minute.'

He was glad to have an excuse to leave Mary for a while. As he collected the tin bowl from the porch and filled it with water from the outside tap, he wondered why she had been on the intake. She rarely went further than the yard. The house was hers, the rest of the farm Hartley's, and they stuck to their separate domains.

Putting the bowl down in a corner of the barn and scattering some straw, he whistled, imitating Hartley, a thin, piercing noise that he breathed out between his teeth. Shadow came running and lapped at the water thirstily.

'Good girl,' he said, stroking her.

Back inside, Mary had made tea. She was sitting, still pale, her hands wrapped around a mug, gripping it tight. He sat down opposite and poured tea into the mug she had left for him, adding milk from the jug. As steam rose from it, he thought again of the thick smoke, remembering the acrid taste that it had left in his mouth, and left the tea to cool down.

He looked across the table at Mary.

'A-are you all right?'

Slowly she raised her head. There was fear in her eyes.

'It was me, Spencer,' she said. 'She nearly died because of me.'

He blinked, not understanding. 'W-what do you mean?'

'I nearly killed her. Alice. My own little girl.'

Spencer waited, trying to suppress his growing sense of unease.

'I was so angry. I can't stand him like this. He used to love us, you know, in his own way. He called her Apple, for the apple of his eye. He'd take her along with him when he was working to show her how to run a farm. At night they'd sit and talk about how the sheep were coming on and when to bring them down from the fell. He said she'd have to know all that for when the farm was hers. He said it didn't matter that she was a girl, that she was as good as a son. Now he just goes to the pub with Thomas, then comes in drunk and falls into bed. He's vicious in the morning. You've seen him. Most of the time I ignore it. I just get on with my jobs and keep going. But today I couldn't stand it when he started picking on Alice. It riled me. I needed to calm myself down. So when you'd all gone up to the pens, I decided to have a cigarette.'

She looked at Spencer guiltily. 'I don't do it very much. Hartley doesn't know. He made me give up. He said we couldn't afford it. But I liked it. It used to make me feel like I was someone else, someone not from round here. Before we got married, I'd go to the pictures and I'd see all those films of what was happening in London. They were all there, drinking and dancing, doing what they wanted. They had long hair and smoked cigarettes and they were having a nice time. I thought of going myself, but it didn't happen. I married Hartley instead and stayed here. But sometimes, when I'm on my own, I like to pretend.

'I had two pigs, a couple of years ago,' she went on. 'I raised them myself from when they were just piglets, and when they were big enough, I sold them. Hartley took most of the money, but I kept some of it back. One day I took myself off to town and I bought myself an outfit: shoes and a dress, the sort of thing I'd wear if we ever went out. But we never do, so sometimes, when he and Thomas have gone off to the pub, I wear it, just to remember that something around here can be nice. I smoke cigarettes and pretend I'm not me.' She glanced at him. 'I suppose you think that's daft.'

Spencer thought of the woman in the red dress leaning against the farmhouse wall in the sun, and of what Alice had said about Mary not wanting her to be stuck in the valley like she was.

'No,' he said quietly. 'I know what it's like to want that.'

'Usually I'd never smoke in the day,' she went on. 'I wouldn't want Hartley to find out. But I was so angry. I went up to the intake and sat behind a tree then I smoked four of them, one after the other, until I felt sick. I'm always careful about putting them out. I've got a shell I brought back from our honeymoon, when we went to the seaside. I put them out in that and then I hide them in the bottom of the rubbish. But I wasn't going to take that up the fell. When I'd smoked the last one, I thought – well, I didn't really think – I'd just let it drop. I wouldn't put it out, I'd just see what happened. So I threw it down. I watched it catch a piece of dead bracken and burn it all the way along. Then it jumped to another piece, this one little flame that just kept spreading. I don't know why I didn't do anything, I just watched until it hit a gorse bush and the whole thing went up. That was when I knew I'd done something wrong. I ran back down the fell, like a little kid in trouble.'

'I saw you,' he said.

Quickly, she looked at him, a swift, nervous glance. 'Did he see me too?'

'I don't think so. I just looked up and you were there.'

'Don't say anything, will you, Spencer? Please?' She leaned over the table, begging him with her eyes.

'No,' he said quietly. 'I won't say a word.'

'Thank you,' she said. For a moment her eyes met his, then she stood up and began clearing away their mugs.

*

That night the muscles in his arms and thighs were taut from carrying Shadow and Alice. He stretched the full length of the bed, trying to loosen them, turning his head from side to side to ease his neck, sore from Alice's grip. He thought of her clinging to his back, and how he had felt her heart thump as they made their way down the hill. It was the closest he had been to another human body for as long as he could remember. He swung his legs over the edge of the bed and sat up, reached for his notebook, and tried to distract himself from the thoughts he knew would inevitably follow.

Eight

On the fell, the peat caught fire and burned on, transforming the landscape into barren emptiness, reducing soil to ash, stripping it back to bare rock. From time to time strange streaks of smoke rose from the ground, a reminder that the fire was still alive under the surface. Back at the farm, the household was subdued. Twice Spencer noticed Mary standing motionless at the window in the kitchen, looking up towards the intake. Hartley became less brusque towards Alice, no longer snapping at everything she said. Two days after the fire had begun, as he was getting ready to go out, he turned to Spencer.

'Me and Thomas are off to't pub.'

Spencer wondered why he was telling him. It was what they did every night.

'You can come with us if you want,' he said, jiggling loose change in his pocket. 'I'd like to buy you a pint,' he said. 'You know, to say thanks, like, for saving me l'aal lass from that fire.'

Spencer felt Mary's eyes on him as he left with Hartley, but didn't look back.

*

The pub was not the one he had passed on his way to the shop. Instead, they turned up a little side road, a bridleway not quite wide enough for a car to pass through. At its end was a low building, its whitewashed walls glimmering in the moonlight and its windows glowing warm. A black ram stared out proudly through its horns on the sign that hung above the door.

'This is it,' said Hartley. 'The Black Tup. I've been coming here since I was a lad of fourteen.'

He pushed at the heavy door and strode inside, Spencer and Thomas following close behind, their boots clattering on the slate floor.

It was one room with a bar, a few tables nestled in corners and old settles fitting snug against thick, uneven walls. A dog was asleep in front of an empty, blackened fireplace as if the fire had been lit. The room was filled with a low, masculine hum, the only woman a barmaid, aged somewhere in her fifties, standing behind the polished brass pumps, her hair a hopeful blonde. As they approached, she took two tankards from their hooks and filled them both with dark, frothing beer. Setting them on the bar she nodded at Spencer.

'And what about you?' Her voice was not entirely friendly.

Hartley spoke for him. 'He'll have what we're having, Sheila, and I'm paying.'

She raised her eyebrows.

'Put it on my tab. He saved me lass from a fell fire. I owe him.'

'Your Alice?'

'That's right,' said Hartley, taking a long swallow of beer. 'She was messing about on't fell. A fire started out of nowhere, then it just spread all over t'intake. It'll never grow back. The soil's burnt off, all gone. Anyway, the lass got up there somehow, right at the top. Spencer here ran through the fire and got her on his back. He brought her down. If he'd left it a few minutes later we'd have been in trouble.'

She shook her head. 'Titch Tyson had a fire t'other day. Everything's that dry, it just goes up. And once it does, you can't stop it. Is Alice all right, then?'

'Oh aye. You know kids. They forget things like that as soon as they've happened.'

A muscle in her arm bulged as she pulled the pump a final time.

'There you are,' she said, now smiling. 'Spencer, wasn't it? This one's on the house.'

*

They sat at a table in the window, the brothers opposite each other, Spencer on a stool at the end looking around the room. Men sat alone at the bar or in pairs at tables, each with his pint of beer in front of him. They talked quietly, playing dominoes, smoking, adding to the fug that filled the air. Spencer watched as they drank, swallowing the beer in long, easy gulps.

At the end of the bar he noticed someone familiar, a man who seemed to be looking back at him. Taking a swig of his pint, he tried to work out who he was. When he glanced over at the bar again, the man was still looking, his expression impossible to read. Spencer suddenly realized where he had seen him before: pushing the wheelbarrow through the neighbouring farmyard. Suddenly feeling as unnerved as he had been that first time, he dropped his eyes and turned to Hartley and Thomas.

After the first few pints, Hartley's face began to relax. He became buoyant, teasing Spencer as they played dominoes.

'I'd have thought you'd be better than this, mind,' he said as Spencer lost for the fifth time. 'Aren't you meant to be the number expert? That's all it is. Matching them up and counting, and that.'

Spencer shook his head, befuddled from the beer and still conscious of the man at the end of the bar. He was thankful that he could stay where he was, seated at the table. Each time he emptied his tankard, Hartley was back at the bar buying rounds of drinks for Thomas and Spencer, and then for the other farmers too. The story of the fire took on a life of its own, the details growing wilder with each pint.

While Hartley was at the bar and Thomas had gone to the grubby urinals tucked away behind the kitchens, Spencer became aware of the man's gaze once more. Trying not to look at him, he focused instead on a stuffed fox head mounted on the wall, its angry eyes staring, pointed teeth bared in a snarl. A dull russet brush hung from the mantelpiece below. He did not like to think of what had happened to the rest of the animal's body.

On the walls were black-and-white photographs of men clustered outside the pub holding up glasses, hound dogs milling around them. Underneath were portraits of single huntsmen, each holding up a dead fox. The photographs had dates written on them in a spidery hand. *Easter 1922, Boxing Day 1962, New Year's Day 1975.*

'Can you spot us?' Thomas asked, sliding back into his seat.

Spencer peered at the photographs. There seemed little difference between them. One man, clearly the leader of the group, was dressed in a scarlet waistcoat under a long coat, knee-length britches and white socks. The other men were dressed in their usual uniform of trousers and jacket, impervious to fashion. Tweed caps finished off their outfits, the same brown as the britches. Hairstyles had not changed over the years – a practical short back and sides for all. The same craggy faces gazed out from the pictures, some smiling, others self-conscious. Eventually, on the picture labelled *New Year's Day 1975*, he managed to spot Hartley and Thomas, standing at the edge of the group, and looking slightly the worse for wear.

'Is that you?' he asked.

'Aye. That was a grand day, last year.' Thomas took a swig of his beer. 'But can you see us in't one above?'

Spencer looked carefully, trying to make them out. 'No,' he said, after a while. 'Where are you?'

Thomas pointed to two men in the centre of the photograph, grinning, their faces easy and carefree. They posed with a reckless swagger, filled with youthful confidence, raising their glasses to the camera, their eyes glinting with anticipation of the chase to come.

'1963,' he said. 'We were twenty-one. We thought we ruled the world.'

Spencer suddenly realized that the brothers were twins. He had assumed that Hartley was the older of the two. He also realized they were only ten years older than him. Before he had thought them forty at least.

Thomas pointed to a tall, stooped man at the back of the photograph. 'That's our dad. He loved the hunt. Took us from when we were lads.'

Fumbling to respond, Spencer realized what was odd about the photographs. 'Where are the horses?' he asked. 'I thought you needed horses for hunting.'

Hartley, returning from the bar, guffawed.

'Horses are for those fancy buggers down south. Who's got the money for a horse? It's Shanks's pony, up here, for us, and you have to be in good fettle to do it.' He clapped Spencer on the back. 'We're out of season now, or I'd have taken you out with us.'

It was hard to get used to Hartley's new, jovial manner. Together with the beer, it made Spencer feel disoriented, as if he had stepped into another world, somewhere far away from either the competition of Cambridge or the tensions of Mirethwaite. Now Hartley was going over to the bar and ordering three large glasses of whisky. He brought them back to the table, his cheeks flushed, eyes bright under dark eyebrows.

'Right then. I'd like to make a toast. Spencer, lad, I cannot pretend I wasn't doubtful when you turned up on that bike of yours. Going over the pass on't hottest day of the year. I thought you were mad. But you've been a bloody good worker since. And, well, you saved me l'aal lass.' He raised his glass. 'Cheers Spence, you're a proper marra.'

'What's that?' asked Spencer, doubtfully.

'Ha!' said Hartley. 'I thought you were an expert? It means mate.'

The whisky burned its way down Spencer's throat, sending waves of warmth through his body. For a long, blissful moment he felt entirely at ease. For once he felt part of things, included, safe within the cosy walls of the pub, tucked away from the complications of the world outside.

As someone came up to the table, Spencer quickly raised his head, thinking it was the man from the end of the bar. Realising that it wasn't, he looked over to where the man had been sitting; he saw that his stool was now empty.

The newcomer nodded at Hartley and Thomas.

'How do, lads?'

'How do, Malcolm?' said Hartley. 'This is Spencer. Our clever bugger from down south. Just saved Alice from a fire.'

'Aye, I just heard. You can't be too careful. It's all dry as tinder.'

'Nowt like that's happened to you?' asked Hartley.

'No. I've been all right so far, apart from the sun drying my hay out too quick. I'd get yours done soon, if I were you. You've got a pair of extra hands to help, at least.'

He looked at Spencer curiously, as if he were assessing his capabilities. 'Seems like there's offcomers all over the place,' he continued. 'We're getting popular.'

'What do you mean?' asked Hartley.

'Have you not heard? There's a load of them down at Titch Tyson's. Hippies, they call themselves. Long hair and trousers tighter than a gnat's arse. They brought a load of clapped-out minibuses over the pass a couple of days ago. I'm surprised you didn't notice – they made enough noise. Anyway, they've pitched their tents in one of Titch's fields, but he doesn't want them staying more than a couple of nights. They want to stay for the whole summer. I don't know who'd want them on their land, not for that long.'

Hartley looked thoughtful. 'Will they pay to camp, like?'

Malcolm nodded. 'A bit, Titch said.'

'How many of them are there?'

'About eight, I reckon, maybe a couple more. Young lads and lasses.'

Hartley nodded slowly. 'I could put them up in Forest End, next to the river. What do you reckon, Thomas? It'd be some extra cash.'

As Thomas shrugged, Spencer digested the news. He liked the isolation of the valley, the way it was detached from the rest of the world. Following the narrow twists of the road from the village to the mountains was like going back in time, twenty or thirty years at least. He felt a strange resentment towards the latest arrivals, knowing that they would bring with them things from outside, reminders of the pressures that he had left behind him.

He knew that Hartley had taken him on for similar, practical reasons. He had known it before, but now he realized it again, more starkly, and felt oddly lonely.

'I'll have a word with Titch tomorrow,' Hartley said.

A bell rang out through the bar. 'Last orders gentlemen, please,' shouted Sheila.

'I'll go,' said Spencer, suddenly in need of another drink.

*

It was two o'clock in the morning by the time they left the pub. The call for last orders had not been quite what it seemed. Hartley had laughed at Spencer's puzzlement when no-one hurried to finish their drink.

'See that feller at the bar talking to Sheila?' said Hartley. 'That's Jackie Wilson. He's our policeman. As long as he hears her call time he's not bothered. After hours it's a lock-in and that's that. No-one else comes in and it's the landlord's private do.'

They wandered back along the road, lit by the moon, an odd, silvery light that turned the landscape from colours into shades of grey. The air was warm, even so late at night, and the day's heat seemed still to be rising up from the road. The only sound was the occasional hoarse cough from a sheep or the rustle of a bird disturbed from its nest.

Hartley led the way, still in high spirits. His tongue loosened by the whisky, he kept up a running commentary as they went.

'That's Malcolm's farm, Malcolm Bainbridge. We were talking to him in't pub about them hippies. This one's Billy Birkett's, he was in't pub too. Looks like he's just cut his grass. Breathe in, Spence, that's one of the best smells of the summer. Reminds me of being a bairn, hiding in the bales from me dad, with Thomas. Hey Thomas, d'you remember?'

'Aye,' said Thomas quietly.

'This is Titch Tyson's. The hippies must be in his back field. I'll go over tomorrow for a word.'

They came to a house built on the side of the road, and next to it a wooden building almost as big, surrounded by a high barbed-wire fence.

'Norman Naylor's spot,' Hartley said. 'He runs the hounds. They'll be asleep in't hut. Best not wake them up though, they make a right unholy racket.'

'Look,' said Thomas suddenly. 'See that in't field.'

A fox ran from one corner of the field to the other, darting, quick.

'Sly beggar!' said Hartley, almost admiringly.

He started to sing, very quietly:

'D'ye ken John Peel with his coat so gay?
D'ye ken John Peel at the break of day?
D'ye ken John Peel when he's far away?
With his hounds and his horn in the morning.'

As they moved further away from the house he sang louder, his voice echoing around the mountains. He began to dance a little jig, hopping from foot to foot as he sang.

'For the sound of his horn brought me from my bed
And the cry of his hounds which he oft times led,
Peel's "view hulloo" would awaken the dead
Or the fox from his lair in the morning.'

'It's a good 'un, isn't it?' he asked Spencer. 'Cracking song.'

'Yes I ken John Peel and Ruby too,
Ranter and Ringwood and Bellman and True,

From a find to a check, from a check to a view,
From a view to a death in the morning.'

He broke off. 'This is where he came from, you know. John Peel. But people sing that song all over the world.' 'That's a hellish big reputation, isn't it?'

Spencer's head was spinning from the whisky.

'Yes,' he said faintly.

'I like a good song,' said Hartley. 'A real belter. I always sing on't way back from the pub. Don't I, Thomas? I can do poems too. Willie Wadsworth and all that. They were the only thing I liked doing, really, at school. They meant something, you know, they were talking about what I knew.'

He caught Spencer's look of surprise.

'Ha! I wasn't thick, you know. I could have been like you, Spence, off to university. But there was the farm. Someone had to keep it going.'

'What about Thomas?' Spencer asked. 'Couldn't he have done it?'

Hartley shook his head. 'Has to be the eldest son. Always has been, seven generations. Dad would never have let us change that.'

Spencer caught sight of Thomas, who was chewing down hard on his lip.

'But aren't you . . . I mean, from the photograph . . . the dates? Aren't you twins?'

'Doesn't matter, lad. I came out first. Twenty-three minutes before him. No: born, bred, married and died at Mirethwaite, lad, that'll be me.'

'And pickled too,' muttered Thomas.

But Hartley was warming to his subject. 'Aye, I brought me bride back to the bed I was born in. All the lads in the valley were after Mary. She was beautiful. I'd known her all my life. There was always summat different about her. It was like she wasn't from round here.

She was always dressed so nicely. And the way she smelled! I used to follow her about sometimes, just to get a sniff of it. Like flowers, I don't know if it were roses or what, but it smelled grand.

'When we were first married we lived at Mirethwaite with Mam and Dad. And Thomas. It was hard to find time alone. But we had our ways. We'd go off up the fell together . . .'

He staggered a little, then steadied himself.

'We'd go up to Blackbeck Dubs and lie down by the side of the river. My Mary—' His voice trailed off. 'Ah, forget I said owt. I shouldn't have, anyway.'

*

By the time they arrived back at the farm the sky had lightened behind the jagged tops of the mountains, hinting at dawn. They took a short cut across the fields, their trousers quickly growing sodden and heavy with dew.

'Ah well, it's good for the grass,' said Hartley. 'Looks like it's going to be hot again tomorrow. It's driving me mad, this weather. They were talking on't radio about all kinds of things the government's going to ban to save water.'

His voice was loud. As they entered the yard his words bounced off the walls, eerie in the early-morning silence.

'Don't wake the dogs,' said Thomas. 'They'll make a fair racket if you do.'

'Then they'll feel the side of my boot,' Hartley muttered, suddenly belligerent. 'Now then. What about this water ban?'

They had reached the porch. He gestured towards the trough with the marigolds. 'There'll be nowt left for Mary's flowers.' He stood for a moment, swaying gently. 'I'll fix it,' he said.

Reaching into his trousers, he fumbled with his flies, turning his back on the others. There was a pause and then, to his horror,

Spencer heard the patter of urine hitting the flowers. As it continued, he and Thomas avoided each other's eyes.

'There we are,' chuckled Hartley. 'That'll sort them out.' He began to sing again:

> 'A farmer's dog came up to town, his Christian name was Pete,
> His pedigree was two yards long, his looks were hard to beat,
> And as he trotted down the street, it was beautiful to see,
> His work on every corner, his technique on every tree.
>
> 'He watered every gateway, he never missed a post
> For piddlin' was his masterpiece and piddlin' was his boast,
> The city dogs stood looking with deep and jealous rage,
> To see this little country dog, the piddler of the age.'

'It's another cracker, isn't it?'

He was about to go on when the window above the porch flew open and Mary looked out, her hair dishevelled and her nightdress open at the neck.

Hartley didn't move. 'Look, me lovely, I'm watering your plants for you.'

She said nothing, staring at him in disbelief.

'There's going to be a water ban. There'll be nowt left for them.'

Mary slammed the window shut.

Hartley staggered back from the trough, looking up blearily. 'Eh? There's no pleasing her these days.'

*

When Spencer went into the house the next morning, tongue furred and head thick, Alice was standing in the doorway to the kitchen, looking solemn.

'Why's everyone so cross this morning, Spence?'

He moved past her to the kettle.

'Was Dad drinking last night?'

He nodded.

'Were you drinking too?'

He nodded again.

'Dad and Uncle Tom have gone to talk to some people, I don't know who they are. They went off early. Dad didn't even want any breakfast. Mam said she didn't care so I ate his bacon. She's sad today too.'

'Where is she?' he asked.

'In the yard.'

*

Mary was on her knees, stabbing a trowel into the trough. A small pile of uprooted marigolds lay on a sheet of newspaper next to her. She looked at Spencer briefly, then went back to what she was doing.

'Mary?' he said.

She carried on digging, ignoring him.

'Mary, are you all right?' Tentatively he reached out to touch her shoulder. She flinched, shrugging him away.

'I'm s-sorry about last night,' he said.

Her face was flushed, her eyes swollen.

'Why did it have to be my flowers?' she demanded.

Spencer couldn't think of an explanation. 'I d-don't know,' he admitted. 'He'd drunk quite a lot, I suppose.'

She shook her head sadly. 'He's always drunk. The hotter it gets this summer, the more he drinks. I can't stand it. I wish it would rain. Maybe that would stop him.'

'He said he was trying to help,' said Spencer, feeling ridiculous for trying to explain Hartley's drunken logic.

'Help? He pissed on my flowers. He *pissed* on them, Spence. I can smell his piss on their leaves.'

He flinched at hearing the word, ugly on her lips.

'He doesn't like me to do anything just for pleasure, or to make the place look better. He thinks a farm's for making a living and that's it. Well I won't keep my flowers there to be pissed on. I'm moving them to the vegetable patch. He won't ever bother going there. He's probably killed them, anyway, with all that beer in his system.'

'I'm sorry,' said Spencer, again.

'Oh I know you couldn't have stopped him. When Hartley wants to do something he'll do it and that's that.'

She jerked another marigold from the soil.

They were silent for a moment, then she turned to him.

'Spence, do you remember that time you said you'd pay for Alice's ballet lessons. Before the fire?'

'Yes.'

'Do you still mean it?'

'I thought you were worried that Hartley wouldn't like it.'

'He doesn't like anything much,' she said. 'But we don't have to tell him. I'm tired of him throwing his weight about. I won't have Alice miss out because he's got some stupid idea about sticking to where you come from. Why should she? It hasn't done me any good. I want to give her a chance to get away, to have a life that's different from the one I've ended up with.'

She looked at Spencer, no longer timid. 'Will you help?'

'Yes,' he said. 'Of course I will.'

*

That evening it was unbearably hot, the air heavy and still. Spencer took his notebook and climbed up into the hills behind the hut in search of a breeze. He had been working for about half an hour when he glanced up, his eyes drawn to a movement on the other side of the fell.

He blinked at the sight of the tiny figure making rapid progress over the mountainside. Squinting, he tried to make it out. As his eyes grew accustomed to the distance, he realized it was running, racing along, leaping over rocks and other obstacles. He wondered what was behind such urgency. As the figure disappeared behind the brow of the hill he went back to his notebook, trying to lose himself in its formulae, but the image of the runner stayed with him, sprinting through the heat of the night.

Earlier that day, the temperature had reached new heights, defeating even Hartley and Thomas. They had retreated to the shelter of the farmhouse, huddled around the table in their shirtsleeves, drinking cold coffee and discussing the need to shear the sheep.

'We'll have to do it this week,' Hartley said. 'We can't put it off any longer. Them sheep are gasping.'

Thomas had nodded.

'And we'd best get someone in. No offence—' he had nodded at Spencer '—but we need someone who knows what they're doing. Clipping takes a bit to get used to. Two of us'll clip, t'other two can be rolling fleeces. I'll ask about in't pub tonight. We'll gather the fell on Wednesday and clip until the weekend. Should be able to get it done by then.'

Spencer had thought of the walk that he and Dorothy had taken back from the vicarage, and of how the Sunday peace had been shattered by Thomas's bellows of rage.

'Right,' he had said. 'Of course.'

Now, as he scanned the fell, idly staring at the sheep that would provoke such excesses of temper, he heard a quick, rhythmic thud, accompanied by hard, heavy breathing. The next minute, the runner came over the hill, arms pumping, head down, face set. He wore blue shorts cut high, a vest, dark with sweat, and a pair of cheap plimsolls with fraying laces. Spencer stared at him, wondering how he managed to move at all in the sticky evening air. He realized with a jolt that it was the man from the neighbouring farm, the one he'd seen again in the pub. As if he felt his eyes upon him, the runner looked up and grinned. Slowing to a jog, he came towards Spencer. Chest heaving, he nodded.

'How do?' he said.

Spencer scrambled to his feet. 'Hello.'

They stood looking at each other, the runner trying to catch his breath. 'Hang on,' he said. 'I'll be able to speak in a minute. I've been running for the past hour, give or take, so I'm a bit hot.'

This was confirmed by the sweat pouring off him, little rivulets making their way down from his temples, trickling across his face to his throat, thrown off course by his chest hairs just above the neckline of his vest. Spencer counted them, five blond spirals.

'I – I – I'm Spencer Little.' He held out his hand and regretted it immediately, feeling absurd.

The man wiped his hands on his shorts and took Spencer's in a clasp.

'Edmund Lutwidge.'

He was older than Spencer had originally thought, but still young, barely twenty. Although slight, he was muscular from running. A tousle of fair hair the colour of damp straw fell into his eyes and now he flicked back his head, shaking out the moisture like a dog.

'I don't know how you can run like that in this heat,' blurted Spencer.

Still breathing hard, Edmund grinned. 'It's not that bad at this time of night. That's why I do it then. I'm training.'

'What for?'

'The show. It's—'

'Yes,' Spencer said eagerly. 'It's at the end of August, isn't it?'

'Right. I've been fell-running champion these last five years. I want to hold on to that.'

'Fell running?'

'You know, a race. Over the tops of the fells.'

Spencer could not think of anything to say. His knuckles were still damp from where Edmund's hand had clasped them.

'It's just a bit of fun,' Edmund went on. 'But it's a grand feeling when you win. And I've got a reputation to keep up.'

There was a pause.

'Anyway,' said Edmund, 'what're you doing up here? It's not often I come across someone this late at night.'

Spencer shifted his feet. 'I – I like it. It's quiet. I'm working for Hartley Dodds, at Mirethwaite. Just – just for the summer.'

'I know,' Edmund said. 'I know who you are.'

He stretched his arms above his head. 'Well, I'd better be off. I've a way to go before I'm finished. Maybe I'll see you up here again, one of these nights.'

Spencer watched as he ran towards the horizon, blond hair rising and falling with each step. Gradually he became smaller, until he was a speck again, lost in the evening haze.

Nine

'HAIL THE CONQUERING HERO!' SAID DOROTHY, DRILY, AS they came face to face on the top of the fell. Spencer had taken to going up there most nights, to think about his work.

'What do you mean?' he said, startled.

She smiled, exposing a row of crooked teeth. 'Haven't you heard? You're the village's new blue-eyed boy. Everyone's talking about you.'

'Why?' He tried to keep his voice even.

'Because you saved Alice Dodds from the fire. The vicar made you the subject of his sermon last Sunday. Or partly, at least.'

'What?'

'Oh, it was one of those ridiculous leaps that the clergy seems to take these days, always trying to make things relevant to the rest of us hoi polloi. He was talking about Moses and the burning bush and linking it to what you did. A bit trite really, I thought, and it didn't really work, but there we are. He put it in the parish magazine as well. Let me have a look . . .'

Shrugging off her knapsack, she began to rummage through it.

'Here it is,' she said, extracting a crumpled pamphlet from a side pocket. Smoothing it out, she passed it to Spencer.

On the back page, between an engagement announcement and an advertisement for a jumble sale, was a paragraph with the headline *Cambridge Man to the Rescue!*

As Spencer read on, his cheeks grew hot with embarrassment.

Cambridge Professor Spencer Little, who's currently working for Hartley Dodds at Mirethwaite Farm, put his own life at risk when he dashed through a ring of flames to save ten-year-old Alice Dodds, trapped on the fellside by a flash-fire. Thank you, Spencer! The blaze, started by unknown causes, has caused significant damage to the fell. This is just the latest in a string of fires in the valley. Our policeman John Wilson urges walkers to be careful and to avoid dropping any matches or cigarette ends.

'I'm not a professor,' he mumbled. 'And I was never at risk.'

Dorothy giggled, a surprisingly girlish sound.

'Don't worry,' she said. 'It's like I told you, it's because of Cambridge. The vicar's decided he approves of you. But it won't do you any harm. Better to be known for doing something like that than being gossiped about for other reasons. Believe me, I know.' She looked at Spencer closely. 'Maybe you do, too.'

Before he could respond, she shook her head. 'What I'm worried about is the effect on the fell. If it's gone down too far into the peat the earth won't ever recover. It can smoulder away for weeks under the surface. You don't see anything, but it's there, sucking everything out of the soil.'

She pointed to the intake. 'You see that? It's as if the mountain-side's been rubbed out.'

He looked over at the fell, charred and lifeless, the darkest patch of night.

'It's awful,' she said. 'Tragic.'

There were tears in her eyes as she stared at it. 'And to think how many animals lived in that bracken, everything from woodlice to rabbits. They won't all have escaped.'

He imagined an exodus of animals, frantically scurrying along the intake's paths and passages, fruitlessly trying to find a place of safety, feeling the heat of the fire on their backs as they ran.

'No,' he said to Dorothy. 'Not all of them, but some will.'

*

That week, Mary asked him to take Alice to her ballet lesson. She was easier with him now, less hesitant, as if she had decided he could be trusted.

'It's better for you to go than me,' she said, as he helped her clear away the dishes after lunch. 'If he notices you're not here, I'll say I sent you to the shops and she wanted to go with you.'

He nodded. 'Good idea.' A look of complicity passed between them.

Alice sat up very straight in the Land Rover, her feet, resting on the dusty dashboard, encased in a pair of grubby ballet shoes whose scuffed pink leather was worn to grey. As they drove along, the smell of cut grass drifting in through the open windows, she kept up a constant stream of chatter.

'Mam said I was to say thank you for my lessons, Spence.'

He turned to smile at her. 'That's all right. I know how much you like them. I didn't want you to have to give them up.'

'And we're not allowed to tell Dad. But I think when he sees me dancing at the show it'll be a surprise and he'll be proud, won't he? And then he'll let me keep doing bally, even after you've gone.'

Spencer nodded slowly, hoping she was right.

'We're learning a special dance for it,' she said. 'I'm in the middle row. We're going to be wearing tutus, like proper ballerinas. Will you come in for my lesson, Spence, like Mam does?'

'I don't know . . .' he said.

'Please. I promise you'll like it.'

'All right,' he said, feeling oddly flattered.

As they drove along the winding road, they passed Malcolm Bainbridge, who nodded to Spencer, lifting a forefinger from the steering wheel in silent acknowledgement. Spencer returned the gesture, surprised and pleased by his friendliness. Perhaps what Dorothy had said was right, he thought – that he might at last have been accepted.

*

At the village hall, little girls were everywhere, their high-pitched voices filling the room with shrill excitement. They swarmed in and out, swooping like starlings, congregating in sudden clusters then breaking apart to form the next. Mothers stood, dispensing tights and hair bands, their perfumes clashing in the dusty room. The atmosphere was intimate and feminine, entirely foreign to Spencer, who shrank back against the wall, trying to make himself inconspicuous.

'I'm going to get changed,' said Alice, and disappeared around the corner, trailing her bag behind her.

Not sure of where to look, he stared down at his boots. They too seemed out of place, ungainly and encrusted with dirt, brutish next to the ballet shoes and flowered summer dresses. He found a spot against the back wall and cautiously looked up again, stealing a glance at his surroundings.

The carpet had been rolled back and lay fatly next to stacks of chairs pushed up against a low stage, in the corner of which stood a piano with a stool upholstered in green velvet. On the walls were paintings: bright, messy splashes of colour with wobbling letters underneath spelling out the names and ages of the artists. Beyond the stage, through a door in a partition wall, he could see a woman pouring orange squash into plastic cups.

A small hand patted his arm. Alice was back, dressed in a knee-length tunic. A pink sash trailed from her belt loops, and thick white tights gathered in folds at her skinny ankles. The outfit made her glasses look incongruous, like a frame too heavy for a picture.

'Can you tie my bow?' she asked. 'I can't reach behind my back.'

She turned around and stood, waiting. Spencer held up the ends of the sash, uncertain of how he was supposed to do it.

'Hurry up,' she said impatiently, 'we're starting in a minute.'

Hastily, he looped it like a tie.

'Now can you do my ribbons?' said Alice, pointing to her grubby satin shoes. 'They came undone. You probably need to kneel down, that's how Mam does it.'

Sinking to his knees, Spencer waited for further instructions.

'You cross them over at the front, then bring them round and go once around my leg again and tie them at the back. You can do a knot or a bow. Mam usually does a knot, then a bow on top.'

The fraying satin ribbons slipped through his fingers, but it was less complicated than it had sounded and soon he had managed it.

'There you are,' he said.

She beamed at him. 'You'll stay, won't you? Just so you can see me do my dance?'

He nodded, and she ran off to join the other girls, all identically dressed and standing in two giggling, straggling lines.

'That's Mary Dodd's daughter isn't it? Alice?'

The woman standing next to him was smiling at him.

'Yes,' he said.

'And you must be Spencer Little?'

He nodded.

'I read about you in the parish magazine.'

Lightly she touched his arm. 'I'm Angela Armstrong. Come and sit with us over there, won't you? It takes the girls ages to get to the actual dance. You may as well have a seat.'

To his surprise, he found himself following her across the room to a group of other women.

'This is Spencer,' she said. 'From Mirethwaite Farm. He brought Alice.'

'Sit down,' said one of the women, patting the chair next to her. Angela took a seat on the other side.

Two short claps diverted everyone's attention to the stage, where a tiny woman in her sixties was waiting for silence. She stood very straight, shoulders back, her black silk dress falling gracefully to the knee. When she spoke, her voice was suited to another era, her enunciation precise and refined.

'Good afternoon, girls.'

'Good afternoon, Miss Mannering,' they replied.

'Now, we're going to have to work very hard to be properly prepared by the day of the show. How many weeks away is it now?'

Hands shot up.

'Yes, Karen?'

'Three, Miss Mannering.'

'That's correct. It's not very far away at all. So today you need to work as hard as you can, and then you need to practise at home as well. Will you do that for me? It's the first time we've danced at the show, so we need to give the best performance possible. Can I rely on you all?'

'Yes, Miss Mannering.'

'Very good. Now, let's warm ourselves up. Joan, when you're ready?'

The bulky woman sitting at the piano was also dressed in black, but to different effect, the material straining over ample hips. Lifting a pair of reading glasses to her nose, she put her fingers on the keys and began to play.

It was a simple tune that Spencer recognized from his earliest piano lessons, and he began to tap out the notes against his thigh. Joan's body swayed as she played, making liberal use of the soft pedal, the notes reverberating around the hall. Miss Mannering talked over the music, punctuating her instructions with a stick that she tapped on the floor as she paced the stage, watching her pupils closely.

'First position.'

Twenty pairs of feet posed, heels together, toes turned out.

'Second position.'

A sliding sound as leather soles swished sideways, spreading apart.

'Third position.'

Shuffling and stifled giggles as the girls tried not to lose their balance.

'Fourth,' said Miss Mannering severely, 'and fifth.'

From where he was sitting, Spencer could only see Alice from behind, but it was clear that she was trying hard, her effort evident in the way she held her back rigid, forcing her shoulders down. She was not naturally graceful, and her limbs stretched awkwardly, as far as they could go. As the girls repeated the five positions, this time adding arms, he felt a sudden protective pride.

'Now girls,' said Miss Mannering, 'take your starting positions for your dance.'

There was a flurry of movement as the girls flitted about, exchanging places. At last they were ready and stood in formation, arms held low. All attention was focused on Miss Mannering, who stood at the very centre of the stage, silhouetted in her black dress, her feet immaculate in dark silk ballet shoes and turned out in first position.

'Remember, when you're dancing, try to keep yourselves light. No prancing elephants. Ballet should look effortless. I don't want to see any frowns, or wobbling, is that clear? The most important thing is to keep smiling. What are we aiming for?'

Hands shot up again. Alice waved her arm, desperate to be the one to answer. 'Alice?'

'Grace, Miss Mannering.'

'That's right. Grace. And poise.'

Alice peeped round at Spencer, who smiled back.

Miss Mannering gestured towards the piano. 'Joan?'

The other woman sat up, held her hands above the keyboard for a moment, and then brought them down to produce one long chord. Then she began to play, her fingers moving lightly over the keys in their own dance, sure and perfect and quick. The music was incongruous in the village hall, something wild and Russian, overflowing with emotion, but the girls seemed not to notice and began to dance, spinning off from the group, two by two, in little pirouettes.

'Lead with your fingers,' called Miss Mannering. 'Arms first, feet to follow.'

They were trying hard, heads lowered in concentration, looking at their feet as they twirled and spun, small bodies straining. The effect was more clumsy than graceful, and punctuated by thuds.

'Remember girls, weightless and flying, not bouncing. You are not kangaroos.'

Dividing into pairs, they danced a pas de deux, taking turns to play the part of the man, then, forming a circle, stretched out their right hands so that their fingertips were just touching, They moved together, skipping around, slowly at first, then faster, until their skirts twirled into a blur. As the music slowed, they peeled off, one at a time, taking long, gliding steps, their arms held low, hands cupped. Kneeling, they leaned forward, gently resting their foreheads on the floor. Soon all twenty girls were there, curled like infants, eyes closed.

The music was very quiet now, slow minor chords leading to the end of the piece. As they slowed even further, becoming almost funereal, Spencer looked at the small white shapes huddled on the dusty floorboards. Alice was easy to spot among them, her messy hair sticking out in contrast to the smooth ponytails of the other girls. Looking closer, he saw that her shoulders were shaking, and wondered what was wrong; then he noticed the next girl, her shoulders shaking too, and the next, and realized that they were trying to suppress a fit of giggling.

He was not the only one to have seen them. Stepping down from the stage, Miss Mannering daintily made her way through the group until she was standing in the middle. As the music stopped she rapped her stick hard on the floor. All shoulders were instantly still.

'Get up.'

They scrambled to their feet, looking sheepish. Miss Mannering's eyes narrowed. When she spoke, her voice was terse.

'This is not good enough. I thought we agreed at the beginning of this rehearsal that we only have three weeks before the performance.' She banged her stick again, hard. 'Ballerinas have to be serious about dancing. They have to be dedicated. They are *professionals*. So I don't want to hear any more giggling. Is that clear?'

'Yes, Miss Mannering,' they mumbled.

'I can't hear you.'

'Yes, Miss Mannering!'

'Better. Now, I want you all to go home and practise. Joan?'

Sliding off the piano stool, Joan picked up a cardboard box and, puffing slightly, brought it over to where they were standing.

'Sarah, will you open this for me?' Miss Mannering asked.

A small red-headed girl ran over and pulled open the flaps.

'Show us what's inside.'

The girl reached in and pulled out a cassette.

'Give it to me, please. Now girls, Joan has very kindly recorded the music for our dance. There's a cassette here for each of you. I want you all to go home and practise until you're perfect. If you can do it in front of a mirror, so you can see what you're doing, all the better. If not, ask someone to watch you and be honest about how you look. By the time we perform, I want no wrong moves. And absolutely no giggling. Is that clear?'

They nodded.

'And mothers—' she raised her voice '—please make sure the costumes are ready in two weeks' time. We'll need to rehearse in them once at the very least.'

*

The next day Alice brought Spencer a drawing of two stick figures, one dressed in a tutu, the other in tights.

'I did it this morning,' she said. 'Can you tell who it is?'

'Is that you?' he asked, pointing to the one in the tutu.

She nodded, pleased.

The other figure was more indistinct – although unmistakably male.

'Who's the other one?'

She took the picture from him. 'Can't you guess, silly? That's you. It's us together, dancing with proper costumes and everything.'

*

He balanced the picture on the mantelpiece, next to his books and the collection of skulls that he had gathered on his night wanderings, arranged in order of size: the ram's horn that had been there on his arrival, the rotten-toothed jaw of a sheep, a delicate rabbit's cranium, a sparrow's skull and, smaller still, a tiny vole's head, perfectly preserved.

That night he lay on his bed and looked at the picture for a very long time.

Ten

Spencer stood watching from his hut as the convoy of dilapidated vans edged its way onto the forest field, jolting along one
of the well-worn sheep trails. They looked out of place in the
valley, an incongruous slice of modernity, covered with enormous,
swirling flora and fauna, giant blooms wound around strange
and fantastical animals, birds flitting across windows, colossal
insects crawling from hubcaps. A scarlet bumper clashed happily
with a roof the colour of sunshine, rainbow streamers cascading
down from it. Music blared from radios, announcing the hippies'
arrival.

They parked haphazardly, drawing to a standstill near a clearing
next to a stream. The figures that climbed out were dressed in clothes
as bright as their vehicles. Spencer stared in fascination as they milled
about with no immediate purpose, wandering through the trees, then

made themselves comfortable on the grass, settling down to roll cigarettes.

An hour passed before they began to set up camp, after one of the men stood up and took off his shirt. The others followed his lead, revealing lean chests. Their stripping seemed to signal a change of mood, and there was a flurry of movement as the group began to pull a jumbled collection of bags, tent poles and bedding from the vans. The clearing was soon a mass of paraphernalia strewn over rocks, wispy dresses hanging from the branches of old oaks.

Making a space in the middle of the clearing, they fitted the poles together, laying them out on the ground. It seemed a complicated process, and it was a while before they had a structure, slightly precarious, held up by a person at each corner. A covering was flung on top, guy ropes untangled and pegs hammered with rocks into the hard ground. The tent was khaki canvas, its military appearance at odds with the slogan daubed across one of the vans:

Make Love, Not War.

Next, they gathered firewood, bringing armfuls of sticks to add to a pile by the side of the tent. Spencer bit his lip as he watched them take rocks from the dry stone walls, remembering long hours spent building them with Hartley and Thomas. The rocks went to form a circle around the fire, and soon steam was rising from two pots sitting in the coals.

He retreated to the hut, trying to work, but found it difficult to concentrate, distracted by the sound of laughter and the smell of smoke that rose up the mountain. Going back outside, he sat on his usual boulder, resting his chin on his knees. It was almost dark, and the figures had become shadows huddled around the fire, which flickered and danced, competing with the sunset that stretched crimson across the horizon.

They passed around bottles, taking swigs, arms draped over one another's shoulders, blankets covering their knees. Someone began to strum at a guitar. The singing soon began, more tuneful than Hartley and Thomas's efforts, with harmonies, a woman's voice lilting over the others.

Watching the dark shapes below him in the firelight, and hearing their laughter, he felt a sudden urge to run down the hill to the group, to be one of them, safe in the darkness, away from doubt. Next to them he felt old, stagnated, as if he had passed something by that was important. He longed to be as easy as they were, to be able to throw his head back and laugh without reservation or shyness, to do something irrational, something new. But feeling old brought back familiar fears that whispered to him, reminding him how little time he had left.

He stood up quickly and took his notebook back into the hut. Lighting a candle, he placed it on the ledge above his bed and turned to a new page. It was when he was working late at night that he most strongly felt the presence of other mathematicians, the ones who had succeeded, who had created a perfect truth. Most had made their mark young. When at last he slept on those long and difficult nights, his dreams were of losing his capabilities before having had the chance to properly use them. The dreams were vivid, and filled with the incurable pain of regret.

He had lived so many years in the world of faculties and common rooms: odd solitary places, suffused with endeavour and paranoia, the shared and ever-present fear of failure. There was no time left for singing around campfires. If he stopped now he knew he would never get his talent back. After the setbacks of the summer term he was determined not to allow any distractions. Sighing, he forced himself to concentrate, marching, step by dogged step, back into the world of numbers.

Soon he was utterly absorbed, working quickly, with confidence, oblivious to anything outside his own small circle of candlelight. Long sequences of letters and symbols fell into place, covering page after page with almost magical ease. He worked late into the night, then fell asleep immediately, his usual insomnia gone.

*

'You'll have noticed yon hippies in Forest End?' said Hartley the next morning at breakfast.

Spencer took a gulp of coffee. 'Yes, I saw them arriving last night.'

Hartley nodded. 'I went down to talk to Titch Tyson t'other day, after we spoke about them in't Tup. He wasn't keen on keeping them in his field. His missus complained about the noise at night. Music, and all the rest of it. I thought, well there's no-one to get upset all the way up here, so I went and had a word.'

'What's hippies?' asked Alice, poking her spoon into a boiled egg.

Hartley shook his head. 'They're what'll be staying in't bottom field for a few weeks. They've got no jobs to go to, they just go round the place in their vans, all painted up, and they like living in tents. They don't look much like folk round here, I can tell you that for nowt. Hard to tell the men from the women, everyone's hair's that long. Anyway, you can see for yourself. You can make yourself useful and go with Spencer to collect their camping money.'

'W-what?' Spencer asked.

'Aye. I've got too much on in't mornings. Anyway, I thought it'd be better if you do it. They're more your age. And they sound like they're from down south. Posh sods. Besides,' he went on with a smirk, 'you'll be good at adding up what they owe me.'

Spencer saw that any argument was futile. 'When do you want me to go?'

'After breakfast, every day, in case they get any ideas about running off. I'll charge them twenty-five pence apiece. And Alice can see if she can sell them some of Mary's eggs. We might as well, if we can.'

'Can we go now, Spence?' said Alice. 'I want to see what they're like.'

*

They walked together down the lane, Spencer reluctant, Alice hopping with anticipation. Shadow, her belly huge now, followed them, her tongue hanging out, panting.

'Are there hippies in Cambridge, Spence?' Alice asked.

'No,' he said. 'I don't think so.'

'Do you think they'll like us?'

'Perhaps.'

'Do you think we'll like them?'

He shrugged, still unsure how he felt about the new arrivals – an odd combination of envy and intrigue. 'I don't know yet.'

It was not yet hot, the dew still clinging to the grass. Birds sang in the hedgerows as they passed, calling to each other, starting off the day. Spencer opened the gate to the forest field and they went through it, following the grooves of the sheep track.

As they approached the camp, Alice grew excited.

'Look!' she said, pointing at one of the vans. 'Look at that! It's a lady with no clothes on!'

He looked at the giant painting of a woman, statuesque, lolling along the side of the van, and felt a flush of embarrassment. But Alice was soon distracted.

'And see those flowers going all the way to the roof, as if they're really growing all the way up there! I've never seen flowers like that before, not that big and not in all those colours. Aren't they lovely?'

Running over to the van, she traced the psychedelic petals with her fingertips, standing on her tiptoes, reaching high. Smiling with delight, she shook one of the bells that hung from a wing mirror.

'Listen, Spence, it's like fairy music.'

The fire from the night before was dead, its flames replaced by charred stubs of wood. Bottles lay discarded around it, green glass clouded with ash. Nearby were rolls of bedding, blankets patterned with Indian prints. At first glance they seemed abandoned, but on looking again, Spencer saw one of them twitch. He stepped back quickly, noticing the tangled hair that protruded from it. Carefully he moved past to the tent, which sagged in the middle, its heavy canvas thick with dew.

The only sound from inside was a deep and rhythmic snoring.

'It's like that book about the giant,' said Alice, coming up behind him. 'The one who slept for a hundred years. Do you think the hippies are really big?'

He smiled at her. 'No, I think they're just asleep. We need to wake them up.'

'I'll do it,' she said eagerly, and before he could stop her she went close to the tent.

'Hello, is anyone awake? Hello?'

The snoring rumbled on.

'Hello,' called Alice, louder. 'We've come for your money.'

'Alice!' said Spencer. 'You can't say that!'

'Why not? It's why Dad sent us.'

'But—'

A rustling sound came from within, a groan, and then the sound of someone sniffing. The rustle grew louder, and suddenly a grubby arm appeared through the front flap of the tent. Alice shrieked and grabbed Spencer's hand. Next came a man's head, his long hair hanging down over naked shoulders, his beard straggling to his chest.

Alice looked at him with interest.

'Are you a hippie?'

He squinted into the sunlight. 'What?'

'Are you a hippie? Dad said the hippies had come to stay in the field.'

He glanced at Spencer. 'Did he now?'

'This isn't my dad,' she said. 'He's my friend. He's Spencer. And my name's Alice.'

'Well, you can call me a hippie if you like. Or you can call me Mick.' He coughed, a spluttering hack. 'What time is it?'

'It's half past seven,' said Alice.

He groaned. 'Christ, that's early.'

'Dad sent us to collect the money. For camping. It's – how much is it, Spence?'

'Twenty-five pence each. How many of you are there?'

'Twelve. Any chance of a group discount?'

Spencer shook his head. 'It'd be up to Alice's father, but I don't think so.'

'Maybe we can talk to him about a spot of bartering. Do some work in return for rent.'

'There's not much on at the moment,' said Spencer uncomfortably.

Mick nodded. 'Well, have a word with him, will you? None of us has much cash, if you know what I mean?'

He disappeared back into the tent. Through the gap in the canvas Spencer saw bodies huddled together.

Returning with a bag of coins, the man squinted up at them.

'So that's how much?'

'Three pounds,' said Spencer.

Mick gave a stack of coins to Alice.

'There you are, darling.'

Carefully she counted it, then handed it over to Spencer.

128

'I need a lot more sleep,' said the man. 'See you later.' And he vanished back into the tent.

*

Alice skipped back along the lane.

'I met a hippy!' she said, triumphantly. 'He was nice, wasn't he? And he called me darling! No-one's ever called me darling! Their vans were brilliant too. When I grow up I'm going to have one like that. I'll paint it all over with flowers and I'll put bells on the mirrors so they make a lovely noise. Then I'll be able to go wherever I want, all over the country or even abroad.'

'I thought you wanted to go to Cambridge,' Spencer said.

'I could drive to Cambridge too. Or I could drive around in the holidays, like you, before you came here.'

'What would you paint on the van, then?' he asked, knowing she would like the question.

She stopped skipping and frowned, thinking it over.

'I'd paint it mostly pink and green,' she said finally. 'With pink bits at the front and the back, and green bits on the side. I'd paint a picture of Shadow and her puppies, and I'd do you as well, next to them. That's what I'd paint. What about you?'

'I think mine would be quite plain,' he said. 'I'd paint the most beautiful equations I know, the most perfect ones.'

'What's an equation?'

'It's like a picture, in a way. A maths picture, I suppose you could call it. When you talk about maths, you use signs to show what you mean. You can use a letter to stand for something else, just one thing or a set of things, and you join them up with symbols. When you get a sequence of letters and symbols that means something important, it's very beautiful. It's as if hundreds of thoughts, ones that have taken you hours to think about, have all been put together and made into something that's very simple.'

'Like what?'

'Well, when your teacher writes "two plus two equals four" on the blackboard you know what she means, right?'

'That's easy.'

'Well, two is a number, and so is four, but "plus" and "equals" are symbols. You know what they stand for?'

'Adding and makes. Two add two makes four.'

'That's right. Or sometimes equals just means "is". So you see, if I had equations on my van, I'd be very happy.'

'That does sound nice,' said Alice doubtfully. 'Maybe you could do the symbols all in different colours, though, like a rainbow.'

'Look,' said Spencer, 'I'll show you.'

Taking his penknife from his pocket, he went over to a thicket of beech trees. The blade eased out from the handle smoothly. Alice watched as he began to carve into the ripples of the bark.

$$AD = AD$$
$$SL = SL$$
$$AD + SL = \cup$$

'What does it mean, Spence?'

'Well, try to think.'

She frowned, looking hard at the carving. 'I might know some of it.'

'Go on.'

'AD is me, isn't it?'

'That's right.'

'So if equals means is, then AD = AD means Alice Dodds is Alice Dodds.'

'Very good!'

He was rewarded with a smile.

'And SL is you, so Spencer Little is Spencer Little.'

'Yes.'

'So AD + SL . . . Alice Dodds and Spencer Little—' Her face fell. 'I don't know what that last bit is. That thing that looks like a U.'

'Are you sure?'

'If it isn't a U, I don't know what it is.'

He smiled. 'I cheated. That isn't a mathematical symbol. It's a smile. It means Alice and Spencer equals happiness.'

'Wow! Let's never tell anyone what it means! I won't, and you mustn't either. It's our secret. Only we know it. Do you promise?'

He nodded. 'I promise.'

*

Emerging from the trees, they caught sight of the vicar, walking along the path next to the river.

'Let's run away before he sees us,' said Alice.

'We can't,' said Spencer. 'He'll notice.'

Just then the vicar looked over and waved. As they waved back, he began to approach.

'Hello!' he said, his broad face beaming.

'Hello,' they replied, without enthusiasm.

'How *are* you?' he asked Spencer. 'We haven't seen much of you recently.'

Spencer flushed, aware of how he had avoided the church after that first, tense experience.

'I – I've been busy,' he said. 'There's a lot to do on the farm.'

The vicar nodded. 'Ah, yes,' he said. 'I imagine you'll soon be making hay.' He began to sing in a quavering tenor:

'*Come ye thankful people, come, raise the song of harvest home,*
All is safely gathered in, 'ere the winter storms begin . . .'

Alice looked at him with the same frank stare that she often directed at Spencer.

'I do like a good hymn,' said the vicar. 'Will you be with us for harvest festival?'

'I don't think so,' Spencer said. 'Term starts at the end of September, but I need to go back earlier. I've got some work to finish by then.'

'Ah, Michaelmas term. I always liked it. Going back with a sense of purpose. Mist on the Backs in the early mornings, cycling to lectures . . .'

Thinking of his lack of application over the summer, Spencer gave a weak nod.

'And building up to carol concerts at Christmas. Wonderful stuff. I led the chapel choir, you know. Are you musical, Spencer?'

'S-sometimes I play the organ at college, but not for services. I'm allowed to go into chapel and practise when it's not being used.'

The vicar's smile grew wider. 'Oh! Then you must know the chaplain Hugh Webster. Old friend of mine from Peterhouse. I haven't heard from him for years. I must give him a ring sometime.'

He paused, noticing the look on Spencer's face. 'You did say you were at Jesus, didn't you?'

'Y-yes,' said Spencer, immediately anxious. 'But I didn't know him very well. I never really saw anyone when I went to the chapel. He probably wouldn't remember me.'

*

Hartley grunted with satisfaction when Spencer gave him the coins, dropping them into his pocket.

'There's my beer money for tonight.'

Spencer decided not to tell him if the hippies ever bought any eggs.

'How were they, anyway?'

'They're really nice, Dad,' said Alice eagerly. 'Well, actually we only met one of them. He's called Mick. And he called me darling! And they had pictures on their vans of ladies without any—'

'We didn't see much of them,' Spencer said. 'They were asleep.'

'Lazy beggars.' Hartley gave Alice a sharp look. 'Now don't you go hanging around them, do you hear? They don't want you getting in the way. And I don't want you having owt to do with them. They can stay as long as they pay, but that's it, understand?'

'But Dad—'

'I'll not tell you twice. Or you'll feel the back of my hand.'

As she slid out of the room, Shadow at her heels, Hartley said, 'She's got too many ideas in her head, anyhow, that lass. All them books she reads. She likes anything that's different from here. She gets it from her mam. You'll look out for her round them hippies, though, will you, eh?'

He looked out of the window as he spoke, avoiding Spencer's eyes.

'Yes,' said Spencer. 'I'll do what I can.'

*

That afternoon they worked together, clearing out what Hartley called gutters; small streams that ran through the fields. They had dried out in the heatwave, becoming boggy ditches, choked with weeds.

'Aye, it's a clarty mess, all right,' said Hartley. 'It'll be good to get them running clear.'

Water skaters slid over the surface, hunting for prey, midges hovering above in clouds.

'Cleggs are what you want to watch out for,' said Hartley.

'Cleggs?'

He shook his head. 'Thank your lucky stars you don't know.

They're big buggers. You find them around shit mostly, that's where they like to feed. But when we clear this muck out, they'll come for us. And when they bite, you know about it. Right, Thomas?'

'Aye,' said Thomas. 'They're big, like.' He held his finger and thumb an inch apart. 'And they hurt.'

They stood up to their knees in stagnant water, raking at the tangled weeds, worrying at the roots and scooping up great dripping shovelfuls to deposit on the banks. They left a trail of dark mud in their wake, and as Hartley had predicted, the cleggs soon came: fat, buzzing horseflies that swooped on the slime. It was hard work, dirty water running down their arms as they lifted their shovels, each disturbance of the surface releasing a dank, rotten smell, but Spencer felt oddly content. Hartley was less abrasive than usual and they soon fell into a rhythm, the three of them working together, bending and lifting in unison.

As they moved downstream, carving out their way along the gutter, the water began to flow more freely, a trickle here and there, making its way around broken stalks and blockages, swirling in small eddies, making the surface ripple and shimmer. It ran brown at first, then slowly became clearer, exposing smooth pebbles at the bottom of the stream. As Spencer stood, feeling the weight of the current against his boots, he noticed little glints of light.

'What's that?' he said to Hartley.

'What's what, lad?'

'There's something in the stream, it's glittering, like something precious.'

He bent to look. 'Ah, it might well glitter. That's fool's gold, lad.'

'Fool's gold?'

'Iron pyrites,' said Thomas.

'That's it, aye. Gets washed down in't beck from the old iron-ore mines at the top of the valley. Worth nowt, but it looks nice enough.'

Reaching into the stream, he picked up a rock and held it out to Spencer, who took it, turning it over in his hands.

'See?'

The rock was a mass of grey crystals fused together, winking in the sunshine, an odd combination of dark and light. The water on it dried instantly in the heat of the day and Spencer slipped it into his pocket.

'Right,' said Hartley, 'when we've sorted out these gutters, we'll gather the rest of the fell and get on with the clipping. Them sheep are too damn hot.'

Spencer looked over to where a line of ewes lay, panting, in the shade of a wall.

'I've already spoken to't lad who's coming to help. We'll get that out of the road and then it'll be just the hay left to do. It's all a bit later than it could have been.' His voice was regretful. 'Fleeces won't make owt when they're sold. But the sheep should feel a hell of a lot better, that's for sure.'

*

Dorothy sat on a rock, drinking coffee from a flask and looking at the scene below. Small figures moved about slowly, unpacking things from their vans. From where she sat she could see the tops of the vehicles, painted with multi-coloured mythical creatures cavorting with half-naked girls.

'Very pre-Raphaelite,' she muttered.

One of the men took a tall cylindrical drum from a van and carried it over to the blackened remains of the fire. Putting it between his knees, he began to tap out a rhythm with his fingers, tripping and hypnotic. Another man joined him, his drum slightly smaller, using the heels of his hands to produce a pulsing beat. For a minute the rhythms were separate, then they came together, syncopating, rising to the tops of the trees. The others drifted over, summoned by the music, some settling at the drummers' feet, nodding their heads to the rhythm, others still standing, swaying, shifting their hips in time. Someone picked up a guitar and strummed along.

As the rhythms changed, speeding up, chasing one another, the guitar player strumming faster, two of the women began to dance. It was not like anything Dorothy had ever seen, as they stretched out their arms and lifted their faces to the sun, then began to spin, their wispy dresses blurring as they moved. Those left sitting began to clap along to the beat of the drums. The group appeared to move as one, whooping and calling, everyone caught up in the music.

Dorothy looked at the little knot of energy, a burst of noisy life in the silence of the valley.

'You've surpassed yourself this time, Hartley,' she said quietly. 'Yes, indeed you have.'

Eleven

THE VALLEY GREW HOTTER, ONE GASPING DAY AFTER another. Sheep moved as if drugged, staggering through the fields to collapse in the shade of walls. Dogs panted, tongues protruding, resting their heads on their paws. Patches of ground had begun to show through the yellowing grass, cracked soil turning to dust. Only Alice seemed unaffected, her energy cutting through the narcotic haze.

'Listen to this,' she said excitedly one morning. 'We're not allowed to use water any more. They've been talking about it on the radio.'

She turned up the volume.

'And this is Radio Carlisle, back with the latest news and views on another sunny day! Here in the studio it's hot, hot, hot, but we're loving it. That's not how they see it down south though. Sunny Jim Callaghan's making the rules, and we're all going to have to do it his way. That's right, the government's new Drought Act brings back rations, and this time it's water. No hosepipes for the gardeners. Toilets are trouble too! So put a brick in the cistern to cut down on flushing. Or use what's left after the washing up instead. As for baths, we're back to how we did it in the war. No more than five inches at a time. Here's our favourite suggestion: save water, bathe with a friend!'

'That's a silly idea,' said Alice. 'Having a bath with a friend. You wouldn't get very clean.'

'Here's Sacha Distel singing an old favourite, Burt Bacharach's "Raindrops Keep Fallin' On My Head" – just to keep you all cool as cucumbers . . .'

*

Hartley snorted when Spencer mentioned the water ban.

'I knew it would happen,' he said. 'We'll get round it. We're not on the mains, so we've got a bit of leeway. All our water comes off the fell. There's not much left, mind. The tarns and becks are all drying up. But I can't imagine there won't be rain before the end of August. I've never known it like this before.'

He and Thomas still made no concession to the heat, continuing to wear their heavy boots and shirts, keeping their jackets with them always. It was as if the weather was something simply to be endured, something they knew would pass in time. Working next to them, Spencer was acutely aware of how quickly his breath became laboured and shallow, his shirt blackened with sweat.

One afternoon, as he was working alone, repairing a wall at the side of the hayfield, Alice came running towards him. He heard her before he saw her, puffing as she scrambled through the tall grass. When she arrived at the wall her face was flushed, her shoulders heaving.

'Spence!' she said. 'The hippies have taken all their clothes off! Come and see!'

He stiffened. 'What?'

'I wanted to go and see them again, but I didn't want to get into trouble with Dad, so I took the path at the back of the wood. I just wanted to play with the bells and look at the paintings of the ladies. But when I got to the gate, I could see them lying there with no clothes on. Boys and girls! Next to each other!'

She looked up at him expectantly, waiting for his response.

'R-really?'

'Come and see! Now!'

Taking his hand, she pulled him back through the grass to the path.

'Alice, I don't know . . . I – I've got this wall to do.'

'Oh, come on! Quick!'

*

As they approached she turned to him, raising a finger to her lips.

'Look,' she whispered, 'they haven't got any clothes on, have they? I was right!'

Turning his eyes to the field, he saw them, men and women, naked on the blankets, sprawled together without a hint of self-consciousness. Each body was different: some brown, others paler, some rounded, some thin. He saw shadows, curves and angles, all exposed to the sun.

'I've never seen grown-ups without their clothes on,' said Alice.

'We shouldn't be looking,' he said uncomfortably. 'Come on, let's go.'

'But if they're lying there like that, they mustn't care who sees them.'

'Still, we should go.'

'What are they doing?'

'I think they're sunbathing. Trying to get brown.'

She stared at him, incredulous. 'They'll get burned. I think they look silly. Like they're dead.'

'Well, never mind,' he said, firmly. 'Let's go.'

*

The image of the naked bodies stayed with him all afternoon, making him clumsy and distracted. That night in the hut he stripped down to his underwear and looked at himself critically, examining his body. He stretched out one arm, then the other, tentatively flexing his muscles. His back was broader, he thought, filled out by farm food and lifting stones, his legs defined from nights spent tramping the fells. For a moment he stood very still, standing up straight, pushing back his shoulders. He hesitated, then pushed down his underpants, stepped out of them and stood naked, feeling the warm air caress his skin. He wondered how he might look in comparison to the bodies he had seen on the blankets, whether he would be out of place or would merge into the group. Lying down on the bed, he closed his eyes, trying to imagine how it would feel to be unconcerned enough to lie naked next to someone else.

Over the next few days, as the temperature rose still further, he was constantly aware of his body from the inside out, feeling sinews gliding smoothly over bone, his muscles snap to attention at the least exertion, chest hairs brushing against the rough cotton of his shirt. The pressure of his belt against his skin was a distraction. Occasionally, he caught the smell of himself, the blunt tang of sweat and dust.

He was, he thought, quite unlike the person who had arrived on his bicycle a month before. He felt excitement stir in his stomach, a rumble of possibility, as if he were emerging from a cocoon. The prospect was both daunting and a thrill.

*

Mary seemed to sense the change in him too. She was less distant with him now, allowing him to help her clear the table after supper, or do the dishes in the old stone sink. Sometimes in the evenings, when Hartley and Thomas had gone to the pub, he joined her outside as she smoked. Like Alice, she asked him questions about his life in Cambridge, tentative at first, then probing, storing away the information in her head. He managed to push away his habitual anxiety, telling her stories that he knew she would like, about punting and May Balls, eccentricities and traditions, then gently steering the conversation back towards the farm and things that had happened during the day. He liked to make her laugh with anecdotes about Alice, little things that she had said or done.

'It's Alice's birthday on Friday,' Mary said one evening as they stood leaning against the window ledge.

He nodded. 'She said she's going to have a party.'

'That's what I wanted to ask you about. Will you help me get ready for it? It'll be the first one she's ever had. I want to get it right.' As she exhaled they watched the plume of smoke curl away through the still air. 'I managed to get Hartley to say yes to it, but he's not going to be here.'

'Where's he going?'

'He's off to auction with Thomas to sell his champion tup.'

'But I thought he always wins with it at the show.'

'He does, but he's got it into his head that he's got to sell that tup. It's about money, again. But I know what'll happen – he'll just pour it down his throat.' Wearily she shrugged. 'Anyway, will you help?'

'Of course I will.'

Later that day, going into the farmhouse for a glass of water, he came across Hartley sitting at the table surrounded by paper; scraps torn from catalogues together with bills and yellowing receipts. Brown envelopes spilled out final reminders printed in red. Hartley was hunched over a ledger, his fingers stained with ink, stabbing figures down onto the page. He jumped when Spencer came into the room, and crooked his arm protectively around his work.

'Oh,' said Spencer, 'I'm sorry. I just came to get a drink.'

Hartley shrugged. He looked defeated, his skin grey and drawn.

'Never mind, lad. I'm just trying to make sense of these damn accounts.'

Spencer hesitated. 'I heard you're going to sell your tup.'

Hartley's face remained impassive.

'Aye.'

'I'm sorry. I know – you always win at the show.'

'There's nowt else to be done. It'll fetch more if I sell it now.'

'Oh.'

'So some other bugger can show it.'

There was a pause.

'If you wanted, I – I could help with the accounts,' said Spencer cautiously. 'I mean, I could help with the maths bit of it.'

Hartley shook his head. 'No lad, there's nowt to be done. They won't get any better, whoever gets their hands on them.'

'Right. Of course.' Spencer turned to leave.

'Put wood in't wall on your way out.'

'I'm sorry?'

Hartley raised his eyebrows. 'I mean, shut the door behind you.'

Bright balloons, red and yellow, bobbed from the garden gate. Large purple letters on a bed sheet hanging from the windows spelled out *Happy Birthday Alice, 11 today!*

Spencer had come across Mary spraying the letters after breakfast, the sheet spread out on the ground. He had smiled to see her with her tongue between her teeth like Alice when she was trying to concentrate. She had jumped when Spencer came up behind her.

'Oh! You gave me a shock! I thought you were Hartley.'

He squatted down next to her. 'No, he's gone off to the auction.'

She sprayed a large A onto the sheet. 'Good. He wouldn't have liked me using this.'

'What is it?'

'Formaldehyde. It's for spraying on sheep hooves when they've got foot rot. I took the can from the dipping shed.'

He sniffed the air. 'It stinks, doesn't it?'

'Yes, it's making me a bit dizzy.'

'Let me do it.'

Taking the can, he sprayed the rest of the letters, trying to match her writing. Then they stood back, admiring their handiwork.

'She's going to love it,' Spencer said.

Mary nodded, pleased.

He brought an old door from the side of the barn and they made a table, stacking breeze blocks to rest it on, fiddling with it until it lay flat.

'I'll put a tablecloth over it,' she said. 'The girls can sit on the ground. It's dry enough.'

The table was quickly transformed as they brought out bridge rolls fanned on plates, arranged according to colour: white and yellow egg with salad cream, orange cheddar, pale pink tuna topped with slices of cucumber. Crisps curled in bowls next to tinfoil hedgehogs bristling with cubes of pineapple and sausages on sticks. A collection of fairy cakes took pride of place, topped with startling blue icing.

'I made those,' said Alice, who had joined them. 'Well, I helped. And I chose the colour of the icing.'

'It's a good spread,' said Mary. 'Just as good as anyone else's.'

'It's brilliant, Mam.'

*

Half an hour later, little girls were everywhere, flitting about the garden in long pastel party frocks, squealing as they chased each other through the washing that hung on the line. Alice was wearing a red dress tied at the back with a bow. She had presented herself to Spencer before the party, suddenly shy as she came downstairs.

'Do I look nice, Spence?' Her voice quavered with hope as she took off her glasses and polished them on the hem of her dress.

He felt a sudden rush of emotion. 'You look beautiful,' he said.

Mary and Spencer stood together, watching as Alice and the others raced around the garden, flushed and excited.

'I sometimes wish I'd had another one,' Mary said. 'Alice would have liked a brother or a sister.'

'Is it . . .' He couldn't think of how to put it. 'Too late . . .?'

She gave him a quick, sad smile. 'No, Spence. That's not the problem. You know that.'

*

Before tea there was a treasure hunt. Spencer had spent hours the night before after Alice had gone to bed writing clues on bits of paper and hiding them around the farm. Her friends scurried from place to place, screaming when they worked out the answers. As the clues became more cryptic, he found himself at the centre of a mass of little girls.

'Give us another clue, go on Spencer, please!'

When it came to the last clue of all, his eyes met Alice's.

'What's the secret of happiness?' read out a girl with long blonde plaits.

Alice's face lit up.

'Got it!' she yelled, and then she was off, racing across the field, her red dress flapping as she ran.

The other girls went after her, noisy flashes of colour in the parched grass. Spencer followed at a distance. As Alice reached the little cluster of trees, she looked back at him for an instant, then ran to the biggest beech and dropped to her knees. There, under the great gnarled roots, she found what she was looking for: a little package, wrapped up in newspaper. She began to unwrap it, the other girls gathered around.

When he heard her squeal, he knew he had chosen well. The iron pyrites that he had found in the gutter sparkled in the palm of her hand. He had cleaned it up, chipping away at the rock so it glittered and shone.

'What's that on the tree?' asked one of the girls.

'It's a secret thing,' said Alice loftily. 'Only me and Spence know what it means.'

'It looks like the love heart my sister and Billy Braithwaite carved when they were going with each other. I saw them kissing next to it. After he dumped her she cut it all up with a knife.'

'Is Spencer your boyfriend, Alice?'

'Is he? Is he?'

Alice looked from girl to girl, flustered.

'That's what he is, he's your *boyfriend*!'

For a moment she looked as if she were about to cry, then her chin went up, her shoulders squared.

'Don't be silly,' she said. 'He's not my boyfriend. We just talk about things that's all. Things none of *you* would understand.'

Back at the barn, the girls fell on the food, devouring the sand-wiches, which they customized according to taste, adding crisps to tuna, pineapple to egg. Mary and Spencer leaned against the wall of the farmhouse, watching.

'She's having a nice time, isn't she?' said Mary. 'That's why I wanted her to have a party. Children remember things like that.'

Spencer nodded. 'I think she likes having other people around.'

Mary sighed. 'Hartley said she's been hanging around the hippies. I know they're probably harmless but, well, sometimes she does get some funny ideas in her head.'

Spencer thought of the naked bodies on the grass. 'I think she just likes the paintings on their vans and the music. The radio's always on.'

'Sometimes I wish I'd done something like that, leaving every-thing behind and driving around with nothing to do except have a good time. I'm not that much older than them. Actually, Spencer, I'm not that much older than you.'

He glanced at her rough hands, gripping the paper plate.

'I know,' she said quietly. 'My face feels like the ground over there, all cracked from the heat. When it rains the ground will go back to how it used to be, but I won't ever be young again. That's the difference.'

As she went indoors to put candles on the birthday cake, Spencer looked across at the table and the little girls around it, as serious about their conversation as professors in a Cambridge dining hall. Again, he thought of his thesis, wondering if he would ever be admitted into that tiny enclave of extraordinary minds.

When Mary came out with the cake, squeals rose from the table, the loudest of all of them from Alice.

'Mam! It's Shadow!'

There, reclining on a layer of marzipan straw, was a replica of

Shadow made from dark chocolate cake, pieces of flaky chocolate carefully stuck on as fur. Her paws were frosted with white icing and a long, red liquorice tongue protruded from her mouth.

'She's even got her pups!'

Six small chocolate marshmallows nestled, feeding, at her side.

'Do you like it, love?'

Alice smiled up at her. 'It's the best cake ever! Come and look, Spence.'

As he went over to the table, Mary lit the candles and the girls began to sing *Happy Birthday*, their voices filling the garden, sweet and high.

'Now blow, and make a wish,' said Mary.

Alice reached up and took her hand. The next moment Spencer felt Alice's other hand slipping into his. As she closed her eyes he curled his fingers around hers, looking down to hide the sudden tears that filled his eyes.

She blew hard, extinguishing all the candles, and the girls cheered.

'I did it all in one go,' she said, looking up at them both. 'That means my wish will definitely come true!'

*

When the mothers came to pick up their daughters at the end of the afternoon, Spencer was surprised to see Valerie Horsley. It was as he helped Mary slice up what was left of the cake, wrapping it in napkins for the girls to take home, that he noticed her, leaning against her car, a rather flashy red Mercedes-Benz, which looked somewhat out of place in the farmyard next to the dusty tractor and trailer.

She too looked out of place as she sauntered over to him, dressed in a tight halter-necked dress and high-heeled sandals, sunglasses perched on top of her head.

'How are you, Spencer Little?' she said, standing close. 'We haven't seen you in the village for ever.'

He managed to smile. 'Hello.'

'I hear you've become a bit of a hero since I last saw you. Terribly brave of you.'

'Really, it wasn't—'

'I thought I'd come all the way up here and congratulate you myself. My daughter's never been to play at Mirethwaite before, but this time I thought I'd say yes.'

She looked at him, tilting her head, assessing. 'It suits you, this new-found fame. You look quite different to last time I saw you. And in a much better mood, I must say. Drop in if you're ever in the village. We're the big house next to the village hall. Come for a sherry. I seem to remember you like it.'

'I – I'd better get to the kitchen,' he said. 'I need to bring more cake.'

She smiled. 'Come one afternoon. Whenever you fancy. But don't leave it too long, will you?'

Twelve

The household rose early on Wednesday, ready to bring the last remaining sheep down from the fell. After breakfast, they set off up the intake, Hartley leading the way, followed by Thomas, with Mary, Spencer and Alice bringing up the rear. Hartley's dogs slunk close to his heels. Shadow, despite Alice's protests, had been shut up in the barn. It was a clear, brilliant morning, the heat still just a promise on the breeze. The mountain reared up in front of them, charred to the intake wall, bracken green beyond. Sheep stood in clusters, a motley collection of grey ewes, brown yearlings and black-faced lambs. Crows perched, silent, in trees, watching and waiting.

When they reached the gate at the top of the intake, Hartley stopped them. They stood, chins resting on crooks, listening as he explained his strategy like a general addressing his troops.

'We'll start at the top and work down. I'll go straight up the middle rake with Fly. Thomas, you go left and take Jip; Spencer and Mary to the right with Jet. See how many are about, and then we'll bring them down together, closing in. We don't want to lose any in't waterfall—' he pointed with his crook '—but there's hardly owt left in't beck so I reckon we'll be all right.'

'Who should I go with, Dad?' asked Alice.

'You stay with your mother.' He nodded in Mary's direction, off-hand. They separated, climbing quickly, heads down. Spencer thought of the first time he had climbed the mountain, his first day in the valley, as Hartley had taken him to the hut. Then he had panted, exhausted by the climb. Now, a month on, he was fitter, easily able to push his way through the bracken. Alice followed, grumbling at the fronds that sprung back, hitting her in the face.

'I still wish we could have brought Shadow,' she said. 'She always comes on the gather.'

'You don't want her to get into any more trouble, do you?' asked Spencer. 'Anyway, she needs to rest.'

'I wish she'd hurry up and have her pups. I've already been thinking about names for them.'

'Have you? What are they?'

Jerking her head in Mary's direction, she put her finger to her lips. 'I'll tell you later.'

Spencer looked up to see Hartley and his dog in the distance. They had made much faster progress than him and Alice, almost reaching the dark pillars of rock at the top of the mountain. Spencer quickened his pace, bashing hard at the bracken with his crook.

Soon he was also at the summit, looking down. The sun was still rising, opening up the day, casting soft light over the fields. Tractors stood idle in farmyards and the road that snaked along the valley bottom was empty of cars. The hippies' camp was deserted, everyone still sleeping. He felt a particular pleasure in being awake at such an unusual hour, in seeing the valley so tranquil, caught in a pause, a hush, before the day began.

The tranquillity didn't last long. At Hartley's signal, they set off down the mountainside, shouting to rouse the sheep.

'Hoo!' yelled Hartley, and they followed his lead, whooping and calling as they made their way back through the bracken. It was a strange, almost joyful sound, and it was odd to hear it from Mary and Thomas, who seemed to have abandoned their usual reserve. Alice joined in happily, jumping up and down, her whoops high and clear above the others.

Startled sheep rose to their feet, bleating their surprise, and soon the fell poured with streams of animals. The dogs herded them, running quickly around the flock, doubling back to marshall strays. There was no logic to the movement of the sheep, who seemed to have little idea of their destination, just a stubborn determination to escape.

As they inched towards the gate, the farmers closed in, stretching their arms out wide and using their crooks to form a barrier. Hartley's commands to the dogs were quiet now; warning whistles squeezed between his teeth, telling them when to hold back, and a single low word, repeated over and over again:

'Fly . . . Fly . . . Fly . . .'

The little dog never lost his concentration, his eyes narrowed, ears pricked, attuned to every change in Hartley's tone. Together they brought the sheep to the open gate, white heads bobbing together as a crowd.

'Stand back, Spencer,' shouted Mary. 'Don't go too near. If they know you're there they'll run for it.'

Spencer stepped back and the sheep surged on, closer. The only sound was from Hartley; the others were tense and silent, waiting to see if the flock would go through.

One of the sheep began to inch forward, taking high, almost dainty steps. The dogs stayed still, their noses to the ground, watching. Spencer willed the animal forward, holding his breath. It moved another inch, then paused, sniffing at the air. That moment a lamb broke from the group, dashing under Spencer's crook and hurrying down the side of the wall, bleating loudly. Its mother gave an answering call and ran after it, parting the crowd. Immediately, the others turned and veered in the same direction.

Hartley let out a howl of rage.

'Stupid sodding animals! I'll bray the hides off the lot of you!' He shook his head violently. 'Get after them!'

Thomas launched himself down the mountainside. He moved easily, suddenly agile, crashing through the bracken and leaping over rocks. His dog went with him, ears flattened as she darted through the undergrowth, and together they managed to get to the front of the flock. The sheep all stopped, confused, then began a messy stampede, turning from left to right and back again, calling to each other in a bleating mass, panicked lambs separated from their mothers, running against the current.

'Go round,' shouted Hartley, and Spencer found himself sprinting through the bracken, his heart hammering, trying to reach the sheep before they went any further.

*

For the rest of the morning they continued to round up the sheep, keeping them together, shifting them forward a few yards down the mountain, then losing them as a single animal made its break for freedom, scattering the flock. As the sun rose higher and the temperature soared, Hartley's fury grew.

Around midday, after another fruitless dash down the fellside, Thomas lost his temper. When another sheep slipped away at the last minute, just as the rest were about to go through the gate, his face turned puce. A torrent of invective poured out of him, the images conjured up so vilely obscene that it made Spencer flinch to hear them. Thomas tore after the animal, arms flailing, his yells of rage echoing across the valley. Pulling its head back, he straddled it, bringing down his crook at the point where its thick fleece met the short hair on its neck. Wood cracked against bone. Mary winced as he lashed out again and again. Alice turned away. Urine began to gather in pools on the ground as the other sheep emptied their bladders in terror.

It was Spencer who carried the battered sheep down the mountainside. Hartley sent him to retrieve it once they had finally managed to get the flock through.

'Put it over your shoulders,' he instructed. 'And hold its legs. There won't be much struggle left in it by now. And don't go getting sentimental,' he added. 'Animals don't feel pain, not like we do, remember that.'

As they trudged through the charred wasteland of the intake, Spencer felt the weight of the sheep on his neck and the scratch of its grimy wool against his skin. The animals were quiet; exhausted perhaps, or intimidated by the dogs that circled, hackles raised and growling, ready to pounce. When they reached the bottom intake gate, the dogs moved closer, intent on preventing another escape.

When the last animal was on the other side, the gate closed firmly behind it, they all breathed a sigh of relief. Stooping close to the ground, Spencer unhooked the sheep from his shoulders and, giving it a little push, watched it stagger away to join the others.

Shutting the flock in the dipping pens, they walked back to the farmhouse, ignoring the mournful cries of mothers separated from their lambs.

'Well, they can want,' muttered Hartley, a muscle flickering in his cheek, 'after the run-around they've given us. They'll stay in there 'til we've had our dinner, and that's that.'

When they got back to the yard, Alice dashed to the barn to free Shadow, who trotted out, belly swinging, panting heavily. Falling to her knees, Alice flung her arms around her dog's neck, letting her face be licked in welcome.

'Good girl,' she said happily. 'You were a good girl to wait for me at home. It wasn't very nice up there anyway. Uncle Tom hit a sheep and everyone got cross.'

After lunch, Hartley gave Spencer the afternoon off.

'It was a hard morning, lad,' he grunted. 'And the next couple of days won't be much better. Put your feet up for a bit.'

*

On his way back up to the hut, Spencer came across one of the hippies sitting on a rock, languidly sucking on a long, intricately carved pipe.

'Hey,' he said, as Spencer approached. 'How're you?'

'It's been a busy morning. We've been gathering the fell.'

'What for?'

'I'm sorry?'

'What were you gathering?'

'Oh – sheep.'

Looking more closely, he realized it was the man he had woken to pay for the camping. 'It's Mick, isn't it?'

'Yes,' he answered, blowing out a smoke ring. 'It is.' There was a pause. 'And did you get them all?'

'All what?'

'All the sheep.'

'Oh. Yes. We did, by the end of it.'

'It must be a pretty lovely life up here, away from all the rush. Surrounded by nature, making your living from the land. Peace and quiet. All good.'

Spencer thought of Thomas's fury that morning and inwardly grimaced.

'That's why we're here,' Mick continued. 'Trying to find a bit of that for ourselves, you know?' He sucked on his pipe for a moment, nodding slowly, then exhaled. 'Want some?' he asked, holding it out.

Spencer was puzzled. 'What? Oh, no, thanks, I don't smoke.'

'It's not tobacco. It's grass.'

'Oh.' The few times he had gone to parties at Cambridge he had always held back, not wanting to clutter his thoughts, but now a sudden recklessness flashed through him. 'Well then, perhaps . . .'

Taking the pipe, he put it to his lips. The smoke was thick and heavily perfumed. He coughed.

'Try and hold it in. It's pretty strong, but it's good.'

He tried to do as Mick said, feeling the smoke fill his lungs.

'Smoking it up here blows your mind. Now I get what those poets were doing tucked away in their little cottages. All their stuff makes sense after a bit of this. You know, Wordsworth and Coleridge and Thomas de Quincey . . . They all lived together just over there, past those mountains. They smoked stuff way stronger than this. Opium. They wrote poems about nature and imagination. Dreams. All the shit we're into. They were just like us, two hundred years ago. Pretty amazing.'

Leaning back, he began to recite:

'In Xanadu did Kubla Khan
A stately pleasure dome decree;
Where Alph the sacred river ran
Through caverns measureless to man
Down to a sunless sea.'

He sighed dreamily. 'It's the best thing in the world; smoke a little bit of weed, or take some mushrooms, then lie back in the sun and get someone to read that poem out loud while you look up at those mountains.'

A warm drowsiness had begun to settle over Spencer. He glanced over at the grey crags, making a vague promise to himself to explore them.

'Pass it over,' Mick said. Holding a match to the pipe, he sucked in hard, then held his breath for a moment. Blowing out a long stream of smoke, he closed his eyes and stretched luxuriously, like a cat, exposing his lean, suntanned belly.

Feeling slightly dizzy, Spencer looked away.

'I'd better be going,' he said.

Mick took a moment to respond.

'Where to?'

'The hut. Up there. It's – it's where I live.'

Mick opened his eyes.

'Cool. Very cool. I like that. Man on his own, camping out in the elements. Thoreau. Whitman. D.H. Lawrence . . .' He took another long drag. 'I'm wondering, you know, who are you?'

'My name's Spencer. I think I told you . . .'

'Yeah, I remember, but Spencer, who *are* you? You're not from round here, I can see that. You don't look like it and I can hear it in your voice.'

He repeated his question. 'Who *are* you?'

Spencer said nothing for a moment, unsure of what to say. 'I'm just staying for a while,' he said finally. 'Passing through, like you.'

*

When he went back to the farmhouse that evening he found Alice sitting on an upturned bucket with Mary bending close to her head, combing through her hair with her fingers.

'Hello Spence,' said Alice cheerfully. Her hair stuck out even more than usual, teased to a tangle by Mary's endeavours. 'I've got ticks.'

'She'll have got them on the gather,' said Mary. 'The bracken's full of them. Oh—' her hands stopped moving '—here's another one.' Carefully she pulled it from Alice's scalp, pinching it hard between her finger and thumb, and depositing it in a margarine tub filled with water.

'There's loads,' said Alice. 'They were all in my shorts and under my arms and on the back of my knees. Shadow's got them too.'

A dozen black corpses floated on their backs, dark streaks of blood leaking into the water.

'It hurts like mad,' she said. 'You can feel them sucking on you, and when you try to pull them out, they don't want to come and they stick bits into you to try and hold on.' She lifted up her arm. 'Look.'

He saw that her armpit was dotted with small red lumps.

'Have you got any, Spence?'

'I don't think so,' he said. 'I haven't noticed them, anyway.'

He was in no state of mind to notice anything much. He had spent the afternoon lying on his bed, sweating in the heat, passing in and out of troubled sleep. His dreams had been arousing and vivid, leaping between centuries and locations, peopled by a cast of characters which included Coleridge and Wordsworth chasing sheep through the caverns of Kubla Khan, spurred on by Mick the hippy as a genial ringmaster, watched by Edmund – the man he had met on the top of the fell, in his singlet and shorts – and Mary in her red dress, holding a cigarette, which then became a hookah pipe. He had woken up gasping, unsure of who or where he was.

Thirteen

THE FIRST OF THE CLIPPING DAYS BEGAN WITH THE SOUND of bleating: an ill-matched medley, nasal and discordant. As the men brought the flock down from the dipping pens, driving them along the narrow lane, the smell of animals filled the morning air; six hundred unclean fleeces, greasy and hot.

'Stop your blethering,' muttered Hartley.

He looked battered from the past night's drinking, eyes small and bloodshot, the veins on his nose an angry vermilion, each breath a blast of stale beer and bad digestion. As they pushed the last sheep into the yard, he paused, leaning heavily on his crook, looking as if he were about to retch.

The clipping station had been set up in the big barn. Two electrical cables looped precariously over a beam led to large red clippers, steel teeth glinting, jaws wide. In the corner, hanging from another beam, was a giant sack made of coarse brown cloth.

Mary brought out a tray with mugs of steaming coffee and the three men stood sipping it, looking at the yard, packed with a grey mass of sheep.

'It'll take all of two days,' Hartley said morosely. 'Even wi't lad to give us a hand. What time is it, Thomas? Should he not be here by now?'

Thomas looked at his watch. 'It's half past eight.'

Just then, a ripple of movement spread through the yard. Looking up, Spencer saw someone slipping through the gate at the far end. The sea of sheep divided noisily, tripping over one another in order to avoid the source of the disturbance.

Making his way through them, the newcomer raised a hand in greeting.

'How do?' called Hartley. 'This is the lad who's coming to help with clipping,' he said to Spencer. 'He's good and he's fast.'

It was Edmund. Spencer remembered back to the running clothes he'd been wearing on the fell and in his dream, and felt himself redden. This time Edmund was dressed in tight jeans and denim shirt, a duffle bag dangling from his shoulder.

'This is young Edmund Lutwidge,' Hartley told him. 'And this is Spence, who's with us for the summer,' he said to Edmund. 'Thanks for giving us a hand, lad, at the last minute. I didn't think you'd be free.'

'Aye,' said Edmund. 'Lucky, wasn't it?'

'Now then,' said Hartley, 'you and Thomas can take care of clipping. Me and Spence'll get the sheep moving through, smit them and wrap fleeces. That sound all right to you?'

Edmund nodded. Picking up a pair of clippers, he flicked a switch. Immediately a loud buzzing noise rang through the barn. He turned the implement over in his hands, testing its weight, then flicked the switch back again.

'Right,' he said, 'let's get started.'

Striding over to the nearest sheep, Hartley grabbed it by the scruff of its neck and dragged it to Edmund, who manoeuvred it onto its back. Pulling the animal close to his crotch and gripping it with his knees, he took the clippers, switched them on, and touched them to the sheep's breastbone. Gently, he started to push out to the side, moving down slowly to the belly. The fleece fell away easily, startlingly white against the dirty grey of the outer wool.

As he worked, the sheep stopped struggling, as if soothed by the strong, careful strokes. Spencer stood for a moment, watching the clippers glide. Edmund was methodical and confident, working his way around the sheep's body, his hand firm, head down, focused on what he was doing.

In less than five minutes he had finished, the fleece lying at his feet like a cast of the sheep, which staggered like a toddler in the direction of the woolsack.

'Oh no you don't,' said Hartley, straddling it. 'Spence, bring that bucket quick, that one there, with the smit in it.'

The bucket was filled with a thick red paste. Pulling out the stick that was jammed into it, Hartley daubed two rough streaks over the sheep's backbone.

'It marks them as ours,' he said to Spencer. 'Two lines, rib to rib. About three inches between them. Got it?'

Spencer nodded.

Hartley released the sheep. 'Right, then. Off you go.'

The clipped sheep wandered off through the pen that Spencer and Thomas had built that morning and out into the neighbouring field, dazed like a newly freed convict. Without the bulk of its fleece it was scrawny, its bones clearly visible under its skin.

Spencer gazed at it, counting its ribs as it moved, staggering, over the grass.

'Spence!' shouted Hartley. 'Stop dreaming, man. Come here and I'll show you how to wrap.' Taking the fleece, he laid it flat on the ground. 'First thing to do is tease the neck out. You want it good and long. Then you twist it, so it's strong. See?'

Spencer nodded.

'Then you put the sides in, like this, so you've got two straight lines, and you roll it up, from the bottom. If there's any daggings, you cut them off. When you've done, you get the neck and wrap it round the whole thing, so it stays together. Got it?'

The wrapped-up fleece was bigger than Spencer had expected, its soft, new wool on the inside, the dark, greasy coat facing out. Hartley threw it into the woolsack.

'Five hundred and ninety-nine to go.'

*

They worked on, breaking only for a lunch of sandwiches – great hunks of bread with meat and pickle between them – accompanied by glasses of foaming beer. As the sun beat down on the barn, the temperature inside it rose and the sheep grew restless and fretful. Hartley and Thomas kept to their usual shirtsleeves, sweat pouring down their faces, but Edmund took off his denim shirt, stripping to his vest, dazzling white against his tanned face and chest. Spencer wished he had the confidence to do the same.

Halfway through the afternoon, the brothers swapped places, Hartley taking over from Thomas at the clippers. Thomas paced about, stiffly swinging his arms.

'It gets you in the shoulders,' Edmund observed to Spencer. 'That's the worst bit. And the bottom of your back.'

'Don't you want a rest?'

'I'm not bothered. I'm used to it. I like to keep going 'til the end of the day, then I stop for good and stretch out.'

He continued, never slowing his pace, a steady stream of sheep passing under his clippers. He seemed unperturbed by the wriggling animals, taking even the most recalcitrant in his stride.

As the afternoon wore on, the woolsack began to bulge with fleeces. Unable to contain herself any longer, Alice, who had been sitting on a stool in the corner reading *Ballet Shoes*, jumped up and ran over to it, flinging herself against it, bouncing off the wool.

'Give over,' Hartley said testily. 'If you want to make yourself useful, go and fetch the needle.'

She went off to the farmhouse, returning after a while with a long, rusty implement. Threading it carefully with coarse twine, Edmund closed the woolsack with large, crooked stitches.

At six o'clock Edmund switched off his clippers.

'I reckon that's me done for the day,' he said, straightening up.

'Aye,' said Hartley. 'We've got through a good fair few. Nigh on a hundred and fifty between me and Thomas. How about you?'

'Knocking on two hundred.'

'We'll be all right to finish tomorrow if we keep going like this.'

'Yep. I'll be off then.'

Nodding at Spencer and Thomas, he shrugged on his shirt and strolled through the yard, which was now half empty, doing up the buttons on his shirt as he went.

*

The next day, Edmund was already at the barn when they arrived, lying on a woolsack, his eyes closed, hands behind his head.

'What's all this?' said Hartley suspiciously. 'Why're you early?'

Edmund opened one eye and grinned. 'Dunno, Hartley, maybe I'm just in the mood for it.'

'Well,' he grunted, 'sooner we start, sooner we finish. Let's crack on.'

They worked hard, quietly efficient. The sheep were calmer than the day before, as if resigned to their fate. Edmund and Hartley got through them quickly and soon the field behind the barn was filled with shorn animals, calling to each other, ewes reuniting with their lambs.

Spencer found himself enjoying his task of rolling up the fleeces, taking pride in making each one into a perfect cylinder. Very soon the morning was over and it was time for lunch. They ate greedily, sitting on the woolsack. That day the sandwiches were filled with cheese – strong, salty cheddar that went well with the beer. Afterwards, Mary brought out bowls of glistening strawberries, swimming in cream.

'They're from the garden,' said Alice. 'We picked them this morning.'

'You did well,' said Edmund. 'They're grand.'

'Now then,' said Hartley, wiping his mouth with the back of his hand, 'how many are we up to? I've done another seventy.'

Edmund nodded. 'Ninety for me.'

'So that makes—'

'Five hundred and ten,' said Spencer.

Hartley clapped him on the back. 'Ha! So if the company's paying us twenty pence a fleece, by the time we're done, we'll make . . .?'

'A hundred and twenty pounds.'

He shook his head. 'You're quick, lad, I'll give you that. By Christ, though, it's hardly worth doing. Time was, you'd make a whole year's rent from a good clipping. Dad used to rely on it, and we could have done with it this year, too.' Putting down his bowl, he stood up. 'Anyway. We've another ninety-odd to do. And you're here for the rest of the afternoon, Edmund? We'll leave you and Spence to it for a couple of hours. Bill Birkett wants to talk about Thomas helping him out with his hay. I want to get it sorted while he's keen.'

'We'll get through this lot no problem.' Edmund nodded at Spencer. 'Right?'

Spencer nodded back, pleased to be included in his confidence.

As soon as the brothers had left, Edmund put down his clippers. 'OK,' he said, 'let's have a laugh while we're at it.'

Reaching for his duffle bag, he brought out a small transistor radio and fiddled with the dials. 'We can only get Radio Carlisle, but it's better than nowt.'

Music blared out tinnily across the barn.

'I like this one,' he said. 'Queen're brilliant.' Holding the clippers to his lips, he jumped up on the woolsack and began to sing, his voice not pure, but surprisingly deep for someone so slight. The sun shone into the barn, making his blond hair blaze. As he went on singing, giving his all to an audience of startled sheep, Spencer was caught between admiration and embarrassment.

Alice, appearing around the corner, stood and stared. Looking down from the woolsack, Edmund beckoned to her. She hesitated for a moment, then, letting out a little whoop, ran to join him, scrambling up to wobble precariously on the top.

'Come on, Spence,' she said. 'Come and sing with us!'

He refused, shrugging shyly.

'Go on,' said Edmund. 'Doesn't matter if you don't know the words. Just mime.'

But he shook his head. Alice and Edmund danced together for the rest of the song, their voices merging in a jubilant duet. When it ended, they fell off the woolsack, beaming and flushed. Edmund's hair was plastered to his face with sweat.

Alice bobbed a curtsey, holding out imaginary skirts.

'That was dead good,' she said excitedly. 'Let's do it again!'

'Might do, later,' Edmund said. 'But don't tell your dad.'

She shook her head. 'No way!'

'Better get back to it,' he said, switching on the clippers. Their busy hum filled the barn. 'Turn it up a bit, Alice. You ready, Spence?'

The afternoon passed quickly, the music providing a rhythm to their work. Edmund was word perfect to all the songs, singing along loudly. Spencer listened, enjoying the sound of his voice, pleased that there was no need to talk.

After an hour or so, they took a break. Spencer brought out cans of lager from the farmhouse. As he handed one to Edmund he noticed a picture of a topless woman on the side. There was a momentary pause, then Edmund rolled his eyes, and they started to laugh.

'Now we know why Mary puts it in glasses before she brings it out for our dinner,' said Edmund. 'I wondered why she didn't just give us a can.' He looked at Spencer. 'I thought the fancy glasses were because of you.'

'What do you mean?'

'Well you're used to something a bit different, down there in Cambridge, aren't you? Posh dinners? Silver spoons?'

'Shut up,' said Spencer softly, taking a deep swig.

'Cheers then.' Edmund raised the can to his lips. 'Hell, it's hot. Worse than yesterday.'

'I know,' said Spencer. 'I'm quite jealous of the sheep, losing all that wool.'

'I could sort that out for you.' Edmund picked up the clippers, a glint of mischief in his eyes. 'Shall I cool you down?'

Spencer leaped to his feet. 'N-no! I didn't mean that!'

Edmund stood up too. 'Are you sure? It wouldn't take a minute.' He took a step towards Spencer.

'Really, I'm fine.'

Darting forward suddenly, Edmund caught him. They struggled

for a while, neither willing to give way, then Edmund got him in an armlock.

'Shall I switch them on?'

'No!'

'*Bzzz*,' he said, mimicking the sound of the clippers.

Spencer felt the strength of his wiry body holding him down, the clamminess of his bare skin under his vest, and his heart, beating fast and hard.

'What are you doing?' Alice was suddenly at the barn door again, her voice high with curiosity.

Edmund burst out laughing again and let go of Spencer, clapping him on the shoulder.

'I was going to give him a haircut,' he said. 'He was too hot. But maybe it's me who needs one instead.'

Switching on the clippers he brought them close to his shock of hair. 'What do you think? Shall I give myself a bit of a trim?'

'No!' shouted Spencer, louder than he had intended. 'Don't!'

*

By the time Hartley and Thomas returned in the late afternoon, there were just a few dozen animals waiting to be clipped. They huddled quietly in the yard, too hot to bleat. Hartley was in a good mood, his eyes bright, cheeks and nose mottled red, his breath smelling of beer.

'Right then,' he said. 'Me and Thomas'll give you a hand to finish them off. You clip, Thomas, I'll smit.'

They worked on into the evening, the giddiness of the afternoon now gone. Spencer stared at the woolsack as he threw in the fleeces, remembering Edmund and Alice dancing on it, singing into their make-believe microphones.

'We're all off to the Tup later on,' said Hartley. 'Bill Birkett's finishing off his clipping today, and Titch Tyson too. It'll be good crack. They're laying on pie and peas. You'll come with us, Edmund? Spence?'

Spencer looked out at the sun, sinking over the fields.

'Aye,' he heard Edmund say.

He turned round and nodded at Hartley. 'Yes,' he said. 'I'll come. Why not?'

*

The Tup was very different from how it had been the last time he was there. Now the air was thick with smoke, farmers standing two deep at the bar to be served. Despite the crush, the atmosphere was easy and convivial, the room filled with the deep rumble of voices and laughter.

Hartley came over to the table, his hands curled around four pints of beer.

'Take them quick,' he said. 'They're going to drop.' He sank onto the settle.

'Well, cheers, lads. Six hundred sheep in two days. That's pretty bloody good.'

They raised their glasses and drank. Spencer felt the warm beer travel down his throat and hit his stomach. His shoulders, stiff from bending to roll the fleeces, began to relax.

'Sheila said the pie and peas are coming out any minute,' Hartley went on. 'I've got us all tickets. I've worked up a fair appetite this afternoon.'

Spencer hid a grin as Edmund raised his eyebrows very slightly, remembering the colour of Hartley's cheeks when he had returned earlier. 'Are you going to take on the work for Mr Birkett?' he asked Thomas politely.

'Damn right he is,' said Hartley. 'That's a week's haymaking for good money, and we'll manage without him, I reckon, Spence, me and you. You can have tomorrow off, though. You worked hard these last couple of days.' He nodded at Edmund. 'He's a good worker. Like you.'

Spencer felt his own cheeks turn red.

The smell of slow-cooked onions and roasting meat drifted through the pub. Heads turned and the hum of voices grew louder.

'That'll be our scran,' said Hartley, and Spencer was glad of the distraction.

A few minutes later, a bell rang out behind the bar. 'Now then, fellers,' shouted the barmaid, 'pie and peas are on the tables at the back. Don't all rush at once. Anyone who hasn't got a ticket, come and get one from me.'

There was a flurry of movement.

'Let's get ourselves in there,' said Hartley. 'Before it gets cold.'

The tables were laden with dishes of pale green mushy peas and metal trays topped with pastry. As the first slice was cut, the smell of hot meat filled the room. Hastily they joined the queue, picking up cutlery and plates.

Back in their corner, they concentrated on their food; rich, steaming gravy pooled around chunks of tender beef and carrots. They ate greedily, wolfing it down in silence, hungry after the day's work, and washing it down with more beer, its yeasty taste mingling with the meat.

They all went back for seconds, and went on eating until the metal trays were scraped shiny clean, the last smear of gravy wiped away. An air of peaceful contentment settled over the pub, as chairs were scraped back, pipes lit and pints supped. The hum of male voices rose again, discussing the clipping, comparing yields and prices and speculating on when the drought would end.

'That was grand,' said Hartley. 'Let's have a whisky to settle it. I'll get a round in.'

'I'll do it,' said Spencer.

'No, lad. Drinks are on me tonight.'

He stood up and went to the bar. A silence fell over the table. Thomas lit up an uncharacteristic cigarette and Edmund sat back in his chair, looking about the pub and nodding to a group of farmers on the other side of the bar. Spencer tried to think of something to say.

'You're very fast at shearing,' he said to Edmund. 'Have you been doing it long?'

As soon as he said it he cringed, wishing he'd stayed quiet.

You're not at some formal dinner in Cambridge, you idiot, he thought.

But Edmund seemed pleased. 'Five or six years, on or off. I started with my dad's sheep, but then I realized there was money in it. Dad doesn't mind me taking the time off, as long as I give him some of what I make. And I like doing it. You know what you're dealing with. You can see the sheep at the start and you know what there is to get through. You get on with it, then it's finished. The sheep are in the fields, all clipped, the woolsacks are full, and you can see the results, you know?'

'Yes!' said Spencer eagerly. 'It's like that with maths. I see the problem, I know what there is to be solved. When I've finished, I sit back and it's there, and done, and it stays done, because I made it happen—'

Hartley came back with a tray on which were balanced four pints of beer and four generous measures of whisky. He unloaded them onto the table and sat down heavily.

'What's the crack then? What did I miss?'

'Spencer was talking about maths,' said Thomas.

'Ah!' said Hartley. 'We've got our own clever bugger staying with us. Did you know that, Edmund?'

Edmund scratched his head. 'Well he was quick at the arithmetic this afternoon.'

'So he should be,' said Hartley. 'Our Spence is a professor. Down south. At Cambridge University. That's why he had the sense to pick us to come and work with.'

'I'm not a professor,' protested Spencer.

'Ah, well, whatever. You will be one day, lad. It'll come, sure enough. Stick with us, we'll show you what's what.' He lifted his glass. 'To the clever bugger!'

Edmund and Thomas raised their pint glasses. 'To the clever bugger,' they said in unison.

Spencer looked at their faces, searching for irony, but found none. Edmund was grinning widely, and even Thomas's face had split into a gentle smile. It all seemed suddenly so simple. A warm flush of happiness spread through him, and he lifted his own glass too.

'Thanks,' he said, and they all drank deep, then picked up their whiskies and downed them in one.

Hours passed, with more pints drunk, each one of them followed by the burn of cheap whisky. Spencer's hazy happiness stayed with him. He sat looking at Hartley and Thomas with sentimental affection. Hartley was in his element, cracking jokes and telling tales, his face brick red, dark eyes glittering. Thomas seemed less awkward than usual, his features relaxed, the top button of his shirt left undone. Now they were his allies, his friends.

He looked around at the pub, a shiver of pleasure passing through him at being part of something. He had been right, he decided, to come away to the Lakes. He could be somebody entirely different, someone with a certain future, rather than an awkward past.

At closing time they wandered along the road in the strange blue half-light, Hartley and Thomas, Spencer and Edmund, accompanied by a handful of other farmers, all of them unsteady on their feet. As they approached a turning, Hartley stopped.

'Wait, lads!' He held up a hand. 'We've got to jump off the bridge.'

Spencer was baffled. 'What did he say?' he asked Edmund.

'We always do it,' Hartley insisted, his voice slurred. 'Every New Year's Eve and every clipping day. Off the old packhorse bridge, into the river. Come on lads.'

'Aye.'

'He's right.'

'Let's do it.'

Half a mile along the narrow track was a humpback bridge, arched high above a river. They stood on it, looking down into a dark pool flanked by great hunks of granite rising out of the water.

'You stand in't middle, Spence, and jump,' said Hartley. 'But get it right, mind. It's narrow. You wouldn't want to hit the rocks. You'd smash up your legs.' He laughed as he saw Spencer's face grow pale. 'You'll be all right. No-one's done that since Jack Porter in 1963. And he was properly drunk at the time. You haven't had that much. Nowt to worry about.'

The men began to take off their clothes, undoing their belts and fumbling with buttons and shoelaces, revealing stocky, muscular bodies, honed from lifetimes of manual labour. There was pushing and laughter and jeering at each other's nakedness, two of them chasing after one another like boys. Spencer hovered on the outskirts of the group, suddenly nervous.

'Come on, man. Get your kit off,' shouted Hartley, his body start-lingly pale in the moonlight. 'We're all the same underneath.'

Edmund, bare-chested but still wearing his trousers, stood on the bridge, looking down.

'I don't know, Hartley. The river's running low. We've had that little rain, it's drying up.'

'What d'you mean, lad? I've been jumping off that bridge for twenty-five years. The pool never gets empty, even when there's no water anywhere else.'

'Look down there, over to the side. Can't you see those bones?'

Spencer looked into the pool at where Edmund was pointing. The skeleton of a sheep was clearly visible just under the surface: eerie, bleached whiter by the moonlight.

'The water's got to be shallow if we can see that,' said Edmund.

'You're right,' muttered Hartley, reluctantly. 'Get your clothes back on, lads,' he said, raising his voice. 'Nowt to do but wait for it to rain. Christ, we've never had a summer like this.'

As the men staggered about getting dressed again, Edmund leaned over to Spencer.

'I'll take you swimming,' he said. 'I know a place that never dries up. I think you'll like it.'

He pulled on his shirt. 'I'll come and find you tomorrow.'

Fourteen

Spencer woke late, disoriented and thirsty. He reached for his flask of water and drained it, feeling the tepid liquid trickle down his throat, then lay back, sweating, piecing together the night before. He had been drunk on whisky and beer, but also with exhilaration at belonging to the pub's easy fraternity.

His elation had dwindled on the long walk back to the farm, turning into leaden drunkenness after he left the others and turned up to the hut. It had vanished altogether by the time he sat on the edge of his bed, breathing heavily, dizzy and anxious. He had looked at his little shelf of books, Hartley's easy confidence about his professorship seeming now to mock him. He had pulled down his notebook, but his handwriting seemed to slide about the page, making no sense. Flicking over his last set of workings, he could see only dead ends, his proof as far away as ever and half the summer gone.

Abruptly, he had shut the book and laid down, closing his eyes as the room began to spin.

Later, in a nightmare, a naked, grinning Hartley had jumped off the bridge, yelling with excitement, then, misjudging his trajectory, crashed onto the rocks below.

When he finally managed to get down the fell and into the farm-house, Alice was waiting.

'Dad and Uncle Tom have gone to take the fleeces to the sorting sheds,' she said. 'He didn't look very well.' She looked at him more closely. 'Neither do you. Are you all right?'

He nodded.

'Dad said you've got the day off. So can we do something together? Can we, Spence? Please?'

He looked at her holding her breath, waiting for him to answer. His head was pounding from the whisky, his throat sore from the smoky pub. He was surprised that Hartley had remembered his promise of a day off and that he'd kept to it. All he wanted was to retreat to the hut and try to get on with some work, but he knew he had no hope of getting his thoughts in order. Besides, the hope in Alice's eyes made it impossible to say no to her.

'All right,' he said.

Her face lit up. 'First we have to go and see the hippies,' she said. 'Dad wants us to collect their money.'

'I thought you were supposed to be staying away from them.'

She blushed. 'Well, Dad said for you to go, but he didn't say I couldn't.'

'I don't know,' he said, remembering his promise to Hartley.

'Go on, Spence, they were really friendly last time. And we won't be long, I promise.'

*

The hippies were up already, drinking tea around the smoking remnants of a fire. They waved to Spencer and Alice as they approached.

'We've got eggs if you want some,' Alice called.

'We'll take them all, my lovely,' said a pretty woman with flowers painted on her cheeks. 'If that's all right with you.'

Alice nodded enthusiastically.

'They're nice and brown. Are they from your own chickens?'

'Well, from our hens. It's my job to collect them, but Spence helps.'

'Is this Spence?'

'Yes.'

'He's good-looking, isn't he?'

Alice giggled as the woman picked up an egg, turning it over in her long fingers.

'Look at those sweet little feathers on the side.'

'They get stuck in the muck,' said Alice apologetically. 'We usually wash them off, but we're supposed to be saving water.'

Hastily the woman put the egg back in the box. 'Well, it's what's inside that we'll be eating,' she said. 'We can have them for breakfast.'

'That'll be twenty pence, then, please,' said Alice.

'Mick,' called the woman. 'Have you got any money?'

Mick came over, pulling a handful of coins from the pocket of his jeans and holding them out to Alice.

'Do you want to count it, darling?'

She took out the coins, counting under her breath, then looked up at him and smiled.

'Thanks!'

Mick stowed the rest of the change back in his pocket, pushing it down into the tight denim.

Feeling mildly embarrassed at the transaction, Spencer tried to think of something to say. 'You're up earlier than usual,' he managed, his tongue feeling thick and slow in his mouth. Catching a whiff of perfumed smoke, he swallowed back nausea.

Mick winked at him. 'We're off to pick mushrooms.'

'You should have them with your eggs,' said Alice. 'We always do.'

His grinned. 'I don't know if they're the same kind of mushrooms. But thanks for the suggestion, it's very clever of you.'

Alice beamed with pride. 'If you can't find them, ask me. I know where they grow.'

He nodded slowly. 'Cool. Do you want to come with us?'

'Oh yes,' said the woman enthusiastically. 'Come! It'll be fun.'

Spencer shifted nervously and put his hand on Alice's shoulder. 'Actually, I think . . . maybe not.'

'Spence and I have got some things to do.' She traced a line in the dust with her toe. 'But thank you very much for asking,' she added, politely.

'We should be going now, Alice,' Spencer said awkwardly.

'Hey!' said Mick. 'I've got something for you, Spencer. It's in the tent. Come with me. I'll get it.'

Spencer looked at Alice. 'You stay here.'

The flaps to the tent were closed. As Mick lifted one of them, Spencer glimpsed two bodies moving urgently together. Mick coughed apologetically, retrieving a book from the pocket in the side of the tent.

'Sorry about that,' he said, standing up. 'They're always at it.' He handed the book to Spencer. 'Here's some Coleridge, man. Read the rest of Kubla Khan. Keep it for as long as you like. It'll lift you up, take you out of your mind. As good as any drug.' He winked again. 'Well, sort of.'

'Th-thanks,' stammered Spencer, backing away from the tent. Alice was waiting impatiently, hopping from foot to foot, her eyes wide. Grabbing her hand, he walked quickly towards the gate in the corner of the field.

'Spence! That was two men!' said Alice in a loud whisper, her voice filled with wonder. 'Kissing! Without their clothes on! I saw them!'

*

On their way back to the farm, Spencer was filled with a rising panic at the thought of Alice telling Hartley what she had seen. Willing his head to clear, he tried to think of a way to distract her.

'So, let's do something fun,' he said. 'What do you want to do?'

Alice clapped her hands. 'Can we practise my dance? Miss Mannering said we had to, and I don't want to get it wrong. I want Dad to see it, and see how good I am. There's that tape she gave us, so we've got music and everything.'

He hesitated, worried about encouraging her in something else that Hartley disapproved of, but uncomfortably aware that he had been paying for her lessons so it was already too late.

'OK, Alice, but we'll have to do it up near the hut. We don't want your dad to see you before you're properly ready.'

'Great! You go now, and I'll come up in a minute.'

She ran into the house. Spencer began to climb towards the hut, glad of a moment alone. A few minutes later, Alice appeared, out of breath from running, a cassette recorder in her arms.

'Here you are!' she said.

'Where did you get it?'

'It's Uncle Tom's. But he never uses it. He won't notice. We don't need it for long, anyway. We'll put it back before tea.'

Alice hadn't been to the hut since Spencer had made it his home.

'Can I see inside?'

Before he had time to answer she had darted through the door, her eyes immediately drawn to the mantelpiece. Standing on tiptoe, she ran her fingers over his collection of treasures: the animal skulls ranked by order of size, his books, and, propped behind them, the picture that she had drawn of them dancing.

'You kept it!' she said.

'Of course. It was a present.'

'Are these your mathy-matics books?' she asked, picking one out at random. 'Trac-ta-tus Logico Philo-Philosoph-icus. What's that?'

He smiled. 'It's not English, it's Latin.'

She flipped it open. 'There's pictures in it. Are these symbols?'

'That's right.'

'Like the U for happiness?'

He nodded. 'Come on then. Let's see you dance.'

*

'You sit here,' Alice said, pointing to a boulder. 'You can be in charge of music. When I'm ready, you press play.'

She arranged herself in first position, feet turned out and hands held low. Pushing back her shoulders, she lifted her chin and gave him a nod. He pressed the button, holding it down until it clicked into place. There was a second's pause, then the piano began, rippling up and down octaves, arpeggios scurrying over mournful chords. The recording was scratchy, and clumsily played, but its Russian wildness fitted its surroundings, somehow perfect against the backdrop of craggy mountains.

Alice began to dance, pirouetting along the edge of the hillside, her hair flying as she went. She was more natural in her shorts than she had been in her tunic. Halfway through a turn she kicked off her sandals. The frown of concentration she'd had during her lesson was gone, her eyes sparkling, cheeks flushed.

'Help me do the circle, Spence' she shouted. 'Come on!'

He slid off the boulder, relieved to find that he was feeling steadier on his feet.

'Put your arm up there, like mine,' she panted. 'So our fingers are together. Then we spin like we're dancing round a maypole.'

Stiffly, he reached out his arm.

'Closer than that, silly,' she said.

He took a step towards her, aware that the music was moving ahead of them, leaving them behind. Alice was hopping from foot to foot, impatient, her hand stretched out towards him. Slowly, he reached out until his fingers touched hers. Her fingertips were tiny.

'Now skip!'

At first he stumbled, then began to find his rhythm. Alice was laughing out loud.

'Spin me with your hands!' she shouted.

Spencer clasped her thin wrists, moving fast, so her body swung out and away from him. She laughed again, throwing back her head.

As the music slowed, changing to a minor key, he let her go. She carried on dancing to the end of the piece, folding onto the ground, curling into herself like a creature from the sea. She stayed where she was, immobile, until the music came to an end, and the tape clicked off.

After a moment she unfurled herself and looked over at Spencer. He clapped enthusiastically.

'Was I all right?' she asked, suddenly self-conscious. 'Was I any good?'

He nodded. 'You were wonderful.'

'It's easier to do it without Miss Mannering around,' she said. 'And I like dancing with you, Spence. You're a really good dancer.'

She took the cassette recorder, pressing the rewind button.

'Can we do it again?'

His head felt clear now, and blood was coursing through his veins. 'Why not?'

*

They were better the next time, moving together more easily, Spencer losing his self-consciousness too. As they went into their maypole position, reaching out to one another, she smiled up at him, a smile of such conviction that he felt the hairs on the back of his neck stand up. They began to spin again, both laughing now, faster than before, dizzy with speed. But as the music reached its peak, Spencer heard a voice.

'Hello.'

Edmund was standing on the path below the hut, smiling up at them. Immediately, Spencer stopped dancing, his cheeks hot with embarrassment. The music was suddenly affected and sentimental. He dashed over to the cassette recorder and pressed stop.

'Hey!' shouted Alice. 'I haven't finished.'

'I don't mind,' said Edmund. 'Carry on. You know I like dancing.'

'N-no,' said Spencer. 'It doesn't matter. We've done it once already.'

Alice, looking hurt, folded her arms. 'But what about the show?'

'Are you dancing?' asked Edmund, 'I've never seen dancing there.'

'It's the first time,' said Alice grudgingly. 'They might let us do it again, but only if we're good enough. That's why I need to practise.'

'Edmund's in a competition, too,' said Spencer. 'He's fell running.'

She looked at him suspiciously. 'Is that why you're up here? Are you practising too?'

'Not today. I promised Spencer I'd take him swimming. We tried to go last night but the river was all dried up.'

'Where are you going?'

'Up on the other side of the fell.'

She clapped her hands. 'I'll come with you!'

'No,' said Spencer quickly. 'You'd better take the tape recorder back to the house. Otherwise your uncle Tom might come back and find out it's gone.'

'But you could wait for me.'

'Edmund hasn't got all day.'

She shrugged, her shoulders suddenly small.

'It's not fair,' she said. Picking up the cassette recorder, she turned and began to trudge back down the path. Spencer stared after her, feeling suddenly guilty about interrupting their day together.

'Are you ready then?' said Edmund.

He turned back. 'Y-yes. You're sure this isn't any trouble?'

Edmund smiled. 'I could do with a swim. Anyway, I said I'd show you where to go, and I will.'

*

Dorothy watched the two figures making their way through the bracken, wondering why anyone would bother in such heat. She had left her cottage early that morning, meaning to be back before lunch, but had become engrossed in tracing the tracks of an old bridleway. Now she was sitting in the shade of a wall, waiting for the sun to fade.

'Like an old sheep', she muttered to herself. 'That's what you are, my dear, just an old ewe who can't stand the sun.'

The figures moved quickly, zigzagging up the mountainside, staying close together. As she watched, tracing their progress, she noticed someone else, smaller, moving with equal speed and purpose, but furtively, following them.

Dorothy narrowed her eyes, squinting. The pursuer was gaining on the other two, someone who knew the fells, anticipating rocks to hide behind, and agile, scrambling up slopes that Dorothy knew to be steep.

Reaching over for her flask, she took a sip of water. When she looked back at the fell, the two figures in front had disappeared. She blinked in disbelief. The small figure seemed to share her incredulity, standing on top of a rock and looking around.

Dorothy was puzzled. Just minutes before, they had been making steady progress up the fell, clear as daylight. Now there was no sign of them. The only way they could go was up the fell or down. But they had done neither, simply vanishing, as if into the air.

*

Edmund and Spencer stood facing each other in the darkness. Here, everything was silent, the only sound dripping water. Spencer felt a sudden calm at being out of the scorching sun. He had not expected it, had been surprised when Edmund said they had almost reached their destination.

They had gone a little way off the track, where the bracken grew high, Edmund looking around intently. Eventually, he nodded.

'See that tree?' he said. 'That's what you have to look out for.'

The tree was lifeless, and entirely smooth, stripped of its bark, its trunk pale against the dense green bracken.

'Must have been struck by lightning,' Edmund said.

Stepping past, he picked his way over a mound of rubble, over-grown with moss and weeds. Spencer followed, wondering where the stones were from. At the bottom of the mound was a clump of bracken, particularly tall. Edmund walked straight into it, pushing through the fronds, and disappeared.

Without hesitation, Spencer went after him, and immediately found himself underground, somewhere cool and dark. The air was old, with an odd, metallic taste to it, and damp. Welcome moisture settled on his skin.

A match scraped against a stone and flared, momentarily blinding. Edmund put it to a candle, which flickered and then caught, its little flame providing soft illumination.

'Here we are.'

As Spencer's eyes adjusted to the dim light, he saw that they were in some sort of cave, not much higher than him, but very long, extending far back, further than he could see. The walls were a strange, dark red, the colour of old blood, reflected in the water that, apart from the shore where he and Edmund were standing, covered the floor of the cave. The water glimmered. As Spencer looked closer, little glints and sparkles twinkled up at him.

'Iron pyrites,' he said slowly. 'Fool's gold.'

Edmund nodded. 'This is one of the old iron-ore mines. It's been flooded since I was a kid.'

'Is it deep?'

'When you go further out it is. There's a bend around to the right that takes you into another cave. It's bigger than this. I'm out of my depth in it.'

They were both silent. Spencer felt the sweat cooling on his body. He could smell Edmund close to him, musky like fresh straw. His heart thudded in his chest as he waited, nervous, unable to move or to speak.

Edmund turned to him, and for a long moment they looked at each other, until Edmund smiled and began to unbutton his shirt.

'Aren't you going to join me?'

'W-w-well . . .'

'We've come all this way. Anyway, we're only doing what they told us.'

'What do you mean?'

Edmund was almost naked now, his slim body pale in the candle-light. He chuckled.

'Save water. Bathe with a friend.'

He slipped off his underpants and stood, waiting at the edge of the water. Spencer looked at him. This time there was no mistake. He grinned with relief and delight and pulled his shirt over his head.

*

Later, Spencer lay close to him.

'You've got soft hands,' he whispered. 'I thought—'

'What? That they'd be rough, like one of those old farmers?'

'Well, yes.'

'So you thought about it then?'

There was a pause, then Edmund smiled, pulling Spencer towards him. 'It's from the clipping. Sheep fleeces are full of lanolin. If you're handling them all day, it gets into your skin.'

*

That evening at supper Alice was in a strange, pensive mood. She sat picking at her food, preoccupied. An odd little smile pulled at the corners of her lips as she pushed her fork around her plate, and she swung her legs from her chair, kicking them slowly forwards and back in deliberate, rhythmic, irksome time. When Spencer tried to catch her eye, she ignored him, looking down at her plate.

As Hartley began to tell a long and complicated story about selling his wool to the company, Spencer let his mind wander, drifting back to the cave and to Edmund. He felt drunk again, reeling, but this time with happiness and hope. When the time had come for them to leave he had been seized by a sudden fear, clutching at Edmund's body, trying to memorize its contours with his fingers. Edmund had ruffled his hair, and told him they had the rest of the summer ahead of them. He felt his breath catch, both at the memory, and the thought that it might be repeated.

Hartley continued his story, complaining about the price he had got for his fleeces.

'It's nowt, hardly worth bothering going to town for. We'll be burning wool before long, to save on wrapping it up. I don't know how much worse it could get. When me father—'

He was interrupted by Alice. 'I saw them,' she said.

Hartley looked at her sharply, then continued. 'When me father—'

'I saw them,' she repeated. 'Two of them, with no clothes on. They were kissing.'

Spencer felt a chill travel up his spine.

'Eh? What are you talking about, lass?'

Panic flooding through his body, Spencer tried to signal to her with his eyes, but she went on looking down at her plate, toying with a piece of potato.

'Spencer knows,' she said.

'What's this?' said Hartley, turning to him.

Spencer shook his head, trying to look unconcerned. His palms were slippery with sweat. Hastily, he put down his knife and fork in order not to drop them.

'It was two men,' Alice said.

His breath was coming fast and shallow. He clamped his lips together, trying to stay in control.

'What?' Hartley demanded.

Alice nodded, looking sideways at Spencer. 'Two of the hippies. We saw them, didn't we, Spence? When we went to get the money? In the tent.'

Hartley looked at him again, his eyes blazing with indignation. 'Well, lad? I thought I told you to keep her away from them?'

Spencer gulped, and took a deep breath. 'I'm sorry, Hartley. Alice followed me over there when I went to collect the camping money. But I – I didn't see anything.'

Hartley's face was red with fury. 'You'd better not have done. I'm not having any of that going on round here. I'll sort them out, I swear it, I will.'

Mary cleared her throat nervously. 'Spencer, is it true?'

'I didn't see anything,' he repeated. 'I think Alice was mistaken.'

Alice stared at him. 'No I wasn't,' she whispered. 'And you saw them too.'

Fifteen

AFTER HIS UNEXPECTED DAY OFF, HARTLEY WORKED SPENCER harder than ever, sending him to the intake to spray poison over what was left of the bracken.

'Can't get up there on't tractor. You'll have to do it by hand.'

Spencer sensed he was being punished for letting Alice see the hippies, but he was glad of the work, which left him on his own. Alice had been avoiding him since that supper, which gave him a vague sense of unease, but most of the time, his thoughts were elsewhere, returning to what had happened in the cave. As he made his way along the sheep trails with a plastic container strapped to his back, slopping liquid from side to side, he relived the moment when Edmund's hands had settled on the small of his back and pulled him close.

His recollections were indelibly imprinted on his mind. Edmund's body had revealed itself to him gradually, inch by inch, as his hands had travelled over it, hesitantly at first, then becoming more certain with each of Edmund's responses. His skin was smooth, a supple sheath for cords of muscle that shuddered under Spencer's touch. Tracing the chest that had filled him with such longing in the barn, Spencer had felt the definition of his ribs, and, with wonder, touched his hard, flat belly. There he faltered, and Edmund, seeming to sense his uncertainty, took hold of his shoulders and gently pulled him to the ground.

As Spencer lay beneath him, feeling the full length of another body pressed hard against his, he realized that a tension older than he could remember had begun to be released. The thing that he had dreamed of, dreaded, hoped for, had become a reality, and that reality was suddenly something uncomplicated, something he could understand and accept.

Now, tramping across the fell, he thought back to that terrible night during May Week, two months before, when he had thought that his dream might at last be realized. The evening had been perfect, spent with his new friend, listening to a Bach Cello Suite in the gardens at his college. Since their first concert at King's, he had been in a state of dizzy pleasure, unable to concentrate on his research, looking forward to their next meeting. There had been other concerts, and long discussions, thrilling and intense. He had gone to his pigeonhole a dozen times a day, checking for the next message, feeling a secret excitement each time he saw the folded piece of paper waiting to be picked up and read.

That evening, as the cello wove its way through the piece, the stately beginning developing into something more complex, expounding on its theme, a feeling of utter happiness had settled over him. A faint smell of wisteria drifted across the gardens and he breathed in deeply, closing his eyes, waiting for the recapitulation, then the rallentando towards the superbly delayed resolution.

Later, they had walked across college to his rooms where Spencer, not sure what else to offer, poured glasses of sherry, bought specially for the occasion. They had talked, as they always did, about maths, pitting their minds against each other, stimulated by the debate, and, Spencer thought, by each other. As the conversation continued, he had felt a growing excitement, his cheeks becoming hot from the sherry and with desire. His attraction had grown since that first evening at King's, when he had sat, trembling, as the other man's thigh pressed against his. Each time they had met, he had found it harder to concentrate on their discussion, losing his train of thought as he gazed at the faultless features opposite him. Once the student had come to a supervision straight from a tennis match, filling the room with a hint of fresh sweat. Spencer had averted his gaze, but that night he had allowed his thoughts to linger on the athletic body revealed by tennis whites.

It was an exquisite pain, but one he knew he could not bear for very long. The effort of trying to decipher the other man's reactions was exhausting, the tension too much to stand. It was almost midnight when he finally cracked. They were sitting in the old leather armchairs, the coffee table between them, sherry bottle half empty. Spencer had spent the last hour in an indecisive haze. Now, he knew, he did not have much time left. He wanted his own resolution. Reaching for the bottle, he let his hand fall clumsily, instead, onto the undergraduate's knee, mumbling words that he had practised earlier, a declaration of desire.

The reaction had been immediate, and not what he had hoped for. As the door slammed he had put his head in his hands, overcome with the shock of it, and the shame. He had spent the rest of the night in a state of despair, sharpened the next morning when, dragging himself to hall for breakfast, he became aware of whispers and looks. What came next had been worse still. The meeting with the Senior Tutor was brief and awkward.

'You know this is a serious matter,' the Senior Tutor had said, not quite meeting his eye. 'As a supervisor, you are in a position of responsibility.'

'I – I – I know. I'm s-s-sorry. I thought—'

The tutor shook his head. 'It doesn't matter what you thought. It was still a breach of ethics. Anyone who wants to teach must be aware of this kind of . . . pitfall.'

There was a pause.

'Luckily for you, the undergraduate in question has not made an official complaint. I heard about this in more informal circumstances.'

Spencer felt a combination of relief and embarrassment at the thought of what was being said about him.

'But if you are planning a career in academia, you understand that this kind of situation cannot be allowed to arise?'

He nodded.

'I've spoken to your supervisor, who tells me he expected you to have made much better progress this term. He says he's already discussed this with you. Am I right in assuming that this matter has distracted your attention away from your work?'

Spencer was scarlet with humiliation. 'A little, yes.'

'I see. Well, let me make myself clear. You are aware that you are one of our finest students. A research fellowship is a very real possibility. But in order to offer it to you, we'll need two things: first, no more . . . incidents such as this; and second, as your supervisor told you, a real breakthrough with your research. Do I make myself clear?'

He had nodded, and left the room as quickly as he could.

Waiting for term to end had been an agony. Hiding himself in the faculty library, deserted after the end of exams, was no solution. For the first time in his life, he was completely unable to work, his mind picking over the previous weeks, trying to understand how he had misread the signs, cursing his stupidity and his recklessness. His meeting with the Senior Tutor had helped him make up his mind. He would escape to a place where he was not known, a place with no memories, where he could become someone new.

It had worked, he thought. He had managed to reinvent himself. What had happened with Edmund was different to the messy disgrace of before. Here was something reciprocated, something he could throw himself into without fear or shame.

Looking down at the bracken, he realized that he had lost track of which part he'd already sprayed. He forced himself to concentrate, surveying the fell, dividing it up into sections, pacing back and forth to cover each area before moving on to the next. The chemicals in the spray made him giddy, the heady smell of bracken increasing his sense of intoxication. As the sun warmed his back, he felt almost drugged, high on the memory of pleasure. His body tingled as he tramped across the mountain, in a state of ease, falling into a rhythm that it recognized. The words of the poem that Mick had given him filled his mind, suddenly bright with new meaning:

In Xanadu did Kubla Khan
A stately pleasure dome decree;
Where Alph the sacred river ran
Through caverns measureless to man
Down to a sunless sea.

The sun felt different from the one that had ruled over the summer, burning and blistering his skin. This sun was benign, caressing, bathing the fells in golden light. He remembered how, when they had finally emerged from the cave, he had turned to Edmund, suddenly bashful, and noticed his blonde hair, lit from behind. He had wanted to kiss him then, and moved closer, but Edmund was more circumspect.

'For a clever bugger you can be a bit thick,' he had said, roughly. 'Do you want to get caught? It's not worth the risk.' His voice softened. 'But soon. I'll see you soon.'

As Spencer made his way through the bracken he hoped that soon would not be long. For two nights he had lain awake on the hard shelf of his bed, waiting. Trickles of sweat made their way across his body, taunting him, following the paths that Edmund had traced with his fingers. He had held his breath as he imagined the two of them together, quivering as a single damp bead of perspiration ran down his chest and made its way between his thighs.

The hut, which had been his nightly refuge from the farm and from the world, was now the place where he went to think about Edmund. The thought of Edmund one day coming there thrilled him. In the cave, he had picked up a stone and slipped it in his pocket as a memento. Now it stood on the mantelpiece next to the drawing that Alice had given him: a solid chunk of dark red iron ore, so dark it was almost purple. On the other side of the drawing were his books, untouched since that day, but now he felt no guilt, just overwhelmingly, gloriously free. For the first time in his life, he did not stop to consider, or examine, or assess. His fears for the future had disappeared; he saw no further than the next time he and Edmund would meet. His desire to find his proof had gone, replaced by desire for Edmund. Every part of him ached to be touched again, to feel Edmund's hands across his body.

*

That evening when he got back to the hut, he saw a piece of paper wedged under a rock by the door. His heart quickened as he bent to pick it up, his hands shaking as he rushed to unfold it.

The paper was torn from a diary, *Cumberland Farm Supplies* printed along the top in green lettering. Impatiently, Spencer scanned the page. Scrawled across it was a message:

Cave tomorrow – 4.

*

The next days passed in a haze. Left by Hartley to finish spraying the fell, Spencer worked quickly each morning, making his way methodically through the bracken, moving closer to his destination, trying to contain the soaring feeling in his chest. By mid-afternoon he was seeking out the pale stripped tree on the side of the mountain, minutes later pushing his way through the bracken into the cool of the cave. There, in the darkness, he would wait for Edmund. There was no sound, nothing to disturb the damp air but the rustle of his breath. Edmund had brought some fleeces to spread over the rocks, and Spencer would sit on them, drinking in the faint tang of animal and lanolin. He came to love those moments, cut off from the hectic sunlight and the sounds of the valley, with nothing to do but savour his anticipation. No-one apart from Edmund knew where he was, those afternoons, and he knew nothing of what was happening outside except that somewhere nearby, Edmund was running along the side of the hill, coming closer to him with every step. He liked the thought of Edmund running, racing to get to him. The moment he burst through the bracken, panting and dripping with sweat, Spencer would scramble to his feet and go to him, feeling Edmund's skin hot against his own.

What happened next was tender and brutal by turn, a revelation that was strangely familiar, as if he had always known it, but which was astonishing. These were moments of blind exhilaration, in which he was oblivious to everything except the body beneath him, on him, in him, encircled by his arms.

Once, afterwards, lying back, the rough wool tickling at his skin, he tried to put his feelings into words.

'It's a sort of churning feeling, as if my whole body's fizzing, and I don't know which I want more, to keep going or get to the end of it. It's like when I'm thinking about maths, looking at a problem, and I start to see the solution. There's a moment when you're working towards it, knowing the proof's there, and you'll find it in the end. Well, that's how I feel when I'm with you. When we – when we're doing this. I'm sorry, I don't think I've put that very well . . .'

'You and your bloody maths, Spencer.'

He tensed, feeling stupid. But Edmund stretched out a lazy arm and pulled him close.

'I know what you mean. I get it when I'm running.'

Then he touched him again, and Spencer fell back into not thinking.

*

One afternoon, towards the end of that first, perfect week, they left the cave and wandered together down the fell. Spencer felt careless and light as they tramped through the bracken, their footsteps crunching on the undergrowth. Birds circled high in the afternoon sunlight, dipping in and out as if they were bathing in it. He lifted his face and closed his eyes, stopping for a minute, following their example. When he opened them again, Edmund was grinning.

'Look,' he said, pointing above their heads.

A bird, vast and solitary, hovered in splendid silhouette, its dark shadow of an underbelly flecked with white markings. The other birds had scattered, leaving it in sole command of the sky, where it soared high, not caring to flap its wings, but riding the currents instead, taking full possession of the heavens.

'It's a golden eagle,' Edmund said. 'Ever seen one before?'

Spencer shook his head in awe.

'There's a pair of them that nest in the cliffs.' He nodded towards a bank of granite at the top of the fell. 'They've been there all my life. I've been watching them since I was six.'

Spencer could think of nothing that had continued from his childhood, apart from things inside his head: numbers and patterns, and the tracks that they had worn into his mind. He imagined Edmund standing, skinny-legged in shorts, like Alice, wonder spreading over his face as he looked up into the sky.

They carried on walking, saying little, easy with each other. As they made their way down the mountainside, the sounds of the valley surrounded them: sheep calling to each other, the rasp of a chainsaw cutting wood, farm machinery, someone shouting after a dog. The sounds were nothing out of the ordinary, the same as any other afternoon, but now they filled him with pleasure, something he and Edmund had in common, an experience shared.

Passing the field where the hippies were camping, he remembered the men in the tent, and reached out to touch Edmund's shoulder.

'You know, there's a couple, I mean, two of the hippies, who are . . .' He hesitated, searching for the word, '. . . like us.'

Edmund shrugged off his hand. 'No they're not,' he said angrily. 'They're nothing like us.'

Spencer was taken aback. 'But I saw them. They were here—'

'Here, were they? That's just it. They can do what they like when they're *here*. And then they can leave. They can go all over the place, wherever they want. They don't work, they don't do anything if they don't feel like it. So they're not like us. Not like me, anyway.'

'But I meant—'

'It's different. It's all different.'

Spencer swallowed. 'What do you mean?'

'Listen. I've always wanted to get out of this place. Can't you see why? It's 1976, for Christ's sake, and it's as if we're stuck in the fifties. We don't look like the rest of the world, we don't talk like them. We don't even think like them. You've seen how it is, working for Hartley. You know it's true. People like those hippies come here, looking for something. They talk about how bloody great it is to get in touch with nature, to be free. Well, try being born here. Try not being able to leave.'

Thinking of Mick's words on the side of the mountain, Spencer realized the truth in what Edmund said. He was also uncomfortably aware of how he had felt at his own escape from Cambridge. He looked at Edmund nervously.

'But couldn't you leave? If you really wanted to?'

'Where would I go?' he asked, his voice bitter. 'What can I do? Clip sheep and run up and down fells. There's not much call for that in the real world, is there?'

'I can add up numbers,' said Spencer. 'There's not much call for that either, outside Cambridge.'

There was a pause, and for a long moment, Spencer was afraid of his gamble, then Edmund's face lightened, and he smiled.

'Well, I guess I like their music, anyway.'

A transistor radio was playing, music drifting over the field. Spencer heard an organ, haunting chords with a melody in counterpoint. He listened intently, straining to catch it.

'I love this song,' Edmund said. 'I remember when it came out. I was only thirteen. I'd just got my first radio. I listened to it all the time.'

As Spencer began to nod his head in time to the music, Edmund started to sing along:

'We skipped the light fandango . . . turned cartwheels 'cross the floor . . .'

'Wait,' said Spencer. 'I want to show you something.'

*

He led Edmund through the field to the path along the river. They followed it until they came to a row of stepping stones rising up high out of the water, which had been reduced to a brackish trickle.

'Where are we going?' asked Edmund.

'Come on, you'll see.'

Despite the absence of water, they used the stepping stones anyway, laughing and balancing, jumping between them.

'Right,' said Spencer, when they had crossed the river. 'Now I'll show you what I mean.'

The church was in front of them, nestled behind its dry stone wall.

'Eh?' said Edmund. 'We're not going in there, are we?'

Spencer chuckled, filled with an uncharacteristic desire for mischief. 'Yes we are, just for a bit.'

'But why?'

'You'll see.'

The door to the church was closed, a sign pinned to it, a message spelled out in shaky capitals:

BEWARE OF THE SHEEP. KEEP CLOSED AT ALL TIMES.

'They get everywhere,' said Edmund with a smile.

Inside, the church was as Spencer remembered it, simply furnished and smelling of polish. Together, they walked up the aisle. The church organ was small, tucked between the choir stalls and the altar rail, its keys yellowed and cracked. Spencer pulled out the stool and sat down.

'It's a harmonium, so it might sound a bit odd, but you'll see what I mean.'

He began to pump the pedals with his feet, the ancient instrument wheezing as it filled with air. Placing his hands on the keyboard, he paused for a moment, then began to play. A melody rose from the harmonium, notes easing into one another, blending and harmonizing. As his hands moved over the keyboard, he looked over at Edmund.

'Does it remind you of anything?' he asked.

Edmund listened for a moment, then began to hum along. 'Got it!' he said. 'It's what we were just listening to – "A Whiter Shade of Pale".'

'Yes! I think they must've based it on this. It's Bach. His "Air on a G String".'

As Edmund continued to hum, Spencer thought again of the concert in the chapel at King's. The pain of those memories suddenly felt less sharp, resolved somehow by this new love affair, which seemed to have fallen into place like the notes coming from the harmonium. He played on, relaxing into the music, feeling a new and certain happiness.

Sixteen

He drifted through the days, only half aware of his surroundings, his mind full of Edmund. When he was with him, everything was brighter, more alive. When he was not, he yearned for him, a gnawing sensation pulling at his stomach. As he trudged over the fell, the drum of poison on his back, he imagined Edmund's skin against his, the faint rasp of his stubble as they kissed. At night he dreamed of things he could not have: a room with a bed and sheets to share, the sight of Edmund, naked as he slept, his face as he woke in the morning.

In his distraction, it was some time before he noticed the change in Alice, who was quiet and withdrawn, no longer brimming with questions, uninterested in everything but Shadow. One afternoon, after lunch, he caught sight of her in the back of the trailer, hunched and disconsolate.

'Alice?'

She sat, clasping her knees to her chest.

'Are – are you all right?'

'Yes.'

He stood for a moment, awkwardly, not knowing how to continue.

'Are you sure?'

A small tight nod.

'You don't look very happy, that's all.'

She said something, so quietly that he couldn't hear it.

'What?'

Shrugging her shoulders, she seemed to shrink into herself, tightening her grip on her knees. Eventually, she looked up at him. The lenses of her glasses were grimy and smudged.

'I thought you were my friend.'

He sat down next to her. 'Alice! I am.'

She took off her glasses and began to polish them with her T-shirt.

'But you don't want to see me any more.'

'Alice! That's not true!'

'I wanted to see you all this week but you haven't been here. You just go off with Edmund, every afternoon, up the fell. And even when you *are* here, like for dinner or tea, you're not really with us. You don't really listen to what anyone says.'

He knew she was right. He could not recall any conversations from that week apart from those whispered between him and Edmund in the cave. Guilt nudged at his conscience.

'All right,' he said. 'Let's do something together, just you and me. You can choose what it is. We can do something with Shadow. Or practise your dance again. Anything.'

She turned to him. 'Do you mean it?'

He nodded. 'Yes,' he said. 'Whatever you like.'

Slowly, she smiled. 'I want to go to the pub.'

'What?'

'I want to go to the pub,' she said simply. 'I've never been and I want to see what it's like. Dad goes all the time, and Uncle Tom. You've been. Even Mam went once, on New Year's Eve. I'm tired of being left out of things.'

'But – I can't take you there!'

'Why not?'

He groped for a satisfactory reason.

'It's – it's just not the place for a little girl.'

'You wouldn't let me come swimming with you and Edmund. Now you won't let me come with you to the pub. It's not fair.'

He flushed at the memory of that first swim.

'Isn't there something else you'd like to do?' he said, to change the subject.

Scratching at the dust with her sandal she shook her head. 'You said we could do whatever I liked but now you've changed your mind. You all do that, Dad and Mam and Uncle Tom and you. I thought you were different, but you're not. You're just the same as them.'

He thought quickly, calculating timings and risks. It was Saturday. Hartley had gone to town and was not expected back until late afternoon. Mary would be busy with the weekly laundry, squeezing wet sheets through the rollers of the old-fashioned mangle, then hanging them out on the line, a job that would take hours.

'All right,' he said, 'I'll take you to the pub. We'll go now. But not for long. Just one drink. And it has to be our secret, OK?'

She let out a whoop of excitement. 'You're brilliant, Spence! Yes please.'

They took his bicycle, Spencer standing up on the pedals, Alice perched on the back, holding on to his waist. Her little hands felt strange compared with Edmund's. Riding along the narrow lane, Spencer willed himself not to think of him, to give all his attention to Alice, who was squealing with glee each time they went over a bump or pothole. As they sped past the fields, over the little hump-back bridge, and past the turning to the church, Alice began to sing, her high, thin voice piercing the heat of the afternoon. She chose the song that she and Edmund had performed on the woolsack, slightly off-key and stumbling slightly over the words, but with conviction, meaning every one of them:

> '. . . *Ooh you're the best friend that I ever had,*
> *I've been with you such a long time,*
> *You're my sunshine . . .*'

Feeling the warm air rush against his face, he felt a surge of affection.

'All right?' he shouted.

Resting her head against his back, she nodded. 'Yes,' she said. 'This is great.'

*

He dared not take Alice to Hartley's territory, the Tup. Instead, he installed her in the beer garden at the back of the Lion and Lamb. Union Jack bunting, faded by the sun, was wound haphazardly about the trees.

'What would you like?' he asked.

'Can I have a dandelion and burdock?'

The bar was quiet after the lunchtime rush and he was glad of it. Cigarette smoke hung in the air, a stack of empty pint glasses crowded the end of the bar. A waitress moved slowly from table to table, clearing away salt and pepper pots and emptying ashtrays into a bucket. He stood at the bar for a while before she looked up and noticed him.

'Oh,' she said. 'Sorry, I was in a world of my own.'

Wiping her hands on her skirt, she went behind the bar.

'What would you like?'

'A pint of bitter, please, and a dandelion and burdock.'

'Straw with that?'

Deciding that Alice would like one, he nodded. 'And a packet of crisps as well.'

Carrying the glasses through the back door, he saw her sitting at the table, alert, taking in her surroundings. The beer garden was small, a scrubby patch of land to the back of the pub kitchens. A vent belched out greasy fumes, filling the garden with the smell of stale chips, but Alice, perched at a table under a blue umbrella, looked happy. She lifted both thumbs when she saw him, grinning broadly. He grinned back, lifting the glasses up high.

'You got it!' she said enthusiastically. 'I've only had dandelion and burdock once before. Dad got me one from the beer tent last year at the show. It's the nicest drink in the world.'

She put her mouth to the straw and sucked at it noisily.

'I got you some crisps as well,' he said.

'Spence!' Tearing into the bag, she riffled through it, pulling out a tiny blue packet in triumph. Ripping it open, she tipped salt onto the crisps, shook the bag, then held it out to him.

'Have some,' she said. 'They're the best crisps ever.'

'Is the dandelion and burdock like you remembered it?'

'Yes,' she said happily. 'It's lovely. Everything's lovely.'

They sat, content, in the shade of the umbrella, sipping their drinks and crunching crisps.

'Now I know why Dad likes going to the pub,' said Alice.

Spencer thought of the crowded bar in the Black Tup, and Hartley's whisky chasers.

'It's not always like this,' he said cautiously.

'Do *you* like going to the pub?'

'Sometimes.'

'Do you go with Edmund?'

He looked at her closely, wondering why she had asked.

'I've only been with him once. After the clipping. Your father was there as well. And your uncle Tom.'

She threw another handful of crisps into her mouth.

'But when you go swimming, you go on your own. Just you and him.'

He felt himself begin to colour. 'We don't go that much.'

'I like Edmund,' she said. 'He's funny and good at dancing.'

'Do you?' he asked, hopefully.

'Yes. But I don't like it when you do things without me.'

She stared at him in the unnerving way she sometimes did, unblinkingly and without embarrassment.

'Isn't it hard to swim when the river's all dried up?' she asked.

He looked at her, trying to read her expression.

'E-Edmund knows places to go,' he said.

'I know places too.' An odd smile curled about her lips, not altogether pleasant.

There was a pause.

'I liked it more when it was just us,' she said.

He stood up. 'I'll be back in a minute.'

In the lavatory, he leaned his cheek against the cool tiles, trying to calm himself, then used the urinal. As he washed his hands he looked into the mirror. He hardly recognized himself, his library pallor gone, replaced by tanned skin, the angles of his face sharper, more defined. He had become, as he had wanted, someone different. It was Edmund who had brought about that change and he would do anything, he realized, to hold on to him, to keep what he had been seeking for so long.

He thought of Alice, sitting opposite him in the beer garden, her eyes wide behind her spectacles, smiling at him. He could not be sure what she had meant, whether her remarks had been innocently made, or were a warning. Running the cool water over his wrists, he resolved to talk to her. He was not sure what she knew, but he had to make sure she said nothing to Hartley.

As he came back into the garden, he saw a woman standing next to their table. Alice caught sight of him and waved. The woman turned. His heart sank as he saw who it was – Valerie Horsley, dressed up for Saturday lunch in a white linen dress.

'Hello stranger,' she said as he approached.

He fought back his dislike. 'Hello.'

'I haven't seen you here before.' She smiled, her lipstick a startling contrast to her dress. 'I would have imagined you'd go to the Tup. You know, like your boss.'

'Well—'

'But Alice tells me you come here all the time.'

He looked at Alice, who returned his gaze, defiant, sucking on her straw.

'I can see why you come here rather than there,' said Valerie. 'I'm sure you wouldn't want to bump into Hartley. He wouldn't want his daughter hanging around places like that. Anyway, your secret's safe with me. And now I know, I might even manage to catch you here again one day.' There was a glint in her ice-blue eyes. 'You still haven't been to my place for a sherry. You promised, remember? Very soon I might start to feel offended.'

He managed to nod.

She took her handbag from the table, red to match her lipstick. 'I must dash. But I'm holding you to that promise.'

As she walked away, Alice made a face.

Spencer gave her a sharp look.

'Why did you tell her we come here all the time?'

She was silent, poking her finger into the empty crisp packet.

'Alice?'

'She came up to me and started asking me questions. She always acts like she knows something you don't, like a secret she won't tell you. So I wanted to surprise her. It made her stop talking and I was glad. I wish people would leave us alone.'

She had started to tremble, her eyes brimming with tears. He decided not to confront her about Edmund. In this mood, he couldn't risk it.

'Come on, let's go home,' he said. 'We'd better get back before your dad does.'

As they left the beer garden he heard someone snicker. 'Isn't that Hartley Dodds's lass?'

'Like father, like daughter,' said another voice. 'They start young in that family.'

A little hand stole into his. He squeezed it tight.

*

It seemed that Alice was not alone in feeling neglected. Spencer was still feeling shaken from their conversation when Mary brought up the subject of Edmund as they washed dishes together that evening after supper.

'I haven't seen much of you these past few days,' she said quietly, passing him a plate.

His heart sank as he began to dry it. He had not thought she had noticed his absence; he had tried to fit in seeing Edmund around his farm work, making up for hours spent in the cave by working hard in what was left of the afternoons, sometimes going back to it after Hartley and Thomas had left for the pub, then falling into bed exhausted, his notebook untouched.

Perhaps, he thought, she had simply sensed what Alice had, that his mind was elsewhere. He did not want to think of the alternative – that Alice had given him away.

'I – I've been trying to get on with my work, that's all,' he said. 'I'm so near to the end, I find it difficult to think of anything else. I haven't got much time left before I have to go back to Cambridge.'

His lie was partly true, he realized suddenly. The summer had passed much more quickly than he had expected. He was running out of time.

'Alice says you've made a new friend.'

'R-really?'

'Yes. Edmund Lutwidge.'

'Oh. E-Edmund. Yes.' The pleasure of saying his name came over him in a rush, swiftly replaced by embarrassment and the fear of giving too much away. 'He's . . . very nice.'

'I've known him since he was born,' said Mary. 'He was such a cheeky little boy. But he always got away with things. It's that smile.'

Thinking back to the last time he had seen it, Spencer found it easy to believe her.

'I – I don't really know him that well,' he said. 'Anyway, I've got to work on my maths.'

She nodded. 'Of course.'

Passing him another plate, she hesitated, then spoke again. 'Spare a few minutes for Alice if you can, though. She's very fond of you. She's going to miss you a lot when you're gone.'

Over the next few days Spencer thought hard. His conversation with Alice had left him nervous, afraid of what she might reveal about him and Edmund, and Mary had done nothing to ease his fears. He mulled over his encounter with Valerie, trying to decide what she had meant. The glint in her eyes as she had mentioned Hartley made him feel even worse. The thought of becoming entangled in secrets, exposed to gossip again, was more than he could stand.

'I don't know what to do,' he said out loud, surprising himself.

He imagined Hartley's rage on hearing that he had taken Alice to the Lion and Lamb. He would not be able to explain himself, he knew. If Hartley sent him away from the farm, he would lose Edmund, and he could not bear the thought of that. He decided to visit Valerie, as she had wanted.

The following afternoon, he pedalled down the valley on his bicycle, slowly, in no rush to arrive at his destination. He found her house easily, next to the village hall. It was not a beautiful house, but deliberately imposing, standing large and solid, proudly alone, in a garden whose green lawns suggested a certain disregard for the water ban. As he walked up the path through a riot of gladioli, he noticed patches of damp, darkened earth at their roots.

Standing at the front door, bracing himself, he pressed the bell. A medley of chimes rang out, but no footsteps came along the hallway. The house was silent, wrapped in the heavy afternoon heat. An atmosphere of sultry lethargy surrounded it, a torpor that seemed to affect even the flies clustered on the window ledge. He pressed the bell once more, but still no-one came. His heart began to lift at the thought of being able to escape, and he turned back, the gate at the end of the path in his sights. But as he set off, a call came – Valerie's voice, suggestive and low.

'Hello? Come round the side.'

For a moment he hesitated, wondering if he could slip away without her knowing it was him. But then the call came again.

'Hello? Anyone there?'

He took the little path to the right of the house, brushing against fleshy hydrangea bushes as he went. At the end was a wooden door set into a wall, a trellis of overblown roses above it, their petals turned to brown. Tentatively he pushed at it, and stepped through.

He was greeted with a sight that made him falter. Valerie was stretched out on a sun lounger wearing only a skimpy bikini printed with large purple flowers, and a pair of enormous dark glasses. Her skin, glistening with oil, was smooth and tanned, apart from two white stripes on her chest where she had undone the straps of her bikini top. A thick novel lay face down next to her, the gold embossing of its title glinting in the sun.

She turned her head to look at him, a sly smile stealing across her face.

'Well, there you are,' she said. 'I was wondering when you might decide to come.'

She was the most naked that he had seen a woman. He was immediately anxious at the briefness of her bikini, a tiny, ineffectual barrier to nudity.

He forced himself to smile.

'I – I – I came to say hello,' he said.

Her smile grew wider. 'Hello.'

He nodded.

'You've just missed my husband,' she said lightly. 'He always goes for a walk after lunch on Sundays. Not really my thing. I prefer to make the most of this sunshine. We built this terrace so I could lie here and soak it up.'

Spencer looked at the patch of crazy paving, just big enough for the sun lounger and a small wrought-iron table with two chairs. The remains of lunch lay on the table: glasses, plates, carelessly crossed cutlery, half a slice of cold chicken, a potato doused in mayonnaise.

Ceramic pots stood around the terrace, planted with red-hot pokers and foxgloves, lupins and more gladioli. Their scent was overwhelming, clashing with Valerie's coconut sun oil. He had a sudden vision of Mary's marigolds in the old stone trough and felt a pang of guilt about not being at the farm.

Valerie sat up, her bikini top slipping precariously. Spencer averted his eyes as she reached behind her head to re-tie the strap.

'Have a seat,' she said. 'I'll get some drinks. What would you like? I know I said sherry, but it feels too hot for that, doesn't it?'

He nodded dumbly as she took a flimsy robe and wrapped it around herself.

'How about Pimm's? That'll be cooler.'

'All right.'

'I won't be long. You stay here and relax. I imagine you might rather like doing nothing for a change.'

He lowered himself onto one of the chairs and sat, straight-backed and awkward. The terrace was, as she had said, a suntrap, and before long he was sweating, little trickles rolling down his back. He longed for the cave, for its coolness and silence, to be waiting for Edmund instead of Valerie.

Ants were beginning to colonize the lunch plates, marching over lettuce leaves and wading through congealed pools of mayonnaise. He watched, fascinated, as they lifted up a shred of chicken, managing to carry it down the leg of the table and off to a mound of earth that was dotted with odd pieces of rock: granite and sandstone, slate, a piece of chalk, interspersed with purple heather and various rather ugly shrubs.

'Do you like our rockery?' asked Valerie, returning with a tray that held a jug of Pimm's, two glasses and a bowl of crisps. 'It's Alastair's, really. He insists on bringing the stones back from holiday. Terribly heavy and not particularly pretty, but it keeps him happy, I suppose.'

She put the tray down on the sun lounger. 'Wretched ants.'

Gathering up the lunch things, she balanced them on one of the rocks. With a sweep of her hand, she brushed the ants off the table.

'Off you go!'

The jug was brimming with slices of orange and cucumber, ice and sprigs of mint. Pouring two glasses, she handed one to Spencer.

'Cheers,' she said. 'To summer days!'

He lifted his glass. 'To summer days,' he said, trying to sound enthusiastic.

They clinked glasses, and drank. The unmistakable taste of it, spicy warmth cut through with cool gin, took him back to Cambridge gardens, tables swathed in white, neat ranks of glasses, strawberries bleeding into cut-glass bowls. He heard again the hum of conversation drifting over lawns clipped short and striped. He remembered feeling uncomfortably hot in a suit, faced with the prospect of girls from the neighbouring college, dressed up in summer frocks and eager to talk. He had been tongue-tied, and aware of it, counting the minutes until he could escape back to his rooms and to his work. Now, sitting opposite Valerie, he felt the same. But the girls in Cambridge had been a simple source of embarrassment, from which he knew he could eventually free himself. Valerie was a danger. She was looking at him, her usual smile of amusement playing on her lips. They were scarlet; she must have painted them, he thought, when she went back to the house, as well as darkening her eyelashes. He had a sudden desire to smear away her smile, which seemed, as Alice said, to hint at some secret, one he could not fathom out. He pushed the thought away, telling himself to keep focused, to play the game, or at least to work out the rules of it.

Valerie took a packet of cigarettes from the pocket of her robe and held it out to Spencer.

'No thanks, I don't smoke.'

Pulling one out for herself, she put it to her lips, flipped a silver lighter and lit it. Inhaling deeply, she held the smoke in her lungs for a moment, then exhaled, a long, determined plume.

'You don't do much, Spencer Little, do you?'

He was taken aback. 'What do you mean?'

She took another sip of her drink.

'Well, you don't smoke. I don't hear anything about you being a drunkard – not like your boss. You take his daughter to the pub, admittedly, but she's just a little girl. You're a bit quiet, but that's not a crime.'

Flicking her ash in the rockery, she shook her head.

'You must have some vices.'

He said nothing, choking back the panic that rose in his throat.

'Who are you, Spencer Little? Why are you here?'

'You asked me to come.'

'No, silly. Not *here*. I mean why did you come to the Lakes? To Mirethwaite? What could you possibly hope to find?'

He watched a bead of sweat roll slowly down her collarbone, inching its way into her cleavage. The outline of her breasts showed through her gown, her nipples clearly visible. He realized that, as well as putting on her make-up, she had taken off her bikini top.

'Peace,' he said, desperately. 'And quiet. I wanted to be able to think.'

She had caught him looking. 'What are you thinking now,

Spencer Little?' she asked. 'You don't seem very peaceful to me.'

Stubbing out her cigarette, she leaned forward and took hold of his hand.

'I'm glad you came,' she said. Slowly, almost tenderly, she lifted his hand and placed it just inside her robe.

'No!' he shouted, leaping up from his chair and backing away from her.

She stared back at him, two red spots of colour on her cheekbones. 'Don't tell me you didn't want it.'

He stumbled down the terrace steps, then over to the door in the wall. Pulling it open, he ran back around the side of the house, not stopping until he reached his bicycle.

*

Later, in the cave, he found himself shaking, in part at Valerie's presumption, but also in fear of what she would do next. The look that she had given him as he left had been venomous. As soon as Edmund came through the bracken Spencer blurted out his story. He spoke quickly, incoherent with panic, and Edmund grabbed him by the shoulders, holding him until he stopped. Lighting the stump of candle, he made him sit.

'What are you talking about?'

Taking a deep breath, Spencer began again, recounting what had happened in the garden. After a while he realized Edmund was shaking too, but with laughter that he was trying hard to suppress. He stopped, halfway through his sentence.

'Why are you laughing?' he asked, hurt.

'Can't you see? It's funny. It's like that film – what is it? The one with Dustin Hoffman. *The Graduate*! You creeping round the side of the house. Mrs Horsley lying there in her bikini. What colour was it again?'

'White,' said Spencer stiffly. 'With purple flowers.'

'And she's bringing you drinks and sitting there just in her dressing gown.'

'It wasn't funny.'

'But what did you expect when you went to her house?'

'I didn't think she would do something like that. She invited me for sherry!' he said, realizing as he said it how naïve he sounded. 'And anyway, she's got a husband. I don't expect married women to act like that.'

Edmund shook his head. 'Sometimes I don't know where you come from, Spencer. What century are you in? Besides, everyone knows Mrs Horsley's up for it. You're not the first, and you definitely won't be the last.'

'Well, I didn't know,' said Spencer. 'And what am I going to do if she says anything?'

'What about?'

'About what happened. Or if she tells Hartley about me taking Alice to the pub?'

Edmund took his hands. 'She won't. She's not going to tell anyone about this afternoon. It doesn't make her look very good, does it? And she won't tell Hartley, for the same reason. She tells him about the pub, you tell someone about her. You're OK.'

Spencer tried to share his certainty. 'I suppose so,' he said.

'You see,' said Edmund. 'Nothing to worry about.'

Slowly, he began to peel off his shirt. 'Now, Spencer,' he said in a falsetto. 'Look how tanned I am! I've spent the whole summer lying on my sun lounger, just dying for a visit from a nice young man.'

Arching his back, he pouted, pretending to take a sip from a glass, puffing on an imaginary cigarette. 'Who are you, Spencer Little? Why are you here?'

Taking Spencer's hand, he placed it on his chest. 'Don't tell me you don't want it,' he breathed.

Spencer was finally won over, his anxiety suddenly replaced by desire. 'Of course I do,' he said, laughing. 'I always do, with you.'

Seventeen

ALL WEEK, PREPARATIONS HAD BEEN TAKING PLACE IN THE show field: tent poles erected, floorboards laid, heavy canvas dragged on top and staked out tight with wooden pegs. Suddenly, a village stood bright white in the sunshine, laid out in neat streets and alleyways. A grid of pens stood waist high, soon to be filled with sheep for judging.

Alice and Spencer had watched men hard at work in the hot sun, carrying stacks of benches into the tents, putting up trestle tables, lashing oil drums to fence posts to be used as rubbish bins, the air thick with the sound of hammering and sawing, interrupted intermittently by the tannoy blaring out test messages from loudspeakers. Trucks had crawled between the hedgerows, crammed with strange cargo: a row of toilet cubicles precariously secured with rope, brightly painted wooden horses, their large teeth bared, ready to be bolted together as a carousel, and, last of all, barrels stacked high on a brewery lorry.

'Better not tell Dad they're here,' said Alice.

Mary had been busy too, getting up early the day before the show to start baking. Later that afternoon, she and Spencer tidied the kitchen together. Next to the window, a row of cakes sat cooling, balanced on wire racks. Wiping drifts of flour from the surfaces, Spencer eyed them hungrily.

'They're for the tea tent,' said Mary, smiling. 'Not now. You're worse than Alice!'

Two bottles stood next to the racks, tightly stoppered, white labels stuck to the front. Spencer stepped forward to read them.

Rhubarb Wine, 1976.

'I didn't know you made wine,' he said, surprised.

She nodded. 'Every year, for the competition.'

'Isn't it very hard?'

'Not if you know how. I get the rhubarb from the garden and I've got a kit that starts all the fermentation off. Hartley doesn't like the taste, so it's safe from him.'

They exchanged wry smiles.

Suddenly Alice dashed into the room.

'Guess what?' she said, excitedly. 'Shadow's had her pups! In the byre where we used to keep the calves! There's five of them. They're so tiny, I can fit them in my hand.'

'You haven't been bothering her, have you?' said Mary. 'She'll want to be left alone with them. She won't like the way they smell if you pick them up.'

'I know that,' said Alice. 'I just held one of them for a minute, then I gave it back. They're sleeping now. All of them curled up next to her. I can't wait to show you, Spence. They're beautiful. Come and have a look.'

'Wait until after tea,' said Mary. 'Shadow'll want a bit of a rest. And Spence is helping me here.'

Alice looked disappointed. 'Mam!'

'Why don't you start making your animal-vegetable? You've not got much time left before tomorrow.'

'All right,' she said, her face brightening. 'I already know what I'm going to make. Guess what it is, Spence.'

'I don't even know what an animal-vegetable is.'

'It's an animal that you make out of vegetables, silly. You stick them together with pins. I'll show you. And guess what animal it's going to be?'

He shook his head. 'I can't.'

'Go on. Try!'

'Alright then, a tiger,' he said, grinning.

'No! I'll give you a clue. It's an animal with a job.'

'A performing bear.'

'Nope.'

'A plough horse,' said Mary.

'Nope.'

Spencer and Mary looked at each other in amusement. 'We give up,' she said.

Alice shook her head in disbelief. 'It's Shadow and her pups.'

*

Alice sat at the dining table, frowning with concentration as she selected the right potato for the body. Back in the kitchen, Mary began to make a stew, chopping up carrots and onions and throwing them into a pan.

'Tell me more about those May Balls, Spence,' she said.

It was her favourite topic. Spencer, who had only been to one of them, feeling lost in a sea of drunken undergraduates, obliged her as far as he could, making up stories of lavish excess and dancing until dawn.

'What did the girls wear?' she asked. 'Ballgowns?'

He thought back, trying to remember. 'Yes. Made of silk, or something. They looked, er, very beautiful.'

'I'm sure they did,' she said wistfully. 'I'd love to dress up like that. Did they have their hair up? Did some of them even wear jewels?'

'I – I suppose so,' he said. 'Necklaces and . . . that sort of thing.'

'What about you?'

'Me?'

Taking a piece of meat from the refrigerator, she held it under the tap to rinse away the blood.

'Yes. What did you wear? A dinner jacket?'

'I think so. It would have been black tie.'

He remembered standing stiffly in a rented outfit, worried about spilling something on his shirt.

She sighed. 'I remember the last time Hartley wore a suit. It was when we went to a Hunt Ball, once, years ago, when Alice was little. But I don't expect it was much like your ones in Cambridge. You'll have had champagne, I'm sure – not like the punch we got – and a proper band?'

He nodded.

'I bet you didn't get drunk, either. You probably stayed up 'til dawn, and gave your jacket to your girlfriend so she didn't get cold. I ended up driving Hartley home—'

'Spence,' called Alice, 'can you come and help?'

He was glad of the interruption, remembering the last ball, that summer. His tutor had been adamant that he should not go.

'Keep your head down and stay out of sight,' he had said. 'I don't want any more scandal.'

From his desk in the library, Spencer had watched the students in their finery coming down the walled approach to the college, laughing, flushed with anticipation of the night ahead. He envied their lack of concern and their easy certainty that they would have a good time, and wondered how it might have been if his advances had not been rejected, if for once he had been able to go to the ball and enjoy it.

The next time he had looked up, he caught sight of the undergraduate, walking with his arm around a very pretty girl in a black dress who was glowing with happiness. As he watched, she leaned her head into his.

A leaden, hopeless feeling had come over him. Gathering his books, he had hurried to his room and crawled into bed, closing the window tight against the laughter and music that had gone on until the early hours of the morning.

He went across to Alice. 'What do you want me to do?' he asked.

'Can you hold the potatoes for me? They keep slipping.'

He took them, keeping them in position as she pushed pins through them, fixing them together.

'Now the eyes.'

She attached two raisins with pinheads for pupils.

Spencer went back into the kitchen. 'What time will you be going to the show?' he asked.

'Early,' said Mary. 'I've got to take the cakes before ten. Maybe you could bring Alice over later?'

'Of course,' he said.

'Come and look!' Alice's voice was high with excitement.

As Mary and Spencer went into the room, she held up the animal-vegetable. She had pinned on five raisins in a row.

'They're teats, so the puppies can feed. What do you think?'

Spencer looked at the odd creation. 'I like it,' he said.

'I've never seen one like that, love,' said Mary.

'Do you think it'll win?'

'I'd say you've got a good chance. What are you going to do about the pups?'

'I don't know,' said Alice. 'Potatoes would be too big, but I can't think of anything else.'

Spencer was suddenly inspired. 'How about blackberries? I saw some growing by the lane. They'd even be the right colour.'

Alice clapped her hands. 'Yes! That's a brilliant idea. I knew you'd have the answer. You're great, Spence!'

As Alice dashed out of the door, Mary shook her head and smiled. Spencer began to tidy the table, picking up stray pins that Alice had dropped onto the floor.

While he was clearing up, Thomas came into the room, his face dark.

'Mary!' he called.

She went to him, wiping her hands on her apron. 'What's the matter?' she asked, noticing his expression.

'Hartley's on his way back from the show field. He's coming to get the pups for drowning.'

'Drowning?' said Spencer, horrified.

'There's nowt we can do about it,' Thomas said quietly. 'He says there's no point trying to sell them. No-one's buying pups at the moment, not this year.'

'B-but what about Alice? She's been looking forward to these puppies all summer.'

'I know. That's why I came back, to give a bit of warning, like.'

Mary's face was bleak. 'I should have known. This is going to break her heart.'

'Is there nothing we can do?' asked Spencer. 'Can't we try to persuade him?'

Mary and Thomas looked at him, and he immediately knew the answer.

'You'll have to take Alice off,' said Mary. 'Do something with her so she isn't around when he does it. Otherwise it'll get nasty.'

'But—' Spencer was distraught at the idea of betraying Alice's trust.

'She'll go with you,' said Mary. 'She won't think it's strange.'

'It's better that way,' said Thomas. 'Hartley won't give in, and neither will she. There'll just be another fight.'

*

Alice came back with a margarine tub full of brambles from the hedgerow, fat berries swollen with sun.

'I've got them!' she said. 'All I have to do now is find a piece of wood and some hay to stick on to make a nest.'

Catching Spencer's eye, Mary nodded towards the door.

'Why don't we go and get some now?' said Spencer. 'I'll come with you. Then we can stick it all together afterwards.'

*

They crossed the yard, Spencer keeping an eye out for Hartley. The barn was stacked high with hay, piled to the rafters with golden bales, the air thick with tiny particles of dust lit up by the light that streamed through the open door. Spencer remembered his unexpected pleasure at creating clean lines out of messy piles of hay, the satisfaction of tossing soft billows of grass into the baler and seeing them come out the other end, compacted into solid, rectangular parcles, neatly bound with string. He had stacked them, fitting them neatly together, devising ways to best fit the space.

'We don't need much,' said Alice. 'Just a bit to make the nest, so it looks real.'

She looked over at him. 'Let's go and see the puppies now,' she said, excited again. 'Then you'll know what they look like, for when we make the animal-vegetable.'

'But didn't you say they were asleep? We shouldn't disturb them.'

'They'll have woken up again by now. Come on!'

'Let's see if we can find the right piece of wood first. That way we'll have everything we need. Your mum said the animal-vegetable has to go over to the show field tonight, not too late.'

'We've got loads of time to finish it,' said Alice. 'And the puppies are so sweet. You've got to see them, before they go to sleep again.'

She began to move towards the door.

Spencer thought quickly. 'Stay here, Alice, just for a minute. I want to tell you a secret.'

'What kind of secret?'

'Well, remember when we talked about square numbers? Well, if you want to get from one square number to the next, you just add—'

She shook her head impatiently. 'Not about maths!' she said. 'I thought it was something important. Something about you.'

His heart lurched as he realized his mistake in mentioning a secret. He thought of Edmund and again he wondered how much she knew.

'Are you going to tell me a proper secret?' she asked. 'Or can we go and see the puppies?'

He thought again. 'All right. I've got one. Come and sit on this bale and I'll tell you it.'

They sat on the hay bale, Alice's thin legs dangling.

'You'll be the only person in the world who knows it. You have to promise – on our friendship – not to tell anyone. Anyone at all. Like with our equation.'

She nodded gravely. 'I promise.'

'OK. Well, the secret is that my name isn't really Spencer.'

Alice looked at him, confused. 'What?'

'When I came up here for the summer I decided to give myself a new name.'

He remembered standing by the roadside at the start of his journey, determined to strip away his old self, leaving no trail to be followed.

'Why?'

'Well – I suppose I wanted to be someone new.'

She thought it over, considering what he had said.

'But then, what's your real name, Spence? Who are you?'

As he hesitated, wondering how to respond, Hartley came into sight, walking through the yard. In his hand was a brown burlap sack, dripping, a small bulge at the bottom.

Alice froze. 'Spence! He's got the puppies in there!'

She made as if to get up. Spencer put a warning hand on her shoulder. 'A-Alice – don't.'

'He's killed them!' she wailed. 'He's killed them.'

She bent over as if in physical pain, her breath coming in little gasps. Tears began to slide from under her glasses, rolling down her cheeks.

'Alice, a-are you all right?' Spencer said, alarmed.

She spoke between great, gulping hiccoughs. 'I should have run away with her again. I could have saved her pups from Dad. Why did he have to do that, Spence? He didn't have to. He's always horrible to Shadow and he's always horrible to me.'

Her tears were coming faster now, dropping from her cheeks onto her shorts. Her grief was unnerving in its force. He hesitated for a moment, then put his arm around her slight shoulders. Tentatively, he began to stroke her hair, smoothing it back from her damp face. She stayed there for a while, a little ball of misery, huddling into him, her tears soaking into his shirt, then suddenly she sat up straight, rigid and trembling.

'I hate him, Spence. I hate him. He killed Shadow's pups. He's a *murderer*.'

*

Later, after the brothers had gone to the Tup and Alice had finally sobbed herself to sleep, Spencer went up the fellside to meet Edmund. He tried to explain what had happened.

'Just when I think he's changing, he does something like this. I don't think Mary can stand it much longer. Or Alice. She's so – I don't know – well, so vulnerable.'

Edmund shook his head. 'She's tougher than you think. Anyone who's lived all their life with Hartley Dodds would have to be.'

'But it was an awful thing to do.'

'She lives on a farm. She has to learn. We all do. I did. Crops die. Animals die, people die. Nothing lasts for ever.'

Spencer felt a sudden rush of emotion. 'I don't think that's true. Some things must.'

Edmund glanced at him, a warning look in his eye. 'Don't go soft on me, Spence.'

'I don't want the summer to end. I don't want to leave.'

Edmund picked up a stick, snapping it over his knee.

'Don't be daft. Your life's in Cambridge. You've got everything you want. You're going to get a fellowship and you'll end up being a professor. You'll stay there for ever.'

'It's not as simple as that. Everything hangs on me getting to the proof before anyone else. I have to show my tutor that I'm nearly there by September. If I don't, I'm finished. I won't get the research fellowship, and I'll have to start on something else. I'll have lost years. I haven't got time. I'm already twenty-four.'

'That's not old.'

'It is for a mathematician. Most of us do our best work before we're thirty. And even the Fields Medal is—'

'What's the Fields Medal?'

'It's like the Nobel Prize, for mathematicians. They only give it to people under the age of forty. I'm nowhere near achieving something like that. Maths is something you've either got or you haven't. I could spend all my life trying, doing work that doesn't mean anything. Or maybe I should just stop. Now. I could just stay.'

He looked at Edmund, trying to read his expression, but he was looking over at the other side of the fell. His face gave nothing away. His hair was golden against his tanned skin, his eyes very blue.

'You'll think different when it rains. It's miserable then. It goes on and on for days, and it's cold, and there's nothing you can do. It gets into you somehow, into your bones.'

He pointed over to where he'd been looking. 'See the fell? Sometimes you can't see to the end of the valley, the cloud's that thick. And then you can't see any way out.'

Spencer looked at the fields beneath them, parched yellow and brown, shorn to stubble the week before, patches of earth showing through like worn corduroy. The setting sun was still warm on his face.

'I can't imagine it ever raining again.'

Edmund shook his head. 'Believe me, it will.' He scrambled to his feet. 'Well, I'd best be off.'

Spencer choked back his disappointment. 'But—'

'I've got the race tomorrow,' Edmund said, holding out a hand to pull Spencer up. 'I need an early night. You're not the only one who's after a medal, you know.'

Eighteen

Spencer woke to the sound of a lone bird singing in the tree next to his hut. Outside, the sun blazed high above the fells, scalding the day into submission.

He stood in the doorway to the hut, looking at the tents in the field below. There was a shimmering intensity to the morning, the valley held in parched stillness. He was suddenly aware that the end of the summer was approaching and that in a few weeks term would begin. The thought of going back to Cambridge was exhausting. He remembered again the conversations with his supervisor and the Senior Tutor. It seemed less likely than ever that he would be able to produce enough evidence of progress. He had meant what he had said to Edmund about giving up his academic ambitions. He had been looking for encouragement, an indication that Edmund might want him to stay. Now he stood looking down, mulling over his response. He would have to make a decision soon, he knew.

In the farmhouse Alice was bent close to the table, writing in her exercise book. When she looked up, Spencer saw that her eyes were swollen.

She smiled tightly.

'Hello,' he said. 'Are you all right?'

She nodded. 'Mam's already gone to the show field. She's setting up the tea tent. She said you'd take me over later in time for my dance.'

'Of course.'

In the kitchen he made coffee, then took it back to the table. 'What are you writing?'

'Things for my school story.'

'Will you read it to me?'

'One day. When it's the end of the holidays. You're in it. Lots.'

'Who else is in it?' he asked carefully.

'Shadow. I went to find her in the byre when I got up.' Her voice began to tremble. 'She was all curled up in the corner. I took her biscuits but she didn't even want them. She growled at me. She's never done that before. I think she hates me.'

He swallowed. 'She's just sad, Alice, that's all. It's not your fault.'

She shook her head, her eyes filled with tears. 'But she doesn't know that. She just doesn't like me any more.'

'Look, let's go to the show field,' he said. 'I bet by the time we get back she'll be back to normal again.'

She looked at him, her eyes red. 'Do you really think so?'

'I promise.'

*

The tannoy was already drifting over the fields as they picked their way across them, a disconnected, nasal voice, squeezing itself out of the loudspeakers. Cars were parked in rows, dirt-splashed Land Rovers next to battered Ford Cortinas and Volvos with grilles between the front and back seats to control dogs. The ground was baked hard from the sun, and the cars drove over it easily, trailing clouds of dust.

Being in the show field was very different from Spencer's fellside view. The white tents were suddenly enticing, their openings pinned back to offer glimpses of darkened interiors, rows of tables draped with white cloths dotted with competition entries. Smells hovered in the walkways: frying meat, the dry, sugary whiff of popcorn, and, as they passed the biggest tent of all, beer fumes, overlaid with the chemical stink from the row of lavatories behind. Chips sizzled in hot fat, hissing and spitting over the hum of generators in strange counterpoint to a more familiar sound, the bleating and coughing of sheep.

At the far end of the field, the pen was filled with a sea of fleeces. Farmers dressed up in moleskin trousers and tweed jackets stood leaning on curved crooks, feet resting on the wooden bars of the pens. The sheep looked very different from the stragglers that Spencer had pursued over the fell, their fleeces long but neatly trimmed, their faces snowy white.

'Look at the sheep, Alice. It's as if they've had a bath.'

'You have to wash them,' said Alice, her voice quiet and flat. 'I used to do it with Uncle Tom. It's hard, they don't like it. They wriggle a lot.'

They passed a set of smaller pens, each holding a single ram standing dignified, horns curling magnificently like an immaculate coiffure.

'This is the first year Dad's not showing his tups,' said Alice. 'He always used to win.'

Spencer thought it best to stay away from the subject of Hartley. 'Shall we go and have a look in the tents?'

As they wandered past coconut shies and hoopla stalls, they came to a crowd, cheering and applauding.

'What do you think it is?' he asked Alice. 'Let's see.'

She wriggled to the front, dragging him behind her.

The spectacle that greeted them was extraordinary. Two men stood facing each other, clad in white vests and long johns that sagged at the knees, black socks and loose, oversized knickers pulled high to the waist. The umpire, a small, wiry man dressed in ginger tweed, stood to one side. At his signal, the two men stepped closer until they were standing chest to chest. Bending their knees, they embraced, resting their chins on each other's shoulders. A ripple of excitement went through the crowd. Intrigued, Spencer leaned forward, craning his neck to see.

Pulling himself up to his full height, the umpire squared his shoulders and raised his hand. He waited for a moment, looking around the ring, and then called loudly, 'Hold!'

The two men began to twist in each other's arms, staggering back and forth like clumsy dancers. Their legs wound together, thighs hooked and collided, knees locked as they made their way across the dusty arena.

The crowd was quiet now, the only sound the grunting of the wrestlers as they thrust and struggled, each trying to throw his opponent to the ground. Under the odd outfits, their muscles tensed and bulged with the strain, their bodies melded together like some strange mythical creature, a beast with many limbs, two heads and two backs.

As they struggled on, their grunts grew louder, their movements jerking and furious. Suddenly one of them was on the ground, lying in the dust, the other raising his hands above his head in victory.

The crowd let out a chorus of catcalls and cheers.

'Fall,' shouted the umpire.

After a minute their arms were wrapped around each other once more, ready to begin again.

Alice turned to Spencer. 'They do it three times,' she said. 'The one who falls most is the loser.'

He imagined holding Edmund hard like the wrestlers, feeling his muscles under his hands, and wondered who would win. He suspected it would be Edmund, and imagined falling, hitting the hard ground, tasting dust. He wanted to see him before the race, to wish him luck.

'Let's stay to see the next one,' said Alice.

'Why don't we have a look around and come back later. We could get you an ice cream if you like.' He was ashamed to resort to bribery, but Alice's face brightened for the first time that day.

'Brilliant!'

The field was busier now, beginning to bustle with families, teenagers skulking, children racing in and out of adult legs, dogs straining on leads. Stallholders called to passers-by, drumming up trade for beef burgers and chips, a ride on a pony, guessing the piglet's weight. All the while, Spencer was looking through the crowds, past the coloured bunting that hung between the stalls, searching for Edmund.

Alice led him to an ice-cream van parked alongside the stalls, dotted with pictures of chocolate sundaes and 99 Flakes, Sky Ray Lollies and Zooms, so bright and sharp that they seemed almost to fly out from the side of the van.

Standing on tiptoe, she called up to the kindly looking man at the hatch, 'Can I have a Raspberry Mivvi, please?'

Spencer gave him the money as Alice ripped off the wrapper. The lollipop was the colour of the foxgloves that grew down by the river. Her tongue darted, curling around its edges. She nibbled, concentrating, precise, making sure to keep the shape symmetrical, licking any discrepancies smooth.

231

They wandered slowly, Alice absorbed in what she was doing, Spencer still scanning the field, looking for a glimpse of Edmund.

Children were taking part in races, jumping in sacks that reached to their armpits.

'Don't you want to join in?' he asked.

As she turned to answer he was startled by the colour of her lips.

'Alice! What have you done?'

She grinned. 'Some of the girls in my class are wearing lipstick for the dance. They pinch it off their mams. But my mam doesn't wear lipstick, so I thought I'd get it from the lolly.'

He thought of the times he had seen Mary in make-up, smoking at the back of the house, but said nothing. Alice's lips were at odds with the rest of her, uncannily adult on her child's face. She wore the colour self-consciously, her mouth parted, as if she were nervous of rubbing it off.

Glancing up, Spencer saw Mary approaching from the tea tent, a basket over her arm.

'Quick, Alice,' he said, 'you'd better wipe that off. Here's your mum.'

Alice grinned, wiping her lips on the back of her hand as Mary joined them.

'Hello Mam!' called Alice. 'Did you bring my costume?'

'It's in the basket,' Mary said. 'Come on, you need to get ready. Miss Mannering wants you there by half past one.'

An announcement came over the tannoy. 'All contestants for the fell race come to the starting line. The race starts in fifteen minutes.'

'I'm going to go and watch,' Spencer said quickly.

Alice's face fell. 'But you'll be back in time to see me?'

'Of course,' he said. 'You know I wouldn't miss that.'

He picked his way along pathways trodden to dust. The beer tent was crammed with drinkers, spilling out of the tent, flushed and talkative, enjoying long swallows of beer and flicking cigarette ash onto the grass. He knew that Hartley would be inside, that he had been there since that morning, and wondered what state he would be in later.

Pushing the thought away, Spencer hurried on, passing the tea tent, sedate and half-empty, and the competition tent, now deserted. As he approached the corner of the field reserved for sports, his heart began to quicken, nervous excitement rising in his throat.

The fell runners were grouped next to the starting line. Their bodies were different from those of the wrestlers, lean and long. Some had taken off their vests in deference to the sun, revealing sculpted torsos ridged with muscle. He looked at them as they paced, waiting to begin, stretching and flexing, shaking their hands to loosen their wrists. When at last he saw Edmund, standing at the end of the line, dressed only in a pair of blue shorts, he caught his breath. He wanted to go to him, to hold him as close as the wrestlers had gripped each other. Trembling with longing, he gazed at him, willing him to turn and notice. When Edmund grinned and raised his hand, he was filled with a rush of dizzy pleasure.

'Young Edmund's quite a champion,' said a quiet voice.

Startled, he looked down to see Dorothy, leaning on a shooting stick.

'I knew his grandfather,' she continued. 'He was a champion too, for years. He was still running in his seventies.'

She looked at him, her eyes shrewd. 'Edmund's always been like his grandad. A bit wild. Of course, with Jim it was always women. He couldn't let a pretty girl go.'

Cold fear pricked up his spine. 'Really?'

'Looks like they'll just get started in time,' she said as if he hadn't spoken, looking off into the distance. 'It's going to rain.'

Spencer looked up at the sky, a clear and brilliant blue. 'Are you sure? It doesn't look like it.'

She nodded. 'I can feel it. I've lived here long enough to know. There's something in the air. And when it comes, there's going to be a lot of it.'

A squeal of feedback came from the tannoy. 'The lads are taking their places,' said the tinny voice. 'There's some fine runners racing today, on the hardest course they've seen so far.'

The runners were poised, their toes against a white line painted onto the grass.

'Good luck, Edmund,' Spencer whispered under his breath.

A man stood by the line, holding an orange flag. 'Are you ready?' he said. 'On your marks . . . get set . . . go!'

They sprang away from the starting line, darting across to the gate that led to the intake.

'They're off!' said the tannoy. 'And good luck to them. It'll be a tough run. We'll expect them back in an hour or so, and I'll be letting you know when we spot the first ones coming down.'

Spencer gazed at the ant-like runners, trying to make out Edmund's blue shorts. He imagined him toiling up the fellside, his arms pumping, chest slick with sweat, and felt a jolt of desire.

The tannoy crackled. 'And now for something completely different, as they say on the telly. There's a dance performance in the wrestling ring, starting in ten minutes' time. It's the first time we've had one here at the show, so go and have a look, and make sure you give the girls a cheer. That's a dance performance in the wrestling ring, starting in ten minutes' time.'

'I'd better go,' he said to Dorothy. 'Alice is in that.'

'I'll come with you,' she said. 'I did ballet myself, as a girl. Hated it. I was never any good. But still, it's nice to watch.'

As they went past the beer tent, Spencer noticed some of the hippies sitting on a bench, glasses of beer in their hands.

'How's it going, Spence?' called Mick. 'Fancy a pint?'

He had dressed up for the occasion in purple bell-bottoms, skin-tight around the thighs and groin and flared at the knee, teamed with a scarlet waistcoat over his bare chest. He was smiling, seemingly oblivious to the curious glances of the passers-by.

'I'm going to watch Alice,' Spencer said. 'She's dancing in a minute.'

'We'll join you when we've finished these. I like her. She's a cool kid.' He grinned at Dorothy. 'We haven't met,' he said. 'I'm Mick.'

Spencer was astonished to see her smile back. 'I'm Dorothy,' she said, holding out her hand. 'How do you do?'

*

A new crowd had gathered around the ring. Women in summer dresses stood chatting, their perfumes mingling in the warm after-noon air as their husbands fiddled with cameras. He recognized some of them from Alice's ballet class.

Angela Armstrong smiled when she saw him. 'Spencer!' she said. 'Hello! Are you looking forward to it? Sarah was so excited she couldn't sleep. I expect Alice was the same.'

He thought of the dark circles under Alice's eyes and her own miserable reasons for them.

'I'm sure they'll be very good,' Angela went on. 'They've been practising for ever so long. You and Mary must be so proud.'

Spencer felt Dorothy's quick gaze settle on him, and blushed.

'We are,' he mumbled.

He caught sight of Mary outside the pavilion, beckoning to him. 'Will you excuse us?' he said.

Mary smiled gratefully as he and Dorothy approached.

'How's Alice?' Spencer asked.

'Nervous. She's all worked up about this dance. She keeps asking when you're coming back. I'll tell her you're here, so she knows.'

Mary disappeared into the pavilion. The next moment, Alice came rushing out.

'You came!'

'I promised I would.'

'You're not supposed to see me in my costume, but I wanted you to in case you can't see it properly when I'm dancing. Do you like it?'

She twirled and curtsied, showing it off; a pale pink tutu, folds of net pinned to a leotard, dotted with twinkling sequins.

'You look beautiful,' he said.

She beamed. 'I feel like a fairy.'

Miss Mannering appeared at the door to the pavilion. 'Alice Dodds! Come back inside. Now!'

Alice turned to leave. 'Oh! I forgot. Miss Mannering said I had to take my glasses off. She said they don't look right. Will you hold them for me, Spence?'

Passing them to him, she blinked like a baby bird, her eyes surprisingly large without the heavy lenses.

'Wish me luck, Spence.'

'Good luck,' he said, patting her arm. 'You'll be wonderful.'

*

Marching music blared as the girls made their entrance, trooping around the ring in order of height. Arms held stiffly by their sides, they picked their knees up high like ponies, shoulders back, looking straight ahead.

'Now folks, please give a warm welcome to the Mannering School of Dance!' instructed the tannoy.

The crowd obeyed, breaking into applause. Broad smiles broke over the girls' faces, and they stood taller, basking in the crowd's appreciation.

Spencer noticed Miss Mannering and Joan standing by the entrance to the ring, dressed in their usual black. They looked out of place in the field, their high-heeled shoes covered in dust. Keeping themselves to one side, apart from the crowd, they watched the girls' performance closely.

As the music came to an end, the girls arranged themselves in a line, their feet in what Spencer now knew to be first position, hands held demurely in front of them. Some were effortless, easily graceful, others nervous, looking at the floor, thin legs trembling as they attempted to hold the pose. Spencer's heart swelled as he looked at Alice, pale but determined, her shoulders forced down and feet turned out to almost ninety degrees. Her skinny body scarcely filled her costume. Despite Mary's best efforts, her hair stuck out in all directions and her ballet shoes seemed even more battered than usual, next to the crisp pink net of the tutu and the feet of the other girls. He found himself holding his breath, waiting for them to start, counting the seconds. The girls held their pose for a few moments more, then the opening notes came; three long chords, a minor key.

They began to dance, twelve small girls pirouetting together. Their skirts flew out as they spun, a sea of net, arms reaching high above their heads. The crowd was captivated, watching them spin; the ring quiet, the only sounds the music and the click of camera shutters.

The girls formed a circle, facing out to the audience. Holding their skirts out wide, they curtseyed and then turned, touching fingertips, and he remembered Alice's small hands against his as they practised. She was frowning now, concentrating hard as she skipped, counting the beats under her breath. Spencer counted with her, willing her forward.

The piano began to crescendo, quickening as the girls separated back out, then ran into the centre two at a time, linking arms in the middle to spin. The first pair met, two little blondes who spun so prettily they earned a round of applause. The crowd clapped for the next pair too, fitting around the rhythm of the music. The clapping continued as the third pair began, Alice and another girl, delicate and dark. Spencer joined in, willing Alice on. All through the dance she had been hesitant, waiting for the other girls to move first.

Come on, Alice, he thought. Dance like you did for me that afternoon on the fell.

As if she could hear him, she dashed into the circle, her arm outstretched. But as she reached her partner she lost her footing and cannoned into her, knocking her to the ground. Immediately the clapping stopped. Alice scrambled to her feet, her cheeks crimson. For a moment she paused, looking blindly at the crowd, her eyes filling with tears, then she turned and ran out of the ring.

Mary and Spencer made their way through the crowd as quickly as they could. At the back of the pavilion, they found Alice sobbing.

'I couldn't see without my glasses. It was all blurry.'

'It's all right, love,' said Mary, carefully unfolding the glasses and sliding them back onto her face. 'It's not your fault. I should have made them let you keep them on.'

She shook her head. 'It *is* my fault. I looked stupid. I ruined it.'

'Listen Alice, the music's still playing,' Spencer said. 'The girls just picked themselves up. They're carrying on. It's OK.'

'It was the first time they've let us dance at the show. They'll never let us do it again.' Her voice rose. 'Miss Mannering's going to be so cross with me.'

'She won't, love,' said Mary. 'You couldn't see. I'll explain. She'll understand.'

Alice shook her head. 'But I made a mess of it. I ruined it.'

'Too bloody right you ruined it,' slurred a deep voice, thick with alcohol. 'Made a right sight of yourself.'

Hartley towered above them, swaying slightly, his face reddened by the day's drinking. Alice shrank back behind Spencer.

Hartley stabbed a finger in Mary's direction. 'And *you*. I told you she was to stop those lessons, and I told you why. But you went behind my back. With *him*. I can see it in his face.'

Mary's own face was white. 'I thought you were in the beer tent.'

'Well you thought wrong. I was, until I bumped into one of them hippies on my way to't toilet and he said me lass was going to be on in't ring and mustn't I be proud? So I thought I'd come and have a look. Nowt to be proud of, though, was there?'

Alice was trembling now. Spencer felt her hand clutch at the back of his shirt. Hartley leaned back unsteadily and then righted himself, jabbing his finger again at Mary.

'Are you happy now? Filling her head with all kinds of rubbish and spending money on airs and graces? Well now you see. Can't make a silk purse out of a sow's ear, can you?'

An odd look passed over his face and his shoulders began to heave. As Spencer stared at him, wondering what he would say next, Hartley began to laugh, a mocking, mirthless guffaw.

Spencer stepped forward. 'Hartley, that's enough.'

Hartley looked at him with bleary eyes.

'What?'

'That's enough.'

There was a long pause as he stared at Spencer, trying to focus, then his eyes narrowed and he took a step forward, squaring his shoulders. As Spencer stepped back, Hartley grunted with scorn.

'You're not man enough to tell me what's enough. She's my daughter. I can say what I like to her.'

Two pink spots had appeared high up on Mary's cheekbones.

'No you can't,' she said. 'Not to *my* daughter.'

Striding towards him, she grabbed his arm.

'For Christ's sake, woman,' he said, staggering backwards. 'What are you doing?'

'We're going home. You're not fit to be out.'

'Don't tell me what I'm fit for.'

'You're showing us up.'

'She's the one who showed us up,' he said, pointing a stubby finger at Alice.

'We're going, Hartley, now.' Her voice was low and furious.

He stood up straight, taking a deep breath, as if preparing to retaliate, but just as he seemed about to speak, he sagged and crumpled, looking around as if he no longer knew where he was. His shoulders twitched in a shrug. Still gripping his arm, Mary began to march him across the field, propping him up as he swayed.

As soon as they had gone, Alice began to silently cry, her arms hanging loose by her sides as she stared at the ground, a solitary, wretched little figure. After a moment's hesitation, Spencer knelt down beside her.

'Alice?'

She turned to him and threw herself into his arms. Her small body was hot from crying, her breath ragged. They stayed there, not moving, as the crowd from the dancing display drifted past, moving on to the next spectacle.

The tannoy began again. 'They're coming down!' said the announcer, excited. 'We've just spotted the first of them coming over the top of the fell. It's looking good. They're pelting down.'

Spencer felt a guilty prickle of excitement.

'Alice?' he said gently. 'He didn't mean it, you know. He was angry with me for going behind his back with the lessons, and he took it out on you and your mum.'

She stifled a sob.

'You were dancing so well.'

She looked at him through glasses smudged with sticky tears.

'I was proud of you, Alice.'

'Really, Spence?'

'Yes, really. You danced like a – a fairy princess.'

She managed a small smile. Spencer stood up and looked over towards the fell.

'What do you think? Shall we go and watch the end of the fell race? They're coming back.'

There was a long pause. He tried to swallow back his impatience.

'All right,' she said eventually, with a shrug. 'If you like. I don't care.'

*

The runners raced down the fellside. In the field there was a buzz of excitement as onlookers chattered, arguing over who would win. Each time Edmund's name was repeated, Spencer felt a secret swell of pleasure. Borrowing a pair of binoculars, he held them to his eyes. Edmund was at the front of the group, his bare chest heaving as he led the way, blond hair dripping with sweat.

'Do you want to see?' Spencer asked Alice, standing small and silent by his side. 'Edmund's in the lead. I think he's going to win.'

'He always does.' Putting the binoculars to her face, she held them briefly steady, then gave them back to him. 'I wonder if Shadow's all right. We should go and check on her.'

The commentator was speaking faster, as if to match the runners' pace. 'And at the front we have Edmund Lutwidge, five times show champion. Looks like today he might make it six. But young Charlie

Dodgson's close behind, and Danny Wilson's in third place. Anything could happen between now and the finishing line. Put a step wrong on the way back down at that speed and it's a broken ankle, or worse.'

Spencer looked up at Edmund, racing towards the gate. He found himself holding his breath, fists clenched.

'They're close now, very close. Edmund Lutwidge through the gate, Danny Wilson up to second, Charlie Dodgson coming through as well. This last hundred yards makes all the difference!'

The crowd cheered as the three men flung themselves down the field, limbs pumping, faces scarlet with effort. Edmund's eyes were screwed up tight against the sun, his teeth bared as he put all he had into the final fifty yards. Suddenly, the man behind him picked up speed. As the crowd cheered, Spencer felt a rush of choking anxiety. The two men raced on towards the finishing line, so close now that he could see the veins standing out on Edmund's neck.

Go on, he willed him, go on Edmund, please!

Pulling away from his rival, Edmund hurled himself over the line.

'And the winner of the fell race is Edmund Lutwidge!' The commentator grabbed his arm and held it high. 'What a race!'

As more applause rippled over the field, Spencer gazed at Edmund, gloriously proud. Feeling the tension drain from his body, he turned happily towards Alice, but when he looked down she was gone.

'Alice?' he looked around, puzzled.

He felt a tap on his shoulder. Suddenly Edmund was there, a white towel around his neck like a boxer.

'Well done,' said Spencer, suddenly shy.

Edmund grinned. 'It was a hard one.'

'But you did it. You got the medal.'

For a long moment, they looked at each other. Edmund's shoulders were still heaving.

'Listen, I'm sorry about last night,' he said softly. 'Let's go some-where now. How about your hut?'

'Not the cave?'

'Too far.'

The tannoy crackled. 'Can Edmund Lutwidge, Charlie Dodgson and Danny Wilson come to pick up their medals?'

'Don't worry, no-one'll know. They'll all be down here. I'll meet you there as soon as I can. Ten minutes.'

As he went off in the direction of the show tent, Spencer watched him, stopped every few yards by well-wishers clapping him on the shoulders, shaking his hand. For a moment, he wondered where Alice had gone, feeling a faint sense of unease at the way she had disappeared. Remembering her comment about checking on Shadow, he decided she must have headed back to the farm. Putting it from his mind, he stole away, up the field, through the gate to the intake, and along the little path that led to the hut.

*

When Edmund arrived, five minutes later, Spencer pulled him through the door and to the bed. He smelled of fresh sweat and exer-tion, his muscles pumped up hard from running. They moved hungrily, with urgency, spurred on by the pent-up tension of the race.

Afterwards, lying close, they lazily discovered each other, visibly naked for the first time in the sunlight that streamed in through the window. Their bodies were patchworked brown and white. Without his trousers, Edmund's skin was startlingly pale, in contrast to his torso, dark from days spent shearing in the sun. He was white from his waist to his feet, usually clad in heavy boots and socks. Now they were bruised from pounding down the mountain-side. Spencer held them between his palms, feeling the heat pulse out of them.

'What do you think about when you're running?' he asked.

Edmund shrugged. 'Lots of things.'

'Like what?'

'Mostly how I'm going to get through the next hundred yards. What's in the way, so I don't trip over it. I nearly fell over a sheep today. A dozy old yow. Didn't seem to notice I was there until I ran into her.'

Spencer ran a finger along the pale strip below Edmund's navel. 'You've got a line. Like those markings that Hartley uses to show which sheep are his. I wish I could be marked like that, with bright red smit, so everyone would know who I belonged to.'

'And who's that?'

'You of course.'

Edmund rolled over onto his stomach. 'You silly sod. Let's go and get a pint in the beer tent. I'd better say hello to the lads.'

Nineteen

BY THE TIME THEY GOT BACK TO THE SHOW FIELD IT WAS deserted, the smell of frying chips gone, replaced by the reek of the chemical toilets as they were lifted onto the back of a lorry. Sideshow owners were dismantling their attractions, unscrewing them into pieces. The carousel horses lay stacked on top of one another, their mouths frozen in wooden grins, waiting to be loaded into a truck, and the warren of sheep pens stood empty, adorned by tufts of wool and little piles of droppings. The ground was crossed with dusty trails worn into the earth by the crowds, and littered with the day's detritus: empty cans, crisp packets, the stumps of ice-cream cones.

One part of the field was still alive: the beer tent swelled with the rumble of voices.

Edmund chuckled. 'They're settling in for the night.'

As they went inside, he was greeted with cheers.

'Up the hero!' someone shouted, and a pint of beer was thrust into Edmund's hand. He drank it down in one long swallow, closing his eyes and tipping back his head.

Spencer stood, awkward, next to him, feeling dazed. Just half an hour before, he had been alone with Edmund, happy in the quiet seclusion of the hut. There had been nothing but the two of them on the narrow bed, content with the simplicity of nakedness. Now he blinked at the sight of a hundred men drinking and laughing, the hum of deep voices filling the stale air with the harsh, quick accent he had struggled to understand just two months before. Wide smiles cracked across flushed faces as new friendships were cemented and old enmities forgotten over pints paid for by wads of notes pulled from back pockets. It was early evening by now, and the sun had lost some of its strength, but in the tent it was still stiflingly hot. Blue smoke rose from cigarettes, the smell of cheap tobacco mingling with yeasty beer, male sweat and the mustiness of canvas that had been packed away for many months.

A couple of farmers nodded briefly to him, raising their glasses. He had won some sort of grudging respect by saving Alice from the fire, he knew, but he knew as well that he would never be one of them, unlike Edmund, who was surrounded by a crowd who had known him since childhood, a crowd now vying to congratulate and crown him as their hero. Suddenly he wanted to be away from the airless tent and drunken conversation, conversation that he had no hope of joining in. He made his way over to Edmund, who had been absorbed into a noisy group that was attempting to shimmy up the tent poles.

'Edmund! I'm going back to the farm.'

'What?'

'I'm going back to the farm. To see if Alice is all right.'

Edmund was unconcerned. 'OK. I'm going to see if I can get myself up here.'

*

The whoops as he left the tent suggested that Edmund had made it to the top, but Spencer's thoughts had turned to the ugly scene outside the pavilion earlier that afternoon. As he walked along the lane, Hartley's cruelty played on his mind, branded into his memory, together with his own cowardice and Mary's strength as little Alice stood there, silent and pale, flinching at her father's drunken mockery. The uneasy feeling in the pit of his stomach grew stronger with every step. Suddenly he was filled with regret that he had not brought Alice home to find Shadow as he'd promised, allowing his desire to lead him to Edmund instead. He imagined her whispering into the dog's ear, burying her cheek in her fur, and hoped she was with Shadow now, and that it would be enough of a comfort.

When he got to the farm, Mary was in the kitchen making tea. Looking at her shoulders, hunched tight, he wished he had been more help to her at the show. He felt for her, pulling the drunk and lumbering Hartley up the lane.

'Hello Mary,' he said. 'Are – are you all right?'

She turned to face him. Her eyes were swollen and she looked exhausted.

'Yes,' she said. 'He's gone to bed. It's better that way.'

'And how's Alice?' he asked. 'Is she OK?'

'I thought she was with you.'

'No. I mean, she was, but then she left. She was a bit bored by the race, I think. She said she wanted to check on Shadow, so I thought she'd come back here.'

'Did she say anything before she went?'

'No. We were watching the fell race. It was near the end, so it was

247

crowded. There was a lot of noise. People were cheering. The last thing she mentioned was Shadow. When they got to the finish line I went to say something to her, but she wasn't there.'

Mary sighed. 'That's Alice. She's always running off. Sometimes I wonder if I've let her go a bit wild. She'll be back for her supper. It'll be just us three.'

She jerked her head in the direction of the stairs. 'He'll not surface before morning. And Thomas'll stay out late. It's always the same on show night.'

But Alice did not come back for supper. As the sun began to sink behind the mountains, Mary carved slices from a leg of ham. She washed a lettuce from the garden and dried it carefully with a tea towel, then arranged the leaves on three plates. The ham went next to them, joined by cold potatoes, wedges of pickled beetroot and tomatoes cut into quarters. A little pool of salad cream settled around the beetroot, staining purple at its edges. Taking cutlery from the drawer, Mary laid three places at the table, then poured boiling water into the teapot to warm it. She worked quietly and methodically, making her task almost a ritual, but there was nothing soothing about it. They were both tense, what had happened with Hartley hanging heavily between them.

The companionable silence of their other evenings was gone now, Spencer lost for something to say as the clock ticked loudly. Mary brought a milk jug, mugs and a bowl of sugar to the table and then they were ready to eat.

The clock struck seven. Alice did not appear.

'Next birthday, I'll get her a watch,' Mary said.

He nodded. 'She'd like that.'

They sat quietly, drinking their tea, waiting. The sun sank a little further behind the mountains and the clock went on ticking, measuring out minutes. They drank a second cup. When the minute hand

248

of the clock jerked to half past, Mary stood up nervously and picked up the third plate.

'Well, let's start. I don't know where she's got to. She's staying out of the way of her father, most likely. I'll keep her plate covered in the kitchen. She might want it later.'

He nodded. 'I expect she will. She only had a lolly at the show.'

The ham was pleasantly salty, the tomatoes succulent and ripe, but very soon supper was over and Spencer and Mary sat with their empty plates in front of them. The clock seemed to tick more loudly than before and Spencer found himself counting the seconds, trying to distract himself from the silence. When it struck quarter to eight, Mary got up from her chair.

'Spencer,' she said. 'It's not right that she's stayed out this long.'

He stood up, pushing back his chair. 'I know. She's always hungry. I think we should see if we can find her. Where shall we look?'

She shook her head. 'You know better than I do. Where do you think she'd go?'

They went outside to the yard, bathed in evening sunlight. Chickens wandered about, pecking at the dust.

'Alice!' Mary shouted. 'Alice!'

Her voice echoed around the yard.

'Alice!' Spencer called.

They shouted together, their voices carried away by the breeze that was beginning to blow through the yard.

'Let's try the barns,' he said. 'Perhaps she's in there.'

The hay barn was warm from the day's sunshine, creeping in through the slits in its walls. It would have been a fine place to hide, Spencer thought, the perfect place to curl up in peace. But it was empty, save for a mouse that dashed over his boot as they stood in the doorway. Pulling the heavy doors shut, they went to the little cow shed where Shadow had given birth to her puppies.

'Alice?' called Mary. 'Are you there?'

Spencer jerked his head in the direction of the stalls and she followed him as he made his way to the end. As they approached, they heard a faint scuffling.

'Alice?' he said, very quietly.

The scuffling grew louder and they moved closer. But when they looked around the stall there was only Shadow, pressing herself into the corner. When she saw them she bared her teeth and let out a warning growl, rumbling and low.

'Shadow, it's us,' said Spencer. 'We're not here to hurt you.'

'Shhh, girl,' said Mary, soothingly.

But Shadow's eyes continued to gleam with suspicion. When Spencer tried to approach her, she growled louder, snarling with menace.

They turned and left the shed. 'She's still hurting over the pups,' said Mary. 'I've seen it before. It can turn them strange for weeks. He was cruel with her, mind you. They usually get a bit of time together before he takes them.'

'It's odd,' said Spencer, unable to keep the anxiety from his voice, 'I thought Alice would have gone to her. Shall we go back to the show field? Just to be sure. They were still packing things away when I left. She might have been hiding there.'

Mary nodded, biting her lip. 'Let's go. Something's not right. She's never stayed out this long.'

They walked down the lane, not speaking, wrapped in thought. The breeze was stronger now, making the leaves shift and rustle in the oak trees, disrupting the air. After weeks of unbroken heat it was an uncanny relief, bringing freshness, but with it, the hint of disturbance.

The show field was even emptier than when he had left it, the carousel horses gone, sheep pens reduced to piles of wooden fencing.

The tea tent had been taken down, a patch of lighter grass marking where it had stood, its trestle tables collapsed and bound under tarpaulin.

'I can't think where she'd be,' said Mary, her hands knotting her skirt. 'There's nowhere to hide.'

They walked past the beer tent, still crowded, now lit up. It glimmered in the twilight, a strange, raucous outpost in the desolation of the field. Inside, a lengthy song was under way, the verses sung by a single, tuneful baritone, the chorus coming from what seemed to be everyone in the tent.

'Hunting songs,' said Mary, bitterly. 'I'd get Thomas out of there to help, if there was any point, but he'd be no use to us, not now.'

Spencer wondered if Edmund was still inside, singing with the others. He wanted to go to him, to ask for help, but he knew not to try.

'I don't know what to do, Spence.'

Mary was very pale, her forehead creased with worry.

Spencer put his hand on her shoulder. 'She's not here, we can see that. Let's think of where else she could be. We'll go back home and phone some of her friends. Maybe one of the mothers from her ballet class took her home for tea. She might be trying to – to keep out of Hartley's way.'

She nodded, and they left the show field, hurrying back along the lane.

As they walked, Spencer looked over at the forest field, hoping for the reassurance of the hippies' fire. They would help, he thought, if he asked them, remembering Mick's fondness for Alice. But instead, what he saw made him blink with shock. The field was empty, stripped of its ramshackle tent, the brightly painted van with its instructions to make love not war now gone. All that was left was the ring of stones that had served as their fireplace.

Cold fear crept into the corner of his mind.

'Mary . . . look. The hippies, they've gone!'

She looked over at the field. 'What? When?'

'I don't know. They were at the show, on the bench outside the beer tent. I passed them. I said I was going to watch Alice dance.'

'I know,' she said flatly. 'It was them who told Hartley, remember?'

He flushed. 'So they must have gone sometime after that. But they never said anything about leaving.'

Mary looked at him. 'Spencer, you don't think . . .?'

'I don't know . . .' he said. 'She likes them. They're fond of her too.'

He remembered Mick's comment by the beer tent: 'We'll join you when we've finished these. I like her. She's a cool kid.'

He knew how Alice loved the paintings on their vans, the tiny mirrors on the women's skirts, the chimes that tinkled in the breeze. He thought of the hippies' casual nakedness, their lazy disregard for convention, their desire to keep moving on. Would they really take a child, he wondered, and realized he did not know the answer.

'I think we should phone the police,' he said, trying to keep his voice even. 'It might just be a coincidence. But we should find out.'

Their pace quickened. When they got to the farmhouse, Mary dashed to the telephone. Spencer stood close as she dialled, three digits that seemed to take an eternity. As she waited she wound the cord around her finger, and he saw that she was counting the rings under her breath. He counted with her, hope diminishing as the number of rings increased.

She put the receiver down and turned to him. 'No answer. What shall I do?'

'Try again.'

As she was slotting her finger into the dial, they heard footsteps coming from above. A door opened, and then stairs creaked, one by one, under a heavy tread.

'He's awake,' she said.

The next minute Hartley appeared, blinking and dishevelled. He looked at the telephone, out on the table.

'What's all this?' he said, instantly suspicious.

'It's Alice,' said Spencer quickly. 'We can't find her.'

Hartley shrugged. 'Is that it? The lass is probably hiding. She's always running off.'

'That's what we thought. We've been looking everywhere. But there's something else. The hippies have gone, too.'

'What? They were at the show. I saw them myself.'

'But now they've left. With their tents and everything else.'

'The bastards,' Hartley said. 'They owe me money.'

'W-we're worried they might have taken Alice with them.'

He shook his head. 'Why would they take her? She's nothing but trouble.'

'They like her, Hartley.' Mary said. 'And she was upset.'

Hartley lowered himself into a chair. For a moment he said nothing, frowning at the table.

'Who were you ringing?' he asked, eventually.

'The police,' said Spencer.

He looked up sharply. 'What for? There's no need to bring them into it. We'll take care of it ourselves. Where's Thomas?'

The clock ticked, three long beats.

'Where the hell do you think he is?' demanded Mary. 'He's in that beer tent, drinking himself silly, like you were this afternoon. Just before you came down and shouted at Alice. He'll be in there, and he'll be pissed and no use, like you.' She picked up the receiver again, her knuckles clenched around it, white against the raw skin of her hands. 'We'll take care of it ourselves, will we?

What do you ever do right, Hartley? I'm ringing the police, and that's that.'

Spencer held his breath, dreading Hartley's retaliation. Mary turned her back and began to dial.

'You needn't bother,' Hartley said in a quiet, certain voice.

She stiffened. 'I've told you, I will.'

'He won't be there. Jackie Wilson's in't beer tent with the rest of them. I saw him there this afternoon.'

He paused for a moment, then stood up. 'I'll go down there and fetch him.'

Mary swung around. 'Over my dead body,' she screamed. 'If you go back to that tent we won't see you again for the rest of the night. I can't believe you're even daring to suggest it. Hartley, Alice is missing! We need to get her back.'

Her shoulders were heaving, her face white. 'Spencer, could you go? Just find Jackie Wilson and bring him—'

'Quiet!' Hartley's voice brimmed with anger. 'Can't you trust me for a minute, woman? I know she's bloody missing. She's my daughter.' He looked grimly at Spencer. 'It'll be me who gets her back.'

He pushed past them to the door, slamming it hard behind him.

*

The policeman was not quite sober, but he was sympathetic.

'It's a bad do, Mary,' he said, putting a hand on her shoulder. 'I'm sorry.'

He turned to Spencer. 'Did the little lass say anything before she went?'

'Nothing. We'd been watching the end of the fell race. I looked down at her when it was finished, but she was gone.'

'How'd she been up 'til then?'

'Well,' he said carefully, 'she wasn't very happy.'

He heard Hartley's breathing, heavy in the silence of the room.

'Why not?'

'She'd messed up a dance she was doing at the show.'

Hartley's face was ashen now, suddenly old.

'She wasn't allowed to wear her glasses, so she made a mistake,' Spencer continued.

The policeman coughed and made a note.

'And what about these hippies? Does she know them?'

'A bit. Not very well.'

'Does she like them?'

Spencer thought of Alice's excitement when Mick had called her darling.

'Yes, she does.'

'And they like her?'

He nodded uncomfortably.

Hartley snorted with contempt. 'I shouldn't have ever let them on my land. Get after them, Jackie, man.'

'We'll do what we can. I'll go and ring round the county. I wouldn't have thought they'd get far in those vans. Someone'll see them. They'll stand out.'

'But what about tonight?' Mary asked. 'What if she's not with them? Can't we keep looking?'

He shook his head. 'We could try, but it's nearly dark. And it's show night. By the time we got anyone out of the beer tent to help, it'd be past ten at least. We'd not find anything. I'll get the county police on the lookout. You call me if she turns up. Otherwise I'll be back as soon as it's light.'

He looked over at Mary. 'Try not to worry, love. She's probably just hiding. You know what kids are like.'

When the policeman had gone they sat in silence, watching the light fade until it was almost too dark to see. Spencer and Mary barely moved, preoccupied with their own thoughts, but Hartley was restless, shifting in his chair, his great hands twitching, flexing his fingers. Suddenly, he stood up, pushing the chair away from him.

'I'm going to bed. Like Jackie said, there's nowt we can do by staying up. Mary, are you coming?'

'I won't sleep,' she said, her quiet voice deadly. 'And not with you.'

For a moment he said nothing, then he kicked the leg of the table.

'It's not me who's taken her. I should have thrashed them queer buggers when Alice told us what they were up to. When I catch hold of them, I'll belt them so hard they'll wish they'd never been born.'

'And belting's the answer, is it? Like it always is?'

They stared at each other, their faces hard with hostility, until Hartley turned and left the room.

Mary pushed back her chair and stood up. 'I can't stand it,' she said. 'I can't sit here while she's somewhere out there. I'm going to go looking.'

Spencer stood up too. 'Better if you stay here, in case she comes back. She'll want you then. I'll go.'

Picking up a torch from the dresser, he quietly left the room.

*

As he made his way over the tops of the fells, as he had done so many nights before, he could see the beer tent still glimmering with light, the strains of hunting songs drifting up the valley. He thought of how unnerved he had been by the eerie singing on the night he had arrived. From the moment they had met, Alice had been his guide to the strange world of the farm, translating words that he could not understand, showing him how to behave. He pictured her, that first day, skinny legs jammed into wellingtons, glasses askew, grinning at him with gappy teeth. Memories of the summer came back to him; collecting the eggs from the garden, their conversations about

Cambridge, sitting together in her den eating strawberries. He thought of her face when she had solved the puzzle of the treasure trail, her satisfaction when she persuaded him to dance with her to the tinny tape recorder.

Where are you, Alice? he thought. Would you really go without telling me?

Heavy guilt settled on his shoulders as he walked, for not standing up to Hartley, for giving in to his desire for Edmund and accepting its reassurance that Alice was all right. He tramped for a long time, shining his torch into crevices and under boulders, calling out her name. But all he heard in return was an empty echo, his own voice in repetition, as if to mock his efforts. The sky was darker than usual at that hour, and before long he was unable to see more than a few feet in front of him. As a cloud passed in front of the moon, plunging the valley into blackness, the beam of his torch began to weaken and fade, and soon gave up entirely. Forced to accept that there was little more he could do, Spencer stumbled down the mountainside and back to the hut.

Eventually, as the adrenaline of the day drained away from him, he fell into a shallow, restless doze. An hour or so later, he was woken by a bang so loud it made the mountains shudder, a vast explosion of noise. He sat up immediately and peered outside. The air was very still, heavy with something he could not identify, which covered him with a sticky film of sweat. As he put up his hand to wipe his face, a second bang came, louder, and then, for a sudden shocking second, the whole of the valley was revealed before him as lightning cracked across the sky.

For a moment, everything seemed suspended in time, and then it came, tiny droplets, fatter splashes, followed by a heavy rush of water. Getting out of bed, he went to the doorway and stood, naked, looking out into the darkness, blurred and thickened with rain.

Dorothy had been right. The summer was coming to an end. He thought of what Edmund had said the night before.

'You'll think different when it rains. It's miserable then.'

He closed the door and lit a candle, its flame lurching and flickering as if it were trying to dodge the raindrops. Wrapping the blanket around himself, he sat back down on the mattress, listening to the downpour. At first it sounded like a wall of solid sound, rain driving hard against the mountain, but soon he became aware of other rhythms, raindrops thudding on the old slate roof, the slap of water over rocks as the stream flowed again, the gush of a gully filled for the first time that summer.

Trickles of water dripped from the roof, making little puddles on the floor. The clammy humidity was gone now, replaced by a damp, insistent cold. He thought of Alice, huddled shivering and alone, and hoped that she had managed to find a place away from the rain. As he pulled the blanket tighter, he remembered what else Edmund had said.

'It goes on and on for days, and it's cold, and there's nothing you can do. It gets into you somehow, into your bones. Sometimes you can't see to the end of the valley, the cloud's that thick. You can't see any way out.'

Twenty

He woke to sunlight, warm against his cheek. For a moment he lay still, enjoying the heat on his face, but then with a jolt remembered, and scrambled out of bed. The earthen floor was slimy from the rain that had leaked in through the roof, mud rising between his toes as he went to the door.

Outside, the sky was blue, the wildness of the previous night transformed into radiance, light reflecting off wet rocks. Spiders had spun their webs between bracken fronds, catching raindrops that shimmered in the sun. The stream next to the hut ran fast and full, tumbling down the mountainside, its gush and splash a happy backdrop to birdsong.

Down in the valley, in the shadow of the fell, things were very different. Mirethwaite lived up to its name, its fields waterlogged and desolate, dry stone walls still wet, darkened almost to black. The river had burst its banks, leaving mounds of grasses and twigs in its wake. It flowed, unstoppable, filled with silent force.

One of the trees in the orchard had been struck by lightning. Hens pecked suspiciously around its roots, ruffling their damp feathers. Picking his way around the puddles that dotted the yard, he saw that Mary's marigold trough was full of dirty water. Steeling himself, he went into the house.

They were all there, sitting at the table, mugs of coffee in front of them, listening intently to the radio. They looked up as he entered, but said nothing, returning their attention to the presenter.

'What a night! We've all been hoping for rain, but that was more than we bargained for. Reports are coming in from all over the county – flash floods all over. It never rains but it pours, as they say.

'Now, the good news is that it's a sunny day, so you can all dry out a bit. Bad news is, there could be more storms on the way. Keep tuned in and we'll keep you up to date. This is—'

There was a click as Hartley turned it off.

'That's no use,' he said. 'Could mean owt.'

Spencer hesitated before speaking. 'Is there any news?'

Mary shook her head. 'We're still waiting.' She was gripping her mug like a talisman, very tight, with both hands. 'The police have got their men out there looking now.'

'And Jackie Wilson'll let us know when he's got summat to tell,' said Hartley.

Mary stood up. 'I'll make us some more coffee,' she said.

Taking the mugs, she went to the kitchen. While she was gone, the men said nothing, Hartley frowning down at his hands, biting his lip. When Mary came back with the coffee, he stood up.

'I can't sit about like this,' he said. 'I'm going to look for her myself.'

Thomas rose to join him.

'No,' he said abruptly. 'I'll go on my own.'

He left quickly, meeting no-one's eye.

An hour later, the telephone rang. Mary leapt to answer it.

'Hello?' she said. 'Yes Jackie . . . yes, it is.'

She listened intently, nodding, pressing the receiver to her ear. Spencer watched her face register hope, then disappointment.

'Oh. Where? I see. And they're sure? Well, thank you. What? Oh, yes. Whenever you can. Yes . . . Thank you.'

She replaced the receiver, looking dazed.

'Mary?' he asked. 'What did he say?'

'They found the hippies near Windermere. They were camping there for the night. But they haven't got Alice. They just said it's the end of the summer so they thought it was time to move on. That's why they left.'

Spencer felt a rush of relief, then anxiety took over again.

'He's coming to talk to us,' Mary said. 'He wants us to tell him more about yesterday.' A tear slid down her cheek. 'It seems so long ago. None of this had happened then.'

He thought of Alice grinning at him, her lips stained crimson from the lolly, and twirling proudly in her costume before the dance.

'I'll go and tell Hartley,' he said.

Mary shrugged. 'If you like.'

He found Hartley in the oak wood, leaning on a crook by the pit where they had thrown the tup. The rain had made the smell of it even stronger, and Spencer covered his mouth as he approached.

'Hartley?' he called.

The farmer was lost in thought, staring down into the pit. Spencer's stomach lurched, suspecting something dreadful.

'Hartley!'

Hartley looked around, hopeful, and Spencer felt relief flood over him.

'Have they found them, lad? Is she there?'

'They've found the hippies. At Windermere. But she's not with them. They didn't know anything about it.'

Hartley's face sagged. He blinked, looking suddenly lost.

'The police are coming up to talk to us, to find out more about yesterday,' said Spencer. 'Mary said we'd be here.'

Hartley nodded. 'Aye. I'll keep looking in't meantime.'

He turned away from the pit and set off through the wood, hitting at the undergrowth with his crook as he went.

*

Jackie Wilson arrived in uniform, and with another policeman.

'This is Sergeant Baines,' he said. 'The station in town thought I could do with a hand.'

Sergeant Baines was taller and younger, with shrewd eyes and close-cropped hair.

'We want to make sure we find the little girl as soon as we can,' he said.

They all sat at the table with more mugs of coffee.

'We just want to go over what happened yesterday,' began Jackie. 'Get an idea of the facts.'

'Hold on,' interrupted Sergeant Baines. 'First I want to make sure I know who's who.'

He looked at Mary. 'You're Alice's mother?'

She nodded.

'And which of you is Alice's father? His eyes slid over the three men.

'I am,' Hartley said quickly.

Sergeant Baines looked over to where Thomas and Spencer were sitting. 'So then, you two are?'

Thomas cleared his throat. 'I'm Hartley's brother, Thomas Dodds.'

'And you live here?'

'Yes.'

'Since when?'

'Since always. I was born here. It was our dad's farm.'

The sergeant scribbled something in his notebook.

'Do you work on the farm as well?'

'Yes.' He shifted in his chair.

Sergeant Baines looked at him for a moment longer, then turned his attention to Spencer.

'And you? Who are you?'

'M-m-my name's Spencer Little.'

His voice sounded wrong under the sergeant's scrutiny, out of place and time, and at odds, he knew, with his appearance. He watched him react to it, a look of surprise, swiftly suppressed.

'And where are you from?'

'Cambridge. I'm studying there. I came here for the long vacation. The summer holidays.'

The sergeant looked at him. 'Why?'

Spencer took a breath, trying to keep his voice steady. 'I – I – I wanted a change, that's all. To do something different, I suppose. Something physical. Usually I'm shut up in the library.'

'And why did you choose Mirethwaite?'

He thought of the eggs, nestled in the rusting biscuit tin. Instinct warned him not to mention them.

'It was the first place I came to,' he said. 'I came on my bike, you see, over the pass. It was too hot to go much further so I thought I'd ask if they needed any help for the summer.'

'He's been a good worker,' said Hartley, his voice gruff.

Spencer had not expected an endorsement. Surprised, he looked over at Hartley. Avoiding his eyes, the farmer lifted his mug, taking a mouthful of coffee.

'And where do you stay? Here in the house?'

'No. I sleep in a hut on the fell.'

'A hut?'

'It's a shepherd's dosshouse,' Hartley said. 'Plenty good enough for summertime.'

There was a pause.

'Let's move on to Alice. Mary, can you give me a description of her – how old she is, what she looks like?'

'Well, she's eleven.' Mary's voice was shaking. 'It was her birthday just a couple of weeks ago. She's got light brown hair and blue eyes. She wears glasses. She's not very tall, maybe this high—' She gestured with her hand.

'Can you tell me more about her? What does she like doing? Does she play with friends? What's she been up to, these holidays?'

There was another pause.

'We're a long way up the valley,' said Mary. 'She's got friends at school, but in the holidays . . .' She brightened. 'We had a party for her birthday.'

Spencer remembered the little girls in their party dresses clustered around the makeshift table, and Alice's delight at being at the centre of it all. But his main recollection was of Alice on her own, standing smiling up at him, Shadow at her side.

'She spends a lot of time with her dog,' he said.

'We've all got work to be getting on with,' said Mary apologetically. 'Alice entertains herself.' She took a quick, nervous sip of coffee. 'She was pleased when Spencer came to stay. She's always following him around.'

Sergeant Baines turned to Spencer. 'Is that right?'

'Well, yes,' he said. 'But she's no trouble. I like her company. We talk about things.'

'What things.'

'Cambridge. Maths.'

'Maths?'

'It's what I'm studying.'

'Isn't that a bit hard for her? If she's only just eleven?'

'She understands a lot.' He thought of Alice's questions. 'She's clever.'

'She's been hard work lately,' said Hartley.

'What do you mean?'

'Answering back. Running off.'

The sergeant was immediately interested. 'Running off?'

'Aye,' said Hartley. 'She got herself all riled up one day and ran off up the fell. Nearly got herself killed because of it. The bracken caught fire and it all went up. She was lucky to escape.'

'What happened?'

He jerked his head in Spencer's direction. 'This one found her. Ran through the fire and picked her up. Carried her all the way back down the fell.'

Mary had sat quietly while Hartley spoke, her head bowed, twisting a handkerchief in her fingers. Now she looked up and gave a short, furious nod, as if she had made a decision.

'Got herself all riled up? That's not what happened, you know it's not.'

'Whisht, woman!' Hartley said sharply.

The sergeant held up his hand. 'Mary?'

'She ran away because she was scared of what you'd do to Shadow. You'd already beaten her half to death. We all heard you. Alice took her away because she knew what you'd do next.'

'She had to learn! You can't let a dog get a taste for sheep. She was getting vicious. It's the way I've always done it. They have to know who's boss.'

'Aye,' she muttered. 'It's all about who's boss, is it? Some kind of

265

boss you've been this summer. Some kind of boss you looked like yesterday, staggering about, blind drunk.'

Hartley's face was purple with rage. 'I was not!'

But Mary was determined. 'You were. You could hardly walk. I had to take you home.'

The sergeant cleared his throat. 'Please, let's try to stay calm. Now, tell me about what happened yesterday. I know it was the show. Start from the morning. Mary, you go first.'

She nodded. 'Well, I went to the show field early, about half past eight, to set up the tea tent, like I do every year. I served teas until about quarter past one, then I went to meet Alice at the ring to get her ready for her dance.'

'What dance?'

She glanced at Hartley. 'A ballet dance. Alice's dancing class was going to do it at the show. Anyway, Spencer and Alice came, and then we went to get her changed into her costume.'

'What had you been doing before then?' The sergeant directed his question towards Spencer. 'Had you been with Alice all day?'

'Yes. When I went to the house for breakfast, she was the only one there.' He swallowed. 'She was unhappy.'

'Why?'

'Shadow – her dog – had growled at her. She'd never done that before, Alice said.'

'And why did she do it then?'

He dared not look at Hartley. 'Her puppies had just been drowned.'

Hartley's hand came down hard on the table. 'Christ! We couldn't keep them.'

'Mr Little, please go on.'

'I took her over to the show. We were early, so we walked through the fields. We looked at the sheep in competition and in a few of the tents. I bought her a lolly, and we went to watch the wrestling. Then we met up with Mary.'

Sergeant Baines made another note. 'And then what?'

'She went to get changed and I went to see the start of the fell race.'

'Any particular reason?'

Swiftly, he decided not to mention Edmund. 'I – I'd never seen it before. I wanted to see what it was like. I did the same with the wrestling.'

'And afterwards?'

'I went back to the ring to see Alice dance. I was with Dorothy, a friend of mine.'

'Dorothy Wilkinson?' asked Jackie.

'Yes.'

Sergeant Baines looked interested. 'Who's she?'

'She's just an old woman,' said Jackie. 'Lives a bit further down the valley. She got into a bit of trouble last year for cutting fences where she shouldn't, but she's harmless enough.'

'So you and this Dorothy went back to the ring together?'

'Yes.'

'And watched the little girls dance.'

'Yes. I saw Alice, though, just before she went on.'

'She wanted to show him her costume,' Mary said.

The sergeant nodded slowly. 'I see.' He made another note. 'And how was the dance?'

Spencer thought of Alice's stricken face as she blundered into the dark-haired girl, her tears behind the pavilion.

'It didn't go very well,' he said. 'They wouldn't let her wear her glasses, so she couldn't see. She bumped into someone and fell over. She took it very hard. She was crying. She thought she'd ruined it all.'

'So she came to you?'

'Well, to me and Mary.'

'And Hartley, where were you? Did you watch Alice dance?'

Hartley said nothing, looking down at the table and breathing heavily through his nose. Sergeant Baines waited a moment, and asked again. 'Hartley? Were you there?'

When he raised his head, his face was tight with guilt. 'Aye.'

'Tell him,' said Mary, coldly.

He let out a long and painful sigh. 'I'd had a few pints. I was a bit hard on her.'

'Why?' asked Sergeant Baines.

'I don't know. I've never liked her dancing. I can't see why she has to do it, prancing about with posh lasses from the village. She's trying to be something she's not.'

He looked at Mary. 'And I'd said so to you. You went behind my back with those dancing lessons. You showed me up.'

She flushed. 'I showed you up! What do you think you did, laughing like you'd gone mad, falling all over the show field? I had to take you home. You were embarrassing me.'

There was a pause.

'Let's try to keep to the facts,' said the sergeant. 'So you took Hartley home?'

'Yes,' Mary said. 'And it wasn't easy, either. Then he went to bed.'

'And what did you do? Did you go back to Alice?'

'No,' she said quietly. 'I was ashamed. I didn't want to see anyone. I thought she'd be all right with Spencer.'

He remembered holding Alice as she sobbed on his shoulder, her little body tight with misery. She had clung to him as if he were all she had left. He remembered, with a shameful stab, his irritation at the prospect of missing the fell-race finish.

He realized that Sergeant Baines was waiting for him to take up the story.

'We went back to the fell race, to see the end of it.'

'Who won?' the sergeant asked.

He tried to keep his voice neutral. 'Edmund Lutwidge. He's a friend of mine. I was pleased for him.'

'And Alice went with you?'

'Yes.'

'Was she happy to do that?'

He pushed away the memory of her small face streaked with tears, her silent shrug in response to his excitement. 'Yes.'

'And what happened?'

'We were at the front, near the finishing line. I borrowed some binoculars and we looked at the runners coming down the fell. There were three of them close together and everyone was shouting and cheering. Edmund won. When I looked around for Alice, she was gone.'

'Gone?'

'Yes. She'd been there the minute before, when she gave me back the binoculars, then suddenly she wasn't.'

The sergeant frowned. 'Did you go and look for her?'

He remembered Edmund, standing in front of him, a towel hanging from his neck, pushing all thoughts of Alice from his mind.

'No,' he said slowly. 'She'd said she wanted to go and check on her dog. I thought that was where she'd gone.'

'And what about later on? What did you do for the rest of the afternoon? Weren't you worried?'

His heart twisted at the memory of Edmund lying naked in the hut.

'I couldn't see Alice anywhere. I thought she'd gone back to the farm to find Shadow. My friend wanted to celebrate so we went to the beer tent.'

Abruptly, he stopped, ashamed of how it sounded, but the policeman was nodding, as if he accepted his explanation. He scribbled something in his notebook, then looked up.

'What was Alice wearing when you last saw her?'

'She was still in her costume. It was pink.'

'It was a tutu,' said Mary. 'With sequins on it. I sewed them on myself.'

'And ballet shoes,' he added slowly, thinking of how shabby they had looked next to the tutu's crisp net.

*

The search party stretched itself across the fields like farmhands bringing in a harvest. Word of Alice's disappearance had spread quickly and now an odd assortment of the valley's inhabitants stood next to each other: farmers, the owner of the village shop and mothers from Alice's ballet class, all searching the ditches and hedgerows, in the woods, amongst the debris strewn over the riverbanks, sweating in the burning sun.

'We want to find out if she's somewhere nearby,' Sergeant Baines had said. 'She might have run off like you thought. We need to know if she's anywhere around here.'

The searchers called, their voices overlapping, bouncing off the mountainsides.

'A-lice,' they shouted, drawing out the first syllable. 'A-lice!'

Even the birds were quiet, as if trying not to detract attention from the search, tucking their beaks into their chests, watching closely. The air was still, as if it, too, were waiting, even the wind holding its breath until she was found.

Slowly the search party moved forward, working its way through the fields, their eyes trained on the ground, looking for anything that might serve as a clue. As the sun reached its peak, they broke for lunch, pulling sandwiches from knapsacks and eating them in the shade of the dry stone walls.

Spencer had no appetite. Sitting with his back to a wall, he rubbed at his eyes, sore from peering into the sun, then let them fall shut. For a moment, golden specks danced across his eyelids, then he was enveloped by darkness. He stayed there for five minutes, maybe more, sitting very still and trying to think, until he felt a small hand on his arm.

Alice! he thought, and his eyes snapped open.

But it was Dorothy who stood there, looking down at him, her face creased with concern.

'Hello,' she said. 'I'm so sorry. I've just heard.'

She lowered herself to the ground until she was sitting next to him, legs sticking out in front of her.

'The police came to my house,' she said, 'asking questions.'

'I'm sorry. I told them I was with you when we went to watch Alice dance.'

'They asked a lot of questions.' She cast him a sideways glance. 'Most of them were about you.'

His heart began to thud hard against his chest.

'I told them we went together to see Alice dance as well,' she said. 'And that we talked about the weather. I didn't mention the fell race. I must have forgotten.'

He turned his head to look at her. For a moment she held his gaze, then dropped her eyes.

'I've known Jackie Wilson since he was a boy,' she said. 'He's never left the valley.'

They both looked out at the mountains.

'You were right about the weather,' Spencer said. 'It rained, just like you said it would.'

She nodded. 'Water, water everywhere, as our Mr Coleridge would say. It had to break. I always know when it's about to happen. Something changes in the air; I can't explain quite what. I just feel it. Summer's almost at an end.'

Their sandwiches finished, people were starting to get to their feet, stowing the empty wrappers back in their knapsacks. The vicar, bustling, caught sight of Spencer and Dorothy and came over to them.

'Hello,' he said, his voice rather less booming than usual.

'Hello,' Spencer replied. Dorothy gave a short nod.

'I haven't been over to the house yet,' he said. 'I thought it was more important to join the search. But are they all right? Mary and Hartley, I mean.'

Spencer thought of Mary's white, stricken face, and Hartley standing, looking into the stinking pit, each of them locked into their own private grief.

'Not really,' he said. 'I'm sorry . . . I don't know.'

A rush of sadness came over him, a sense of loss so profound that he blinked again, this time to ward away tears.

'I'll visit them this afternoon,' the vicar said hastily, and hurried off to rejoin the search party.

Spencer stood up, extending a hand to Dorothy. She took it, hauling herself up.

'Be careful,' she said.

Twenty-one

ON THE THIRD DAY, SPENCER FOUND MARY STANDING AT THE kitchen sink, staring through the window, her hands immersed but unmoving in the soapy water. He had spent another night not sleeping, examining his memory, revisiting the day of the show, searching his mind for clues. Alice's absence was a conundrum that he found himself incapable of solving. He ached with dull fatigue, overlain by a cold and creeping fear.

The radio was blaring out a song. He crossed the room and switched it off. Mary stayed where she was, immobile, saying nothing.

'Mary,' he said softly.

She showed no sign of having heard him. Gently, he touched her shoulder. As she turned, she wiped her cheeks dry with her apron and looked up at him with tired eyes.

'They're talking about her on the radio,' she said. 'She was on the news just before.'

'What did they say?'

'They said she's been missing since Saturday and that the police have been looking for her, and that they're worried. They gave a description. She sounded so . . . I don't know . . . small.'

There was a pause.

'Hearing it made it seem real.' She shook her head, as if trying to deny that it was.

'Have you heard any more from Sergeant Baines?'

'Only that they're talking to people who were at the show. Trying to find out if anyone saw her.' She gestured hopelessly with her hands, still coated in soapsuds. 'It's all so slow. I just want to go to her. I can't stand not knowing what's happened.' Her voice cracked. 'She was so upset about falling over. I shouldn't have cared about Hartley showing me up. I should have stayed with her.'

'You did the right thing,' Spencer said quietly. 'He was making it worse for Alice. You had to take him away. Besides, you didn't leave her on her own. She had me. I was there.'

For a moment Mary was silent, any reproach left unspoken.

'I'm going to go outside,' she said eventually. 'Will you come?'

She took a packet of cigarettes and a box of matches from a drawer and put them in her apron pocket. He followed her to the back door, where they stood looking out at the shabby garden and its clumps of dried-out weeds, parched brown by the drought. The sudden rain had battered them, snapping off their heads, which now lay abandoned in the dust.

Mary pulled a cigarette from the packet and struck a match, her hands shaking as she held up the flame.

She inhaled, held in the smoke for a moment, then let it dribble from her lips, as if she were too tired to exhale, her neck bent like the weeds. Everything about her suggested exhaustion. When the cigarette had burned down almost to her fingertips she let it fall to the ground, then lit another.

'Isn't Hartley here?' asked Spencer, mindful of how he felt about her smoking.

She shrugged. 'I don't care if he knows,' she muttered. 'I don't care what he thinks, not any more. He's going to have to start seeing the truth.'

She looked wretched, her skin raw from crying, hair falling lank to her shoulders. But in her eyes there was a look that he recognized, a look of defiance, a look of Alice.

'Could you do me a favour?' she asked.

He nodded. 'Of course.'

'Will you go to the shop? I used up all the coffee on the police. And we've run out of milk. Some bread, too, if you can get it. I don't want to see anyone. I can't stand the questions and I don't want their pity.'

He nodded. 'Will you be all right on your own?'

'I'm used to it,' she said. 'You know I am.'

*

He took his bicycle, pedalling as fast as he could, hunched over the handlebars, throwing himself into the physical exertion. As he passed Dorothy's cottage, he turned his head to look at the waterfall, now a busy, tumbling torrent roaring down the side of the fell. He wondered what she had meant when she had warned him to be careful, how much she knew. He remembered Alice calling her a witch. Now it seemed almost plausible. He felt a sudden chill, as though he had just passed into a shadow.

The road was as empty as always and he kept to the middle, avoiding the pools of water in its potholes. The hedgerows were spattered with mud from where cars had driven past, and lumps of tarmac lay among the grasses, washed loose by the rain. As he came to the hill just before the village, he heard the faint sound of a car's engine. Pulling to the side, he changed gear and pedalled slowly, hauling himself to the top. For a moment he wondered where the car had got to, as its engine had gone quiet, but then, in a sudden, terrifying moment, it was on him, swerving so close and so fast that he toppled into the hedgerow. As the car sped off, he heard jeers and shouts, then the blare of a horn.

Slowly, he got to his feet and pulled his bicycle out of the ditch. He was shaking, his heart thudding in his chest. The car had missed him by a fraction of an inch. Gripping the bicycle with both hands, he leaned on it as he stood, listening hard, trying to gauge whether the car was coming back. It was tourists messing about, he told himself, remembering Dorothy's complaints about cars not belonging in a place like this.

The road stayed quiet, a blue ribbon stretching out ahead of him. After a while, he set off again, gingerly, cycling slowly up the hill, looking over his shoulder as he went.

It was a relief to arrive at the village. He leant his bicycle against the post-office wall and crossed the road to the shop.

The first thing he saw was Alice's face, smiling out from a poster stuck up in the window next to the other advertisements. It was a small photograph, in blurred black and white, but it was unmistakably her wide grin and heavy glasses. He had been there when the policemen had asked for it. Mary had gone to the dresser and picked out the photograph, mounted in a cardboard frame and tucked behind a tankard.

'It's her school photo,' she had said, handing it to Sergeant Baines. 'From this year. Will that be all right?'

Now the photograph was a poster. Spelled out in large capital letters across the top was a single word:

MISSING

Immediately below the photograph was her name, followed by a description.

ALICE DODDS
Missing since 31st August
Aged 11, height 4'6", brown hair, blue eyes
Last seen wearing pink ballet costume
Please contact Police on 09403 349 with any information

His heart twisted at the sight of Alice's smile. Her excitement at having her picture taken was evident. It was an expression he recognized from their discussions about Cambridge or from when she had answered one of his maths conundrums correctly, one of unreserved hope and delight, and one that never failed to move him. Once again he felt a shiver of shame at how he had chosen Edmund over her.

Steeling himself, he pushed open the shop door, then winced as a bell rang out, announcing his entrance. His heart sank as he saw the group of women standing at the counter. Amongst them were Valerie Horsley and Margaret Vickers. He thought of the last time he had been in the shop, speaking in dialect to keep them at arm's length. Now there was no need for such a tactic; their conversation stopped abruptly the minute he walked into the shop. As he went to the shelves, picking out coffee, milk and bread, he felt their eyes on him and was suddenly nervous.

Going to the counter to pay, he saw that Angela Armstrong was part of the group.

'Hello Angela,' he said.

She looked at him doubtfully, her freckled forehead creased into a frown.

'Hello.'

There was a pause.

'Is there any news?' she asked, awkwardly.

He shook his head. 'No. The police are still looking, but nothing yet.'

'Will you give my regards to Mary? If there's anything she needs . . .' She trailed off, looking embarrassed.

Feeling the weight of the other women's eyes on his back, he paid quickly, nodded goodbye and left.

As he went through the door, he heard Valerie's voice. '. . . always strange . . . I wouldn't be surprised . . .'

*

She went on speaking after he had gone, her voice heavy with suggestion.

'He used to take her to the pub you know. I saw them one day sitting in the garden. Alice said they went there a lot. That's not normal, is it?'

'But they're close,' said Angela Armstrong, uncertainly. 'Mary must have known. He brought her to ballet lessons. He seemed very nice.'

'And how many men do you know who bring little girls to ballet? Your husband? Mine? They run a mile at anything like that.'

'Perhaps he was helping Mary out. I don't think she has a very nice time of it. Hartley's not the easiest man, we all know that.'

'We wondered if anything was going on between those two,' said Margaret. 'Do you remember, Valerie, when he was so strange in here that time?'

Valerie snorted. 'I don't think he's interested in Mary. I don't think he's interested in women, full stop.'

Angela was shocked. 'Valerie!'

But Valerie was unrepentant. 'Normal men don't spend time with little girls. They work, they watch television, they talk to their wives. They don't take eleven-year-olds to the pub. He was there at the show, too, right at the front, watching her dance. There was something in his eyes.'

Angela's face was pink. 'I don't think—'

'Remember those Moors Murders, over in Yorkshire, ten years or so ago. With that couple? You know, Ian Brady and Myra Hindley.'

'Oh, that was horrible,' said Margaret. 'I felt awful for those little children's parents, I really did.'

'But Spencer *saved* Alice!' protested Angela. 'From that fire. He looked after her.'

'He was the last one to be seen with her, though,' said the shopkeeper from behind the counter. 'That's what I've heard, anyway.'

'Me too,' said Valerie. 'And you have to ask yourself – why's he here? Don't tell me it's normal for someone studying at Cambridge to come all the way up to the Lakes. Especially to work on a farm. It doesn't make sense.'

She pulled a packet of cigarettes from her handbag and lit one. 'Actually, I asked him about it once.'

'Did you?' said Margaret. 'When?'

Valerie exhaled. 'He came round for a drink,' she said. 'I was interested in him. I wanted to know what made him tick. But he wasn't giving anything away. As soon as I asked him what he was doing here he got all hot and bothered. Said he was looking for peace and quiet. Then he ran off.' She nodded thoughtfully. 'I should have wondered then.'

*

Spencer cycled fast out of the village, trying to pedal away his growing sense of unease. He had noticed a little gleam of triumph in Valerie's eyes, and was unnerved by it, unsure of how far she would take her insinuations. He remembered the look on her face as he had backed away from her in the garden. She had not forgotten, he knew, and he knew as well that he was no match for her. Putting his head down, he made his way along the road, still rattled by what had happened on his way to the shop. Perhaps, he thought, the jeers and calls had not just been bored tourists having fun on a summer afternoon. Perhaps they had been meant expressly for him. He wondered what rumours had spread in those few short days since Alice had gone missing, what whispers had spread through the village.

As he approached the top of the hill he saw another bicycle coming towards him, pedalled by a bulky figure. As it inched towards him, he realized he had no chance of avoiding a conversation with the vicar. They both stopped, the vicar dismounting to wheel his bicycle across the road. His face was red with exertion, his grey ecclesiastical shirt patched dark with sweat. He stood, gripping the handlebars, panting slightly.

'Spencer! I was hoping I might catch you.'

'Hello.' Spencer remained straddled across his bicycle, keeping it in front of him as if for protection.

'Where have you been off to?'

Spencer wondered if he was imagining the note of coldness in his voice. He looked at him doubtfully.

'M-Mary asked me to go to the shop.'

The vicar nodded. 'She was in a bad way yesterday. Is she any better now?'

He thought of her, smoking and wretched in the scrubby garden.

'Not much.'

'I'll visit again tomorrow. Will you tell her she's in my prayers? Hartley too, naturally. I thought of holding a special service this

Sunday, to pray for Alice's safe return. If, of course, she hasn't already been found.'

'Yes,' he said. 'I'm sure Mary would like that.'

'And you?' the vicar said, with a slight edge to his voice. 'Would you feel able to come?'

He remembered his embarrassment the last time he had been to the church, how heads had turned when the vicar had welcomed him. This time, he suspected they would turn for other reasons, but he knew as well that he would have to go.

'Yes,' he said. 'Of course I would.'

The vicar looked down at the ground for a moment, then back at him. 'Is there anything you'd like to talk about? I'd be ready to listen. It's my job, you know.'

There was something odd in his expression, something not quite sympathetic. Spencer shook his head.

'I'm all right.'

'I was speaking to my friend on the telephone, you remember, the chaplain at Jesus.'

Spencer's heart clenched. 'Y-yes.'

'It was very odd. I mentioned you but he didn't seem to know who you were. He said the name rang no bells with him at all.'

It was almost an accusation.

You too, he thought.

The idea of the vicar checking up, discussing him, made him suddenly stubborn.

'I only went to chapel for the music,' he said, looking him in the eye. 'I wasn't religious.'

*

Riding away, he felt the vicar's gaze burning into his back like midday sun, and tried to suppress the panic rising in his throat.

281

Conscious of having rejected the clergyman's attempts to involve him in village life, he was aware that he had probably made an enemy. This latest confrontation made things worse. It had shaken him, even more than the scene in the shop. The only way to explain would be to tell the vicar he had changed his name, but then the story of what had happened in Cambridge would come out.

Trying to suppress his growing unease, he pedalled on, thinking back to his arrival in the valley, the hostility of the farmers, and his unexpected pleasure at being accepted after saving Alice from the fire. Now he saw that he had simply been tolerated, never liked.

As he approached the lane that led to Edmund's farm, he slowed down, staring up at the house and its cluster of outbuildings. Stopping, he stood for a while, trying to decide if he should take the turning. Edmund had never expressly forbidden it, and although his instincts warned him he might not be welcome, he wanted to see him, to find reassurance in his smile. Suddenly he knew he could not keep himself from going to him. He began to push the bicycle up the rough, pothole-ridden track.

*

The same dog was lying in the porch, as if it hadn't moved since the last time he had been there. He bent to stroke its glossy coat.

'Good dog,' he said, thinking of Shadow. He remembered Alice asking if Cambridge would allow dogs, and once again fear pricked at his heart. She would never have left without Shadow, he knew, but the prospect of her being taken against her will was almost too horrible to contemplate.

At the sound of footsteps he turned to see the man who had given him the chainsaw. His expression was as suspicious as it had been then. Spencer remembered what Edmund had told him: 'It's just my dad and the three of us. Arthur's the eldest, then Billy, then me. Mam died when I was six. Arthur never really got over it.'

'H-hello,' he said. 'We met once before. Are you Arthur? I – I'm looking for Edmund.'

The man frowned. 'Edmund?'

He forced himself to keep smiling. 'Yes.'

'He's fencing. I'll take you.'

*

He heard Edmund before he saw him, the thwock of a mallet on wood rattling around the mountains. He was in a field some way from the house, hammering wooden stakes into the ground along the side of a stream.

As they approached, Edmund looked up and Spencer saw a flash of irritation pass over his face. He swung his mallet again, driving the stake hard into the earth.

'Edmund,' said his brother, 'you've got a visitor.'

Letting the mallet fall to his side, he wiped his brow with the back of his hand.

'I've got three more to do, then that's it,' he said. 'Then I'll put the wire on.'

'Aye,' his brother said. 'Do you want a hand?'

He shook his head. 'Spencer can help. Since he's here.'

They said nothing until he was out of sight, Edmund continuing to hammer while Spencer stood, awkward, waiting. Eventually he stopped. Shoulders heaving from the exertion, he squinted up.

'What were you thinking, coming here?'

There was an edge to his voice that Spencer had never heard before.

'I'm sorry,' he said. 'I had to come. I had to see you.'

Haltingly, he told him what had happened on the road and in the shop. Edmund's face remained impassive as he spoke, but he

283

listened carefully, his blue eyes fixed, intent, on Spencer.

'You haven't got any proof,' he said finally. 'Maybe they meant to drive the car at you, and maybe they didn't. Anyway, Valerie Horsley's a gossiping bitch. No-one believes what she says.'

'They might,' said Spencer. 'This time.'

'You shouldn't have come. It'll only make things worse. My brothers are going to wonder why you're here.'

'Do they know . . .' He could not think of how to say it. 'I mean . . . about you?'

Edmund's eyes widened. 'Jesus, Spencer! Of course they bloody don't. Do you think I'd have survived this long if they did?'

'But—'

'No! You never heard the things they were saying in the pub about the hippies. They wouldn't have lasted much longer, not after people heard what was going on. They probably got wind of it – I bet that's why they left in a hurry. Probably best, too. You wouldn't want to be around after those lads have been in the beer tent all day.'

He picked up the mallet again. When he looked at Spencer, his eyes were cold. 'My brothers aren't ever going to know. Or my dad.'

Spencer felt a tightness begin to spread across his stomach.

'Edmund, I think I'm in trouble. The policeman's already asked me what I was doing for the rest of the afternoon. I said I was in the beer tent, celebrating with you.'

'Well, you were.'

'Not all afternoon.'

He thought of his wonder at seeing Edmund lying naked on the bed, the tenderness he had felt as he had held his feet. That day felt an age away, belonging to his happiness, before he knew Alice was gone.

Edmund shrugged. 'We weren't there that long. We can just say we were in the beer tent all the time.'

'But there were enough people who noticed us come in. They cheered. They bought you drinks.'

'They were pissed,' he said, impatiently. 'They weren't looking at their watches.'

'I – I'm scared, Edmund. I think it's going to get worse. People are suspicious.' Spencer hesitated for a moment, then his words came, in a rush. 'I think we should t-tell the police where we were. At least—'

'Have you gone mad?' Edmund's face had darkened with anger. 'Haven't you been listening? You're supposed to be the clever one. You said your maths was about working out how one thing leads to another. Can't you see what would happen if you told them?'

'But I can see what's going to happen if I don't. It's already happening. And . . . well, they couldn't do anything. We're over twenty-one. We haven't broken the law.'

'It's all right for you. You can tell them about us and then you can leave. You can go back to your university and you'll be all right. But I've got nowhere to go. I'm stuck. And the news would spread, believe me.'

'I wouldn't leave you.' The thought made his heart twist. 'I've told you, I never would.'

'Look, Spencer, can't you see? We haven't got a future. There's nothing ahead. We've had our fun, for the summer, but summer's finished now.' He grinned, a small, weak grin. 'See, it rained. I told you it would. And it was bloody miserable.'

'But Edmund—' Willing himself not to stammer, Spencer spoke in a rush. 'I think – I – I'm in love with you.'

There was a pause. His words hung in the air between them, as Edmund nodded slowly.

'Well then, prove it.'

Twenty-two

That night, for the first time since Alice's disappearance, Hartley went drinking. At supper he was restless, his cutlery clattering as he sawed at his meat, the only sound in an otherwise silent room. As the meal wore on, his agitation grew, and he shifted in his seat, unable to sit still. Eventually he pushed his plate away, his food unfinished.

'I'm going to't pub,' he said, his voice defiant.

Mary did not rise to his challenge. Taking a sip of water, she shrugged, refusing to look at him.

Hartley stood up, scraping his chair over the flagstones. 'Thomas?'

He shook his head.

'Well then, I'll go on my own.'

When he came back downstairs from changing his clothes, he walked past them without speaking, shoulders squared and head held high.

The pub was quiet, with just a few regulars sitting at the bar. Hartley's presence was acknowledged with nods and offers of drinks.

'First one's on the house,' said the barmaid, taking his tankard from its hook. 'Any news?'

'Not yet.'

She put the pint in front of him, spilling a little onto the brightly coloured mat. He stared down at it, watching the beer soak in, turning the cardboard brown. Picking up the tankard, he took a long swallow, draining half of it, feeling relief at the sensation of warm beer sliding down his throat. He went to his usual table and sat down, still holding on to the tankard with both hands, staring unseeingly at the wall.

As he was downing the last of it, he was approached by Titch Tyson.

'Fancy another?'

Hartley nodded.

Titch took the tankard to the bar and had it filled.

'Can I join you?' he asked.

Hartley nodded again. 'Aye.'

They took out a box of dominoes and began to play, falling into the rhythm of a game they both knew well, old competitors taking each other on. They spoke very little as they played, their few words punctuated by the slide and click of the dominoes.

After a while, they were joined by two more farmers, bringing over their pints to watch the game. It was some time before anyone brought up the subject of Alice.

'How's Mary?' asked Malcolm Bainbridge. 'Must be hard on her.'

Hartley inclined his head an inch in agreement.

'And what about the clever bugger? What's up with him?'

'What do you mean?' said Hartley.

'Well, you must know what's being said.'

He lifted his tankard to his lips. 'No.'

'You know he's always been a strange one. You've said so yourself.'

'M-my name's Spencer Little.' Titch Tyson imitated his stutter.

'Well he can't help that,' Hartley said. 'And he's worked hard enough for me.'

'He's not normal, though,' said Malcolm. 'Is he?'

'I'm starting to think no-one bloody is,' said Hartley. 'I don't know what's what any more. Not since Alice went. I thought we'd lost her at the start of the summer, in that fire. It was him who saved her then, you've got to give him that.'

'Aye,' said Titch. 'He did. But how did he know where to find her?'

'Eh? I don't know. They were always together. She was always following him about.'

'That's not right, though, is it?' said Malcolm. 'I mean, my l'aal lass doesn't hang around with grown men. She's got her friends for company.'

'Well he didn't seem to mind it.'

'But that's it. Why not? I would. You would. Kids can be a pain in the arse.'

There was a pause as Hartley considered what he had said. In the meantime, Titch went to the bar and bought another round, his large hands fitting easily around the four tankards.

'All that about the lasses dancing, too,' said Malcolm, as Titch returned. 'How many of us were at the show for that? It was for mams from the village, not us.'

'Aye, but he was at the wrestling earlier on as well. And he went off to see his mate in't fell race after the dancing,' said Hartley. 'He's friends with young Edmund Lutwidge. He won it, then they went straight to't beer tent for a pint. Spence told us. He told the police as well.'

'Hang on,' said Malcolm, slowly. 'I watched the end of that race.

My nephew was in it. I went to't beer tent with him afterwards too, but Edmund wasn't there. My nephew was keen to buy him a drink, like, but he didn't come for another couple of hours. I remember it. Edmund came in with Spencer and got a cheer for being champion. But we'd had a fair few pints before they got there.'

Hartley's face darkened. 'What?'

'He's right,' said Titch slowly. 'I was there too.'

'So what the bloody hell was going on?'

'Why don't you ask Edmund?' said Titch. 'He's over there.'

They turned to see him, sitting alone at the bar. Immediately, Hartley stood up.

'Hold your horses, man.' said Titch. 'Don't lose your temper.'

Giving a short, impatient nod, Hartley went over to the bar.

'How's your fettle, Edmund?'

Edmund looked at him, his eyes faintly bloodshot, as if he had been drinking for a while. But when he spoke his voice was steady. 'All right. Can I get you a pint?'

'I'll have a whisky,' said Hartley. 'And then I want a word.'

Edmund bought the drinks from the barmaid and pushed one of the glasses over to Hartley. 'Right, let's have that word.'

Hartley took a sip of whisky. 'You'll have heard about Alice.'

Edmund nodded. 'I'm sorry.'

'I want to ask you something.'

'Aye?'

'The lads have been talking. They're saying there's something strange about Spencer and Alice.'

Edmund shrugged. 'How would I know?'

'You're his mate. He went to see you win the race. He said that's when Alice went off. And then you and him went to't beer tent.'

'That's right.'

'But Malcolm reckoned that was a couple of hours later.'

'Yes,' said Edmund. 'After the race I went to get washed and have a bite to eat. I bumped into Spencer on my way over to the beer tent.'

'So you weren't with him before then?'

'No,' said Edmund. 'I wasn't.'

*

Hartley left the pub soon after, making his way along the road he had followed so many nights before. It was a still night, the moon round and full, casting a pale glow on the fells and the fields, but he was in no mood to notice. He had drunk a lot, but he neither staggered nor sang. Instead, he trudged, hands jammed into his jacket pockets, head down. A cold, dangerous anger had settled over him, and now it fuelled his every step.

As he got to the farm he veered off sideways, taking the little path that led up the side of the fell. He climbed without effort, not pausing for breath. When he reached the hut he squared his shoulders, then spat once, deliberately, on the ground.

Spencer was sitting on his bed when the door flew open.

Hartley stood, solid, blocking the doorway. 'What the hell do you think you're playing at?' His voice was thick with drink.

'W-what do you mean?'

'Don't play silly beggars with me, lad. You know.'

Spencer heard his own voice, thin and weak next to Hartley's growl. 'I don't.'

'Were you laughing at me, eh? Pretending you wanted to work, saying you wanted a change? I should have known when you said you'd work for nothing. It was too bloody good to be true. Why would someone like you want to do that?'

He took a step towards the bed. 'It wasn't work you wanted, was it? It was me daughter.'

His eyes were swimming with tears. Suddenly Spencer pitied him.

'H-Hartley, what are you saying? I love Alice, but not like that. I—'

'What have you done to her? Where've you taken me l'aal lass?'

In an instant he had crossed the room and taken hold of Spencer by the shoulders.

'You lied to me. You said you were with Edmund Lutwidge. You said you went to the beer tent, but you didn't.'

'I did! I was with Edmund!'

'Not all afternoon you weren't. Don't try to be clever with me. I'm not from Cambridge, but by god, I'm not thick. There was a good two hours between the end of the fell race and you walking into the beer tent. Malcolm Bainbridge told me.'

'But—' Then he thought of Edmund earlier, listening to his declaration of love, and challenging him to prove it, and he stopped.

Hartley's breath was in his face. 'Don't try saying you were with him. I asked him tonight, in't pub. He said he went to get some food and have a wash, but on his own, not with you. You were with Alice.'

The image of Edmund, naked and smiling, flashed in front of his eyes. Then his heart clenched as he thought of Alice in the pub, a strange smile on her lips, saying it must be hard to swim when the river was all dried up. Suddenly, irrefutably, he knew everything.

Urgency gave him the strength to push Hartley away from him.

'I'm sorry,' he said, and dashed to the door.

Running over the intake he thought of Edmund: the first time he had seen him, across the farmyard, his hair golden in the sunlight, then later, sitting at the bar in the pub, and later still, their meeting at night on the fell. He remembered him jumping on the woolsack with Alice, singing into the clippers with the kind of abandon he could never have himself. He thought of Hartley, drunk and swaying on the bridge, ready to jump, and of Edmund's murmured promise to take him somewhere else the next day, away from Hartley and the others.

His hands on his body had been an awakening.

As he ran further he thought of other things, of how Edmund had talked of the rains and his refusal to believe that Spencer could stand them, of the wariness in his eyes, of how he had brushed off Spencer's desire to belong to him. His mind raced, making connections, adding together signs that now seemed obvious. Worst of all, he thought of how Edmund had lied to Hartley in the pub about not being together that afternoon, and he knew at last that Edmund had not loved him. In one horrible moment of clarity, the pattern was revealed to him: one of misplaced infatuation, followed by humiliation. He had fled from Cambridge only to repeat it here, unable to see it until now.

'For a clever bugger, you can be a bit thick,' Edmund had said. Now the phrase rang hollow in his ears as he cursed his own stupidity, the way that he had allowed reason to be overcome by desire. He had misinterpreted Edmund's hints and signals, just as he had those of his undergraduate. The consequences this time, he realized now, were far worse. His desire for Edmund had caused him to betray the trust that Mary had placed in him, his responsibility for her child.

His thoughts circled back to Alice. It was she, he realized, who had changed him, not Edmund. He remembered her, squinting at him from the doorway to the kitchen on his first morning, Shadow by her side, her breathless questions about Cambridge, the way she whooped with pleasure when she answered a maths problem correctly. 'Mathy-matics,' she had murmured, savouring the word. 'Pure mathy-matics.' He felt her breath on his neck as he carried her down the mountainside after the fire, her thin arms holding him tight as they rode along the valley, her tears soaking his shirt as she wept on his shoulder at the show. She had made him capable of feeling, for the first time, something like real love.

She had needed proof of it as much as Edmund had. He had failed her.

*

'I'm sorry Alice,' he said out loud, quickening his pace. 'I'm coming. I'm coming now.'

*

By the time he reached the cave he was sweating, his knees bruised from scrambling against rocks, his legs whipped by bracken and scratched by gorse. He hurried past the stricken tree to the clump of bracken, but when he tried to push through, he hit something solid. A mass of earth and rock had blocked it, carried down the mountain by the rains. In a rush he began to attack it, pulling at stones and hurling them to one side, scraping away the heavy red mud. The sun from the previous day had baked it hard and it was unyielding as he picked and scratched at it, pushing it up under his fingernails. He worked solidly, trying not to give in to the dread that was creeping over him, forcing himself to keep going, then, feeling a draught from within the cave, damp air that smelled faintly of iron, he began to tear at the earth, flinging rocks behind him, trying to create a hole big enough to pass through. His hands were not enough, and he started to kick, using all his weight until the wall began to give. With one last, violent shove, it crumbled and fell and he lurched forward.

It was cold in the cave and a damp chill settled over him. His kicking had made the opening wider than it had been before the rains, and the moonlight slipped through, making the fool's gold glimmer and shine. He blinked, trying to adjust his eyes to the half-light. The water was higher than he had ever seen it, lapping against the little shore. It had been even higher, he could see, from the marks that reached almost to the roof of the cave. The fleeces that he and Edmund had used as a mattress were gone, long since washed away.

As he looked around, peering into the darkness, he noticed something white washed up on a rock. Immediately, he waded in. The water was up to his thighs by the time he reached it. He picked it up with a sinking sense of dread. It was Alice's exercise book, the one she always carried with her.

What I Did On My Holidays

He thought of her, bent over it, shielding her writing with her arm. Now the book was soggy with water, the ink washed from the paper. Dropping it, he began to wade forward, deeper.

'Alice!' he shouted, his voice cracking. 'I'm coming. Don't worry, you're safe. I'll look after you. I promise, I will.'

His words echoed off the glittering walls and he turned his head, anxiously scanning the cave. Then he saw her, a pale shape on a black rock protruding out of the water.

'Alice!'

She lay on her side, curled up, her knees close to her chest, as if she were asleep. As he grew closer he saw her eyes, open and glistening, and he felt impossible hope surge in his chest. But her eyes were still and lifeless, caught in a single, final moment.

He could see it now, so clearly, the sequence of events unfolding itself with horrible inevitability in his mind. She had run away from the humiliation of the show, from the place where she thought she was not wanted, hiding where she knew that only he would find her. He pictured her sitting on the sheepskins, growing colder, waiting for him to come to her rescue as he had done on the fell, then feeling the water inch up her legs, and knowing that it was too late, that he wouldn't get there in time.

Tears began to pour down his face as he stroked her hair, brushing it back from where it was plastered against her forehead. The pink tutu clung to her body, her skinny limbs protruding from its layers of net. He thought of her curiosity, her endless questions, her energy, her unguarded affection. Now she was silent and unmoving. He lifted her and held her close, hugging her tight.

He turned.

Now the silence was broken as he waded, each step forcing the water to ripple out away from him, slapping into hard granite. He felt neither the dark cold nor the pressure of it, moving blindly forward, cradling the little weight in his arms.

He passed from shallows into shadows, and then was claimed by moonlight. He stood for a minute, looking at the vast, sleeping mountains and fields that glittered under silver dew.

'I'm sorry,' he said quietly, and laid his burden down.

Dorothy sat at the kitchen table with her morning coffee, reading *The Times*. Turning to the obituaries as usual, she read through them, stopping as she noticed a familiar name.

Victor Turner, mathematician: born, Godalming, Surrey, 21st June 1952; died, Cumbria, 3rd September 1976.

Victor Turner was one of the most gifted mathematicians of his generation, whose inspired research led to significant developments in the field of mathematical logic. Born in Godalming, Surrey, in 1952, he was educated at Jesus College, Cambridge, where he undertook the Mathematical Tripos, becoming Senior Wrangler in 1968. Having remained in Cambridge to complete his Part III, he was currently working on a PhD, the findings of which were eagerly awaited by his peers and academics alike.

A keen cycling enthusiast, Turner spent this year's Long Vacation in the Lake District, where he worked as a farm labourer under the assumed name of Spencer Little. Sadly, his involvement in the search for a missing girl led to his drowning in a former iron-ore mine, flooded as a result of torrential rain at the end of the summer heatwave.

An inquest recorded a verdict of death by misadventure.

Acknowledgements

Choosing a mathematician as a hero was a somewhat rash decision, given my utter inadequacy with numbers. Thanks to Sharanjit Paddam and Umar Salam for first making me see that maths could be a passion, and eighteen years later having the patience to explain again why. Thanks as well to Annalisa Picciolo for her unique insights and clarifications. Any mathematical blunders are my own. Thanks to Sam Brookes for articulating the beauty and precision of Bach in the way that only he can, to Beth Crosland for her tact and skill in taking author photographs, and to Flavia Krause-Jackson for her daily reassurances.

Thanks also to my father, Ian – the original mathematician-farmer – for his advice and corrections on both subjects, and to my mother, Jennifer, for her memories of the Lakes in the 1970s.

I am very grateful to my agent, Caroline Wood, for getting me started on that difficult second novel, and to Laura Barber at Portobello, the most perspicacious, diplomatic and encouraging editor I could ever wish for.

This book was written under difficult circumstances. Thank you Alberto Masetti-Zannini for sticking with our joint endeavours, and Sandra Davenport for being there always, in just the right way.